Praise for the novels of Anne Frasier

Play Dead

"Frasier has perfected the art of making a reader's skin crawl. . . . [An] exceptional thriller. . . . Frasier's characters are not only fully realized, but fascinating to boot, and she evokes the dark, mystical side of Savannah with precision and skill."
—*Publishers Weekly*

Sleep Tight

"There'll be no sleeping after reading this one! A riveting thriller guaranteed to keep you up all night. Laced with forensic detail and psychological twists. . . . Compelling and real—a great read."
—Andrea Kane

"Guaranteed to keep you awake at night, *Sleep Tight* is a fast-paced novel of secrets, lies, and chilling suspense."
—Lisa Jackson

"Gripping and intense. . . . Along with a fine plot, Frasier delivers her characters as whole people, each trying to cope in the face of violence and jealousies."
—*Minneapolis Star Tribune*

"Enthralling. . . . There's a lot more to this clever intrigue than graphic police procedures. Indeed, one of Frasier's many strengths is her ability to create characters and relationships that are as compelling as the mystery itself. . . . Will linger with the reader long after the killer is caught."
—*Publishers Weekly*

continued . . .

Hush

"This is far and away the best serial killer story I have read in a very long time . . . strong characters, and a truly twisted bad guy. With *Hush*, Anne Frasier slams into the fast lane and goes to the head of the pack. This one has Guaranteed Winner written all over it."

—Jayne Ann Krentz

"A deeply engrossing read, *Hush* delivers a creepy villain, a chilling plot, and two remarkable investigators whose personal struggles are only equaled by their compelling need to stop a madman before he kills again. Warning: Don't read this book if you are home alone."

—Lisa Gardner

"I couldn't put it down . . . engrossing . . . scary . . . I loved it."   —Linda Howard

"Anne Frasier has crafted a taut and suspenseful thriller driven by a villain guaranteed to give you nightmares . . . [ends] on a chilling note you won't soon forget."

—Kay Hooper

"A brilliant debut from a very talented author—a guaranteed page-turner that will keep the reader riveted from beginning to end."   —Katherine Sutcliffe

"Well-realized characters and taut, suspenseful plotting. It will definitely keep you awake to finish it. And you'll be glad you did."   —*Minneapolis Star Tribune*

"A wealth of procedural detail, a heart-thumping finale and two scarred but indelible protagonists make this a first-rate debut."   —*Publishers Weekly*

Other Books by Anne Frasier

Hush
Sleep Tight
Play Dead

BEFORE I WAKE

Anne Frasier

AN ONYX BOOK

ONYX
Published by New American Library, a division of
Penguin Group (USA) Inc., 375 Hudson Street,
New York, New York 10014, USA
Penguin Group (Canada), 10 Alcorn Avenue, Toronto,
Ontario M4V 3B2, Canada (a division of Pearson Penguin Canada Inc.)
Penguin Books Ltd., 80 Strand, London WC2R 0RL, England
Penguin Ireland, 25 St. Stephen's Green, Dublin 2,
Ireland (a division of Penguin Books Ltd.)
Penguin Group (Australia), 250 Camberwell Road, Camberwell, Victoria 3124,
Australia (a division of Pearson Australia Group Pty. Ltd.)
Penguin Books India Pvt. Ltd., 11 Community Centre, Panchsheel Park,
New Delhi - 110 017, India
Penguin Group (NZ), cnr Airborne and Rosedale Roads, Albany,
Auckland 1310, New Zealand (a division of Pearson New Zealand Ltd.)
Penguin Books (South Africa) (Pty.) Ltd., 24 Sturdee Avenue,
Rosebank, Johannesburg 2196, South Africa

Penguin Books Ltd., Registered Offices:
80 Strand, London WC2R 0RL, England

First published by Onyx, an imprint of New American Library,
a division of Penguin Group (USA) Inc.

First Printing, May 2005
10 9 8 7 6 5 4 3 2 1

 REGISTERED TRADEMARK—MARCA REGISTRADA

Printed in the United States of America

PUBLISHER'S NOTE
This is a work of fiction. Names, characters, places, and incidents either are the
product of the author's imagination or are used fictitiously, and any resemblance to
actual persons, living or dead, business establishments, events, or locales is entirely
coincidental.

BEFORE
I WAKE

Chapter 1

In thirty minutes the hooded executioner would administer the initial injection of sodium pentothal. If this were a movie, it would be time for the camera to cut to the black phone on the wall.

If it were a movie.

Every now and then, one of the occupants of the packed witness room glanced at the phone. As if by some kind of silent, primal signal, other eyes automatically followed. It was something that couldn't be helped, even though every person there was all but certain the phone on the wall would never ring.

This was Virginia. Virginia made it tougher than any other state for a death row inmate to win an appeal. Virginia was also quick to administer the death penalty, not believing in allowing an inmate to languish in prison.

Albert French, the man strapped to the table on the other side of the thick glass, had been found guilty for the heinous murders of a Virginia couple. It wasn't his only claim to fame. He'd also committed murder in three other states—that they knew of. Virginia just happened to be the best place to get his punishment dealt with quickly and efficiently. Some thought, a little too efficiently.

Special Agent Nathan Fury had hoped for a delay while the U.S. District Court reconsidered its decision to allow the execution to be webcast. It wasn't just that Fury disapproved of turning the execution into sport and entertainment; he also worried about the impact of channeling a madman's last minutes of life into private residences worldwide.

At that very moment, home viewers were watching a pretty blond reporter, microphone in hand, standing just outside the prison gates, counting down the minutes until they switched to the death chamber camera.

Dick Clark's Rockin' Eve on acid.

Most of the twenty-five witness chairs were filled. People stood awkwardly in the back of the room, arms crossed, staring straight ahead as if the glass were a movie screen.

Someone bumped Fury's arm.

He pulled his gaze from the man on the table to a priest dressed in a black robe and clerical collar standing beside him. Fury had never seen him before.

The priest shook his head. "The medium is the message. That's what it's come down to. Who said that?" the priest asked. "The medium is the message?"

"Marshall McLuhan," Fury told him. "Prophetic, wasn't it?"

"People say it's their constitutional right to view an execution, but they're wrong. I don't even know why they're wrong," the priest said. "The way I see it, a man doesn't have to know the reason. That's why we have a conscience. So we don't have to sit down and hammer it out, look at this view and that view. If something is wrong, you feel it—here." He poked at his stomach. "In your gut."

"My mother was afraid it would be on TV and she might stumble across it while channel surfing," Fury said. "I told her it could only be viewed on her computer, and that she'd have to order it special." He grimaced. Special. What would that look like on next month's credit card bill? Something like *Kill Al*, *$19.95.*

Sick.

The priest kissed the cross that hung around his neck and moved to a reserved front-row seat.

French had refused a visit from clergy. The priest was probably hoping for a last-minute change of heart so he could administer absolution. If not, he would still pray for the murdering bastard.

Some people thought God forgave a killer as long as he repented.

Not Fury's god.

Nothing made sense, and religion just confused the issue.

"My son's eyes are in him," said a voice that was old and shaky and troubled.

To Fury's right, in the spot the priest had vacated, stood a tiny, frail woman with white hair. Her cheeks were crisscrossed with wrinkles. She wore a yellow badge, indicating she was family of one of the victims.

"Pardon me?" Fury leaned closer.

The room seemed silent, but if you listened closely there was a murmur, a nervous, contained panic that translated to a hum. Like a transistor radio tuned to nothing.

"I was sitting down in front, and he looked at me." The woman gestured with a thin arm. "Right at me. When he did, I saw my son. The son he killed, staring back at me." She put a hand to her throat. "I thought I'd die."

Fury searched his mind for something reassuring to say. "This is an emotionally charged situation," he offered. "It's easy to get confused or pick up on things that aren't really there."

"No, it was him," the woman insisted. "My son is in there. Inside that man. I don't know how, but he is. Haven't you heard about that? How a killer takes something from his victims? A trophy. Well, he must've taken a piece of my son's soul." She pulled in an old breath. "Now Albert French is going to die. I wanted him dead. He deserves to be dead." Her arms began to shake violently. "But I didn't know my son was in there! Inside him!"

As Fury looked on in dismay, all words of comfort gone, the old woman's eyes rolled back in her head and she began to fold.

He caught her before she hit the floor. Bending, he hefted her into his arms. She couldn't weigh more than ninety pounds.

All parchment skin stretched across hollow bones.

Two EMTs appeared.

It wasn't uncommon for witnesses to need medical care. Fury had attended an execution where the father of the victim had a heart attack and died at the exact same time the convicted killer's heart stopped beating.

Unsettling as hell.

A physician was on site to examine French's body and sign the death certificate. He materialized from the viewing room crowd. Some people turned to see what was happening. Others continued to stare straight ahead at the man behind the glass.

Someone held the door open, and Fury carried the poor woman to a gurney parked against a wall in the hallway. He stepped back and let the EMTs do their work.

The old woman was already coming around.

They would give her a sedative along with something to help her sleep tonight.

She would be okay. For now. Until she woke up tomorrow and started thinking.

Execution didn't help. That's what most families said. They waited and waited and waited for this day, thinking it would somehow ease the tearing, gnawing pain that never stopped, never went away. But when it was over, when the killer's dead body was stuffed into the plastic bag and hauled off, most people said it didn't help. The pain was still there.

Waiting for the execution had been a carrot, something that had kept them going. A promise of relief.

Fury returned to the back of the viewing room to stand against the wall.

Almost time.

French was alone in the death chamber.

The webcast operators were crouched over their equipment, waiting to switch from the outdoor to the indoor camera.

Five minutes to midnight.

The director gave the signal to begin the indoor feed.

Lights, camera, action.

The warden spoke to the prisoner through the intercom. "Would you like to make a last statement prior to your scheduled execution?"

A recorder was running, documenting the verbal exchange.

"Would you like to make your peace with God?" the warden asked.

French looked out at the crowd, scanning the people one by one, his gaze finally locking on the camera. "I'm not sorry for anything," he said clearly. "I'd do it all again if I had the chance. Never felt more alive than when I was killing someone."

French's wrists were bound with leather straps, but he managed to bend his hand enough to throw the world the finger.

Fury glanced at the black wall phone.

It was time.

The phone wasn't going to ring.

French looked directly at him, directly into Fury's eyes. He smiled.

The first syringe, loaded with sodium pentothal, emptied into French, putting him to sleep. One minute later the syringe of Pavulon, a muscle relaxant, entered his bloodstream.

The room was silent. The only thing Fury could hear was the pounding of his own heart.

Potassium chloride was administered.

Did they suffer?

No one knew the answer to that question. It looked peaceful, because the recipient was paralyzed. If he did feel pain, there was no way to physically respond, no way he could writhe or cry out.

Death was announced ten minutes later, the camera zooming in on Albert French's face.

The killer's dead eyes were open wide, staring into the camera lens, staring out from computer screens around the world, seeming to silently communicate a desire, a want, an evil that could be passed from the dying to the living.

Speaking directly to Fury and everyone out there in computerland.

"Agent Fury?"

A young guard handed Fury an envelope with his name written across it in small, cramped letters. "I was supposed to give you this."

Fury opened the envelope and pulled out a sheet of lined paper, folded three times. A note written in the same cramped letters.

Dear Agent Fury,

Just thought you might find it amusing to know that I didn't kill those people in Ohio. Wish I did, but I didn't. I killed everybody else, but not the lovely Ohio couple.

Yours truly,
Albert French

Fury slowly refolded the letter and leaned against the wall. It was his turn to get dizzy.

French had confessed to the Davis murders. The Ohio murders. It had been his MO from beginning to end.

Fury tended to believe deathbed confessions, but French's little farewell note could simply be a final head game. One final fuck you.

But if it was the truth . . . ?

It meant the real killer was still out there.

Chapter 2

It was good for business to accept drinks from customers. It created a feeling of camaraderie. It kept them buying. Kept them drinking. Kept them from leaving to spend money in one of the other seedy bars in town.

Sometimes Arden Davis would simply open beers and let them pile up in front of her, or dump them when the customer wasn't looking. Other times, like tonight, she would do her best to keep up. Five so far, with two waiting. She would have a headache tomorrow.

The man doing the buying was someone new, someone she hadn't seen before.

That's how it was. The bar drew a lot of locals, but it also drew single men, usually salesmen, on the road and lonely, stopping for drinks and a bed, maybe even sex if they got lucky.

The man buying her drinks was attractive.

She didn't know his name.

His hair was gray, cut close to his head.

He had blue eyes. Amazing eyes. Intense blue

eyes that made her uneasy and a little bit excited at the same time.

When he'd first appeared, she thought he was about forty, dressed in a black suit that was out of place in the dark bar. But then, when he was near enough to slide onto a bar stool, she realized he was younger. One of those guys who'd gone prematurely gray.

The tiny desert town of Artesia was located in southern New Mexico, halfway between Roswell and Carlsbad on Highway 285. On the east side of town was the Aztec Oil Refinery rising out of the desert floor, all black grime and dull metal, towering over everything, producing heavy, petroleum-laden fumes that permeated the town unless the wind was out of the west.

You got used to the smell and the dullness the fumes left in your head.

There was no reason for anyone to stop in Artesia unless forced by an overheated engine or exhaustion. Back in the seventies the town had experienced a brief flutter of unwanted glory and attention when David Bowie came to film *The Man Who Fell to Earth*. The production company had been looking for a desolate landscape and an atmosphere of bleak alienation. They found it in Artesia.

Months ago Arden Davis was cruising for a new life when she took what she thought would be a shortcut to El Paso and ended up in Artesia.

Rent was cheap. The air had been out of the west that day, and the local one-stop Holiday Motel was advertising for a bartender. It seemed like destiny.

"What time do you get off?" the gray-haired man asked.

There were five other people in the bar: two guys playing pool, three people sitting in a booth, keeping the jukebox busy with belly-rubbing country tunes. "I stop serving at one o'clock," Arden said. "And kick everybody out at half past."

He nodded and ordered another drink for both of them.

The portable phone rang. Arden caught it on the second ring, lifting the receiver to her ear. It smelled like cigarette smoke and somebody else's breath.

"Arden?" the voice at the other end said. "It's me. Harley."

Harley Larson. Like her, he'd been recruited for Project TAKE. Through a Killer's Eyes. They'd been FBI special agents not many years out of the academy, and it had been an honor to be invited to participate. It had been exciting as hell.

"I'm going back to West Virginia," Harley said. "To the Hill."

Something heavy landed in the pit of Arden's stomach, and her heart began to hammer. She hunched her shoulders and slipped through the swinging metal doors that led to the kitchen and privacy.

"Why?" she whispered.

"They need my help solving a recent homicide."

For a period of about ten years, the FBI's Behavioral Science Unit had been the star, the darling of Quantico. Profiling and the rise to fame of profilers like John Douglas and Robert Ressler, men who'd gone on to write books and inspire movies, had been the rage. Police departments sent officers to the FBI training grounds to learn the ropes. But as time went on, it was found that profiling had its limitations, and many trainees couldn't put into practice what they'd learned once they returned home. Even the biggest names within the Behavioral Science Unit were making fairly serious mistakes with serious consequences.

So they bumped things up and started Project TAKE.

"Don't go," she begged.

"Hey, you should come too," Harley said with a smile in his voice. "It'll be like old times."

"I could never do that." She tried to hide her panic by taking comfort in the awareness of a landscape of dead neon and a lonely road a few steps away. A foreign, stark world of sorrow that made her chest ache and somehow also made her feel a little bit alive.

New Mexico was so far from West Virginia. So damn far. Almost another planet. Certainly another life. "I could never go back."

I can breathe in this place. At least I can breathe.

"Everything okay in there?"

The gray-haired man. She'd forgotten about him. She'd erased him. That's what she did. Erased people.

Like she'd erased her brother, Daniel.

How long had she been talking to Harley?

Time for her often refused to move in a normal way. It moved so *slowly*. And so *fast*. She finally understood why some people left Christmas decorations up all year. Why take them down when the damn holiday was just going to come squealing around the corner again?

"I have to go," she told Harley.

"Be careful," he said. "There are bad people out there."

She told him good-bye and disconnected.

By twelve thirty, she and the gray-haired man were the only ones left in the building. "Would you like to come to my room?" he asked, not wasting any time. "Have a drink? Talk?"

She gave him a smile. "I'll lock up early."

She was drunk. Lonely. Not staggering-around, slurry-speech drunk, but feeling no pain, which was always a good state to be in.

Arden didn't bother to count the evening's earnings, leaving it in the register. The man helped refill the beer cooler and carry the dirty glasses to the sink. If she wasn't too hungover, she'd wash them tomorrow morning before Linda came in for the early shift.

She shut off the lights. She locked up and turned on the alarm. Together she and the gray-haired man in the dark suit left the bar and headed in the direction of the motel rooms.

His room.

The Holiday had two floors, all with orange doors that faced out. A sprinkling of cars dotted the parking lot, most from out of state. A few families on their way to Carlsbad Caverns. The others salesmen, on their way to El Paso.

At night Artesia seemed different, magical. It was

so silent, the sky a vast blanket of black velvet with more stars than Arden had ever seen in her life. In the far distance, the oil refinery twinkled like a Christmas tree.

Inside the room, the man locked the door, then slid the chain into place. He didn't turn on a light.

That was okay.

Dark was good.

He pulled the curtain open a few inches so light from the parking lot washed away some of the shadows. "Have a seat." He motioned to one of the two striped chairs at a round table with a pole lamp running through the center.

The room smelled like stale cigarettes, with a hint of old body odor. The man looked even more out of place in the cheap motel room than he had in the bar. As alien as David Bowie had most likely looked in the little town.

Arden rubbed her nose and made a mental note to suggest the owner get some kind of plug-in air fresheners. Holding the door open with a chair while the maid cleaned just wasn't cutting it.

She expected the man to remove his jacket and tie. Instead, he sat down across from her at the little brown table.

Maybe he really *did* want to talk.

Silence grew around them. "Do you have anything to drink?" she finally asked.

"I think you've had enough."

What?

She stared at him. Or tried to stare. A rectangle of light cut across the table, enough to illuminate his hand, which rested on the smooth surface, but cast his face in deeper shadow.

No wedding band. But that didn't mean he was single.

"Do you do this often, Arden?" He sounded disapproving. "Go to rooms with men you don't even know?"

What was happening here? She sat up straighter, trying to shake off the alcohol. "That's none of your business."

Through a haze, it suddenly occurred to her that he wasn't drunk. He was sober and alert.

Predatorial.

Her neck hair tingled, and she thought of Harley's warning.

She dropped a hand to her ankle, feeling for the little Smith & Wesson she used to wear. Not there.

He'd called her Arden. Had she told him her name?

Something is very wrong here.

In one swift motion, she jumped to her feet and lunged for the door. Before she could get the chain free, he was there, his hand on hers, his grip hard and forceful.

Chapter 3

Arden jabbed an elbow into the man's stomach, and slammed a heel down on his foot. He let out a grunt and threw his weight against her, pinning her to the door.

She would at least leave a mark on him. Something for the police to see, to question. She reached up to rake her nails down his face. She would dig deep. She would scar him.

His next words stopped her.

"I'm FBI," he said through gritted teeth, his voice edged with pain. "FBI."

A chill moved up her. "Show me your ID."

He remained pressed against her. While her heart thundered in her chest, she heard and felt him fiddling with his jacket. Suddenly something was slapped against the door above her head. A leather ID folder. The kind she used to carry.

She could barely make out the logo. She couldn't distinguish his photo or name. "I can't see it." But she knew he was telling the truth.

"You've seen enough." He released her and stepped back, returning the case to his jacket.

Her legs were weak. She collapsed in the chair, her heart continuing to race.

"Why didn't you just tell me who you were?" She struggled to appear outwardly cool. "Why did you trick me into thinking you were interested in me?"

"I told you the truth. I wanted to talk. In private."

"Oh, come on. You plied me with drinks."

He let out a laugh. "Plied?"

She should have known he was FBI. It couldn't have been more obvious. "I have nothing to say to you or anyone from the Bureau."

He dropped into the seat across from her. "We want you back, Arden."

The way he said her name gave her a weird feeling in the pit of her stomach.

How had things suddenly taken such a turn? "Who are you?" she asked as she stared hard at his undefined shape, unable to make out any features. She reached up and turned on the light attached to the table.

Sharp angles. That prematurely gray hair. Blue, blue eyes.

"Just think of me as a relative," he said. "Uncle Sam. Your friendly recruiting officer."

"I'm done with the Bureau." First they came for Harley; now they were coming for her.

She had no logical reason for the terror and unease that gripped her, but she knew she couldn't go back.

"They aren't done with you."

Was he someone she'd once known?

The FBI liked to play little games, and secrecy for the sake of secrecy seemed to top their list.

You could have known him once.

Had she?

Maybe. Maybe not.

Her memory had been adjusted. Tampered with. Erased.

"We just want you back," he said calmly, practically.

Arden tried to imagine herself in another location other than where she was. The thought scared the hell out of her. "I'm busy. I have a life."

Tomorrow they were getting a new beer cooler. The following night the punk karaoke guy was coming from Las Cruces. Probably wouldn't go over well in Artesia, but Arden had been looking forward to it for a month. "I've promised friends I'd help them move this weekend."

"Do you really have a life here?" He sounded smug. "Have you told any of those friends about yourself? About what you used to do? Who you used to be?"

"I don't want them to know. I don't want that old life to contaminate my new one."

"Then how can they really be your friends? If they don't even know who you are?"

"I'm not an agent anymore." Why had she even tried to explain anything to him?

"How can they be your friends when they will never know the most important facts about you?" he asked. "Never know what imprinted and continues to imprint your life?"

She knew the life she'd built for herself wasn't real. It was cardboard. Full of props that she'd clung to for their very bland familiarity. Boring was what she craved, needed, embraced. Give her boring any day of the week.

"It's like having company every night," the guy she worked for had told her when she accepted the bartending job. "You just talk to people and get them drinks. What a great job. Pretty soon the locals start treating you as if you're family, and you get worried if they don't come in. You call their house to see if everything's okay. Yessirree, we're one happy family around here."

Maybe the idea of family had appealed to her. She didn't have a family. Well, there was her brother, but he hated her.

"We need your help," the man told her.

She let out a loud, sarcastic laugh. Her heart had settled down now that the initial shock was over. *"My help?"* Was he trying to arouse her patriotism with verbal propaganda, or was it simply naive flag-waving on his part? Then again, maybe he knew better but was just doing his job.

"Being a lab rat was fun for a while," she said, "but it doesn't appeal to me anymore."

"You were a lot more than a lab rat. You know that. And the program has been tweaked. Perfected."

What difference had it made in the end? she wondered. Dead was dead.

"They no longer use Cottage 25 or the tanks."

The tanks . . . *Jesus*. She didn't want to think about them.

The idea behind Project TAKE had been straight-forward. Using sensory deprivation and something called psychic driving—a term coined by the late Dr. Ewen Cameron of the Allen Memorial Institute in Montreal—test subjects were inundated with infor-mation about handpicked serial killers, mass mur-derers, spree killers, in an attempt to make them see the world through the killer's eyes, thus making them a crucial component in determining a killer's next step before he made it.

At the Webber Research Institute on the Hill, sub-jects were saturated with every shred of info that could be dug up on a specific killer, including the most trivial childhood stories supplied by relatives and often the incarcerated killer himself. Informa-tion about girlfriends, schools, cars. Home life. The whole package.

In Cottage 25, under the watchful eye of Dr. Phillip Harris, subjects were locked in isolation chambers and fed the recordings of the confessions of madmen. The killers took them by the hand and walked them through their own personal landscapes of death, beckoning them to join their cult of evil.

Adopt him. Accept him as your own personal savior, someone in the program had joked. *Get to know the guy inside and out.*

At least that had been the plan.

Shortly after the project began, many of the care-fully screened test subjects dropped out, some after only a few hours of isolation. The ones who re-

mained experienced sleep irregularities, along with
spatial and tactile shifts, lack of concentration, and
the big one: memory loss.

Instead of stepping into a killer's mind, they'd
stepped out of their own and lost a little of themselves.

She and Harley had stayed. She and Harley had
become poster children for the project. Arden had remained out of sheer stubbornness. Harley . . . She
didn't know what had driven him. Maybe a desire
for fame. Because wasn't it every profiler's dream to
catch the big one?

"We've been watching you," the agent said
bluntly.

His unapologetic admission made her feel uneasy
and exposed.

"We know everything you've been doing."

"I don't think I want to get involved with such Big
Brother mentality."

"You can't keep on like this," he told her softly in
a concerned voice that suddenly made her throat
tighten and her eyes burn.

"What do you mean?" she asked, struggling for
self-control. "I've found my niche here."

"You've been playing a role. Can't you see you've
done nothing more than step into someone else's
life?"

"How do you know what I'm thinking? Feeling?
And isn't stepping into a life what it's all about? Isn't
that what I was taught to do?" She'd learned her les-
sons well.

"I familiarized myself with your file," he said. "I

know who you used to be, and I know who you are now."

"What's wrong with striving for a new kind of contentment? I look at other people doing the same thing. They're happy."

"They are nothing like you. They will never understand you."

In her mind, the flimsy cardboard life receded like a TV show she may have once been addicted to, all the while feeling guilty for the addiction because she recognized it for the fluff it was.

Escapism.

It had been okay for a while. But lately she felt what was left of her identity slipping away. In the middle of the night she would wake up with a sense of panic. Who was she? Who was Arden Davis? What if this really became her life?

She'd wanted to get as far away from who she'd been as possible. But when confronted with the thought of the drudgery and bleakness never ceasing, of her circumstances never changing, the novelty wore thin.

The scent of the gray-haired man seemed familiar, in the way the compressed paper of an old record album found in a cellar was familiar, yet distant.

"Do I know you?" she asked.

"No."

His answer came quickly. Had there been a flash of something in his face? Or was it just her imagination, another false reality?

Somehow familiar, yet not. He reminded her of someone she'd once known from a time she'd forgotten. A time that had been erased from her memory. Not out of cruelty, but to give her a chance at a normal life, because painful, guilt-ridden memories crippled. And now here was the FBI, begging her to come back.

They called it bleaching. Untested, experimental, done only to her, because she'd wanted it. What they didn't know, what she'd never told anybody, was that the bleaching hadn't quite been able to silence the killer's voice inside her head.

Since she'd left the study center in Madeline, a small town in a remote area of West Virginia, a few shadowy memories had returned. Blurry hints of what had been, the bad things she'd seen. She was afraid that one day the memories would all come back.

She didn't try to remember.

She didn't want to remember.

She wanted to be content. She wanted to be one of those people who didn't think, only reacted. Who went to happy hour for beer and free chicken wings. Who laughed at tedious jokes. She wanted desperately to be that person, but all along, in the same way she could never get used to the desert and the refinery puffing out its choking smoke, she knew she'd failed.

Laughter.

Parents.

Family.

Not her. Someone else.

Blood. So much blood.

How many liters in a man? A woman? A child?

"That gray hair ... Where'd you get that gray hair?" she asked, trying to change the subject.

"I'm not here to talk about me."

"I'll bet you were hiding in a dark closet, went for the chain above your head to turn on the light, but grabbed a cadaver's hand instead."

That got a little burst of laughter from him, followed by a reluctant smile. He reached inside the breast pocket of his jacket and pulled out a small folder with an airline logo.

"Ticket." He slapped the packet on the table. "Your flight leaves in two days."

Be there, or be square.

Ten-four, Eleanor.

"Don't worry. We aren't on the same flight. I'm taking off tomorrow morning."

"You bought a ticket without consulting me?"

She wasn't somebody they could push around. She wasn't the kind of person to come running at the snap of someone's fingers. That was one thing she knew about herself. "You're assuming a lot."

"Look at it this way. You can come back, or you can keep hitting on strange men and eventually end up a statistic. The choice seems obvious."

"Don't you get it? We're all statistics."

"Some just sooner than others?"

"Do you work in Behavioral Science?"

"It's called NCAVC now, remember? National Center for Analysis of Violent Crime."

She could smell him again.

The odor of secret things locked up in storage. Boxes of paperback novels that had grown moldy from the dampness. A leather ball glove. Incense and half-burned candles. Faded jeans and flannel shirts.

Someone else's past.

His past, not hers.

She wanted to go back to fifteen minutes ago.

Erase and rewind.

She wanted to forget this conversation had ever taken place. They would go to bed together. He would kiss her. Hold her. Pull her away from the edge.

"French was executed," the man suddenly announced.

"I know." Was he trying to shake her? "The whole country knows."

"Did you watch it?"

She wanted to lie in order to stop the direction of the conversation, but she had the idea he already knew the truth. "Yes." Some people said that seeing the killer die never brought closure, but she'd felt relief when French had taken his last breath. The man who killed her parents no longer existed. Maybe now he would get out of her head.

He nodded. "Thought you would."

She hadn't wanted to. But she couldn't *not* watch it.

"Something interesting happened a week later," he said casually.

"Oh?"

"A murder." He paused. "Of a rural family in northeast Oklahoma. Killed with French's MO."

She looked up sharply. "Copycat? Someone carrying on his work?"

"Maybe."

"That's why you want me back?"

"Yes."

Fear fluttered in her stomach.

Fear.

She'd forgotten what fear felt like.

The worst feeling in the world.

As she watched him, she got the uneasy feeling that he wasn't done, that he had another card to play. "Why me?" she asked.

"You were one of the best."

"*Were.*" Her mouth was dry. She swallowed. "Past tense."

She couldn't go back. Or maybe more to the point, she couldn't make herself leave the safety of the desert. "Arden Davis no longer exists."

Most people would have said, "Yes, she does. She's in there somewhere." Instead, he watched, silently acknowledging that she could be right.

She picked up the small folder and pulled out the ticket.

A flight from Albuquerque to Charleston, West Virginia.

A line from an old TV show popped into her head: *Your assignment, should you choose to accept it . . .*

What was the name of the show? Something her father had liked . . .

Her mind clicked shut.

She returned the ticket to the folder and handed it to him. "No, thanks. I'll have to pass."

"One more thing about French." He stared hard into her eyes, issuing a challenge. For a fraction of a second, something flitted across his face, and she got the idea he didn't want to tell her what he was about to tell her. "He recanted." He paused. "He denied killing your parents."

Nausea washed over her, and her heart flopped in her chest.

No.

She didn't want to believe it. She stared into the stranger's blue eyes, looking for some sign of a lie. She saw none. "But he confessed."

The agent slowly blinked. "I know."

"What about evidence? There must have been evidence."

"The crime scene was compromised by the local cops. It was chaos. They'd never seen anything like what they found that day."

What they'd found was what she no longer remembered. What had been erased from her mind.

"And we didn't need it. We had him on the Virginia homicides. We knew Virginia would take care of him and make sure he didn't kill again."

She could taste her fear. It was metallic. Or maybe she'd bitten her tongue.

Make it stop. Make it all go away.

Arden had been instrumental in catching French. The first time. Her profile had led detectives to him. From there, a DNA match and the murder weapon—a butcher knife—had sealed the case.

By that time, the FBI was feeling pretty proud of Project TAKE, and the media was touting Arden as a superprofiler.

She'd been there for the arrest. With French's

hands cuffed behind him, he'd smiled broadly, his pupils glazed and flat. "You're next on my list, sweet pea," he'd said before being roughly tucked into the backseat of the police car.

Two months later, French escaped while being transported to a hospital for treatment of what they thought was a massive heart attack.

He wasn't caught for three months.

That's when Arden really began to study him in depth. That's when she slipped under his skin and saw the world through his eyes. That's when he came after her family—or so they thought. Shortly after the Davis killings, he was recaptured and confessed to the murder of Arden's parents.

Now he was dead—and the killer was very possibly still out there.

Her palms were sweating. "Maybe he was lying."

"Maybe he wasn't. Maybe the webcast set off the real perpetrator, and now he's killing again."

The agent was watching her closely again. She couldn't stop staring at his blue eyes.

"What if French didn't kill your family?" he asked.

"You want me to come back to work on my parents' case?"

Were they insane? Were they trying to drive her completely, wrist-slitting mad? That was like asking a doctor to perform open-heart surgery on his wife. Or a mortician to embalm his own kid.

The agent just stood there watching her, suddenly looking sad.

I can't do this. I'm not strong enough.

"I'm sorry."

He really did seem sorry.

His sympathy, whether false or real, made her eyes burn. "There has to be someone else." She blinked. "Harley. What about Harley Larson?"

"You were better than Harley."

The agent claimed to know all about her. Evidently, he didn't know everything. *I'm broken now. Don't you get that? Don't you understand?*

The murder of her parents was *her* fault. She'd brought the killer to their house. Her parents would still be alive if she hadn't been involved in the project.

But if French hadn't murdered them . . . ? What did that mean? *What the hell did that mean?* Their deaths still had to be somehow connected to him. And connected to her. It was too much of a coincidence to have been random.

She put out her hand. Her eyes were swimming with tears, and she could hardly see. "Give me that damn ticket."

Chapter 4

Nathan Fury lay on his back across the double bed, computer on his lap, all the while aware of Arden Davis just a few doors away.

He'd hoped to be able to convince her to return without revealing Albert French's final denial. He hadn't wanted to dump that on her. Not now, anyway. Not so soon. He would have preferred to wait until after she'd had time to adjust to being back on the Hill.

But in true Arden Davis fashion, she'd refused to budge, and he'd been forced to take her all the way.

He didn't think he'd soon forget the look on her face when he'd told her. Disbelief. Pain. Denial. Acceptance. Then pain again.

Everybody in the Bureau thought she was a lost cause. A casualty of war. He hoped she'd prove them wrong.

He knew the basics of Arden Davis.

He knew she was thirty years old, five feet, ten inches tall, 140 pounds, with red hair and green eyes.

He knew who Arden Davis used to be.

Favorite books: *Catcher in the Rye* and *Stranger in a Strange Land*.

Favorite movies: *Midnight Cowboy* and *The Birds*.

Favorite music: the Pogues, the Waterboys, Neil Young. She used to know all the words to "Heart of Gold" and "Fairytale of New York."

He knew about childhood injuries like the broken arm she'd gotten while ice-skating on the pond behind her farmhouse. How close she'd been to her grandmother, and how her grandmother's death had sent her into a deep depression that had lasted over a year.

Davis liked both cats and dogs, but was more of a dog person. She'd had a black dog named Zeke that had slept on the end of her bed and kept her company when she had chicken pox. The chicken pox was caught at Sunday school from a girl named Molly. Molly's mother had claimed her daughter was no longer contagious, but she'd arrived in the church basement covered with scabs and smelling of fever. While Molly was in the basement passing the infection around, her mother was caught screwing a guy in the bathroom of a nearby gas station.

Ah, nothing like small-town living.

At one time, Davis could run like hell. She'd won high school track team long-distance awards. She'd always been athletic, and it made sense that she would choose a sport and event like long distance that relied more on the individual than a team. No basketball or volleyball in her history. Group sports wouldn't have appealed to Arden Davis then or now.

He had copies of poems she'd written during times of duress and loss.

First boyfriend. Second and third boyfriends. When and where she'd lost her virginity. A date rape in college.

Copies of the diaries she'd kept on and off through junior high, high school, and a little bit of college. Last December's murders that had led to her present decline.

And then volunteering to be bleached.

She was either extremely gutsy or extremely desperate. Probably a little of both.

If Fury could have been selective, there were things in his past he would have liked to erase. But you couldn't choose what to take out and what to leave in—although he had a theory that Arden Davis's bleaching had something to do with her own subliminal desire to forget, like amnesia brought on by shock and trauma.

She'd forgotten what and who she'd wanted to forget—with a sprinkling of a few additional holes.

His briefcase held photographs of Arden, along with her family, friends, associates, pets—some of the visuals courtesy of the FBI.

He sifted through the photos.

Birthday shots. A photo taken in the front yard of her rural Ohio home, a two-story white farmhouse, an immaculately clean John Deere tractor in the background. Arden at age one wearing a ruffly dress with matching socks. Such a green, direct gaze for such a young child.

Arden at age thirteen posing with Zeke.

An idyllic life. The kind of life Albert French or Albert French aficionados liked to snuff.

In a more recent shot, snapped through a tele-photo lens just a few months ago, Arden's straight, chin-length red hair was so vivid it looked as if it had been colorized.

He stared at the photos, trying to connect the child to the woman from the bar.

Two different people.

He always said, You are what you remember. If that was true, then who was Arden Davis?

He pulled out another photo.

This one of Arden and a dark-haired man, taken near a mountain stream. They were sitting on a blan-ket, a picnic basket nearby, wineglasses in their hands. They'd set the automatic timer and put the camera on a tree stump. Shortly after the photo was taken, they'd made love.

Fury knew they'd made love because he was the man in the photo, the man with Arden Davis. The man she'd erased.

Chapter 5

Arden watched from the window of the 757 as it came in for a landing at Yeager Airport in Charleston, West Virginia, the airplane wheels making jarring contact with the ground.

That morning, Arden had bummed a predawn ride to Roswell from her coworker, Linda. From there, she'd taken a bus to Albuquerque International Airport, where an indirect flight left her with two hours to kill in Cincinnati before the last leg of her journey.

That had been the easy part. Now she had to get to Madeline, a West Virginia town that made Artesia look like a metropolis. There were no airplanes to Madeline. Few buses. From experience, she knew any kind of transportation to that remote locale was sporadic and tended to turn what should have been a two-hour drive into an all-day adventure. Renting a car seemed the logical choice.

Approaching the baggage carousel, she spotted a young man with curly blond hair holding a sign with Arden's name printed across it in large Magic Marker letters.

They'd sent someone to pick her up.

She gave the kid a goofy, *here I am* wave.

His mouth opened and he bobbed his head and grinned in acknowledgment. He lumbered over, still displaying the sign, realized what he was doing, and dropped it to his side. "Hey." He held out his hand. "I'm Eli."

He had a firm but damp grip.

He stared at her for too long, with an expression Arden would call hero worship if she didn't know better.

She had to recheck his sign to make sure her name was really on it.

Her bag shot out of the hopper and she moved into retrieval position.

"Yours?" Eli grabbed the handle of the large green duffel as it came around, letting out a loud, surprised groan as he hefted it from the carousel to the floor.

Eli was one of those tall, thin, geeky types who was all skinny legs and arms. He wore jeans and a two-tone orange T-shirt that was too small. Ten years ago, he would have been into Dungeons and Dragons.

"Sorry it's so heavy." She didn't have much in the way of belongings, but when everything you owned went into one bag, that bag could weigh a lot. "Here." She grabbed the nearest handle. "You get that end; I'll get this one."

Together, the bag between them, they shuffled awkwardly toward the exit doors.

His vehicle was a small, rust-tinged, cream-colored station wagon of some sort, the back plastered with band decals. Mostly Emo bands like Dashboard Confessional and Alkaline Trio.

They hefted in Arden's bag. Eli tossed in the sign with her name on it, slammed the back door, and they were off.

Five minutes into the drive, they hit the hilly, rural landscape of West Virginia, driving down a narrow road that twisted back on itself, winding through thick stands of trees with warning signs that looked like question marks.

Arden checked her watch, hoping her Dramamine hadn't worn off.

"You should have been here two weeks ago." Eli braked for a hairpin curve. "The colors were awesome. But then it rained and now it's over."

It was a gray day, the tree trunks black and glistening, their branches stripped except for a few of the more tenacious varieties. A deep layer of fallen yellow leaves covered the ground. Arden could smell the humid, mulched-earth scent seeping through the air vents.

Eli was nervous and talking too much.

He told her that he and his friends worked at the Hill doing odd jobs, trying to make money for college. He told her that people there were expecting her, and that someone would show her around and give her the scoop on everything once she arrived.

"My friends and I . . . we aren't involved in TAKE. We're guinea pigs for an unrelated, unaffiliated side project."

"What kind of project?"

"Listening to music to see if it improves memory. Stuff like that."

She nodded. He was so young. So enthused and energetic.

About Daniel's age . . .

She'd tried to call her brother a few times. She'd picked up the phone and dialed. Dialed *that* number. A number from her past. From a world and a life that no longer existed.

The first time, she couldn't speak. She opened her mouth, but nothing came out—while Daniel was on the other end, getting more annoyed by the second.

The next time, she was told the number had been disconnected.

I'll just go there, she'd thought. To Lake County, Ohio. It would be better to go there. Better to see him face-to-face. Because a phone call wasn't enough. A phone call wouldn't fix anything.

It can't be fixed.

You can't fix it.

He can't fix it.

Done is done, and dead is dead.

Not her thoughts. Someone else's. Remnants of Albert French lingering in her brain.

She sometimes thought of French as something smoky, something that curled around in her skull, settling deep into cracks and crevices, into places where ideas and egos liked to hide. . . .

Eli's prattle was a hum in her ear, no distinct words that she could turn into pictures in her head. Worse than white noise, but not as bad as Muzak.

Then the signs came.

MADELINE 20 MILES

The signs made it real.

MADELINE 16 MILES

When they reached the five-mile marker, she sat
up straighter, her body tense and bent slightly forward.

Five miles in rural West Virginia were like twenty
somewhere else. Arden had forgotten that. Forgotten
how long it took to get from point A to point B.

Forever and never.

Especially when your heart was racing and you
didn't want to arrive at your destination.

They topped the last hill.

There was the town. There was Madeline. So cute
and cozy and innocuous. Red brick and church
spires peeking out from behind clusters of trees.

The scene would make a nice greeting card.

The town had been laid out in a deep valley surrounded by hills. A teacup, residents liked to say, the
distance from rim to rim only a few miles.

Sheltered. Protected. Isolated.

Her gaze shifted across the valley to the bluff
overlooking the town.

The asylum stared back, causing her heart to
jump.

She put a hand to her chest, and felt the rapid, er-
ratic pumping.

Am I breathing? I don't think I'm breathing.

She opened her mouth and inhaled, then exhaled.

There. Better.

Eli made a left turn, taking a new bypass around town, heading straight for the Hill.

If Arden were driving, she would pull over. Stop.

Hadn't she just left New Mexico a couple of hours ago?

She checked her watch. Not a couple of hours. Eighteen. Eighteen hours since she'd stood under a velvet-black star-filled sky, breathing refinery fumes.

This was a bad place.

She'd known it before, but now that she was here, now that they were circling up the steep drive, the tires on the wet brick pavement making a jarringly familiar humming sound. It took all of her willpower to keep from jumping out of the car.

Everything was happening too fast. She had to slow things down. She had to distract herself.

She spotted a man dressed in a plaid jacket walking a black Lab with a red nylon lead.

Dogs. Would her life ever be that normal again? Dog normal?

Maybe a cat would be better than a dog. More than one cat, so if she went away for a few days the cats could keep each other company.

But I really like dogs. . . .

But dogs were much needier. They expected things of you. They wanted to make you happy, and didn't like it if you stayed in bed all day. Cats, on the other hand, loved nothing better than a bed day.

Dogs like to play.

Arden couldn't see herself playing. Couldn't see

herself tossing a ball, then talking in a high-pitched, enthusiastic voice when the dog retrieved it.

Had she actually done that? Yes. Yes, she had.

Eli's voice brought her back to the reality she was trying to escape. "Do you remember this place?"

His question made her wonder how much he knew about her. "Yes."

The visual impact of the Hill was an imprint that had never blurred, never faded. Bleaching hadn't been able to remove it from her mind.

The asylum was massive. More like a town, or at least a large campus. At its zenith, it had boasted landscaped gardens with fountains, swans, and geese where the townspeople came to picnic on weekends. The brick for the buildings had been fired on site, dug from the very clay they now drove over.

Eli swung the car in the direction of the main building.

Five stories tall, with grand pillars and a sweeping staircase, it looked like something from the Natalie Wood weeper *Splendor in the Grass.*

Mom loved that movie.

Don't think about her. Especially not here.

This main architectural wonder was called Building 50, which never made sense to Arden, since it was the biggest structure and the center of everything. You'd think it would be called Building 1. Here it seemed that the larger the number, the greater the importance.

The asylum was part of a therapeutic movement that took hold in the nineteenth century. During a short span of time, close to two hundred mental hospitals sprang up in small towns around the United States. The stunningly beautiful and serene structures and grounds were designed by Thomas Kirkbride, a visionary and leader in the health reform movement.

Everything was visually aesthetic. Or had been at one time, before drugs became the main avenue of treatment and patients were kicked out on the street and hospitals closed, condemning the buildings to years of neglect.

Tall, thin panes of glass pressed down from above, at once imposing and grand, every window frame different in style and covered with ornate wrought iron, dwarfing and overpowering a person of stable mentality.

On either side of the main entrance were what had once been separate wings for males and females. Beyond that, a person would have once found buildings that contained the blacksmith's shop, power plant, bakery, upholstery shop, doctors' offices, and a separate hospital that had boasted a maternity ward and surgery.

Later in its history, the Madeline State Lunatic Asylum became the Madeline Mental Health Center, but most locals just called it the Hill.

Serene would not now describe the grounds that had once been referred to as an oasis for the mind and spirit. The place was bustling. Dust-covered construction trucks were parked at odd angles. Scaffolding and thick, semitransparent plastic had been set up over outer walls and windows. Men used hammers, chisels, and drills to remove old cement and replace it with new.

Beyond all that, hidden by buildings and landscape, was Cottage 25. . . .

Eli pulled the car to a stop in front of the pillared Building 50, near the old stone carriage steps. Together he and Arden dragged the duffel bag from the back and toted it up the stairs to the double doors.

He let go, straightened, and stood there. Arden waited, expecting him to leave.

The long good-bye was what Arden had always called this awkward moment when it was time for the characters to separate but it seemed something more should be said.

She didn't want him to go. She didn't want to turn and walk through the doors by herself.

A tip. He was probably waiting for a tip. She dug into her pocket and pulled out some bills. He waved the money away.

He was such a sweet kid. Standing there, he reminded her of Daniel.

Here she was, a person bleached, yet everything reminded her of something that hurt. It wasn't fair. It wasn't the way it was supposed to work. Bleaching should have taken away the pain. What good was it if it didn't do that?

Then Eli was gone. Down the stairs to his car.

She watched him go. Instead of making a U-turn, he continued up the road, going deeper into the grounds. There were many ways out.

When she could no longer see his car, Arden grabbed her bag and dragged it across the threshold and through the double doors, where she was met by a woman who introduced herself as Victoria. She was tall and thin, with dark, curly hair and red lipstick.

Arden followed her into a small office adjacent to the lobby.

"We're putting you on the fourth floor in what used to be the women's wing," Victoria explained. "You have a nice view of the park and town from there. I think when you were here before those rooms were closed, but the Hill has changed, and what was the men's wing is now an assisted and independent living facility."

An old-folks' home? The last time Arden had been on the Hill, the participants had roomed in the old Mercy Hospital, adjacent to Cottage 25. She was relieved to find that her new digs would be farther away.

Years ago, in order to save the asylum from crumbling into disuse and disrepair, the city had purchased it for a dollar. In return, the town council agreed to restore it to its original glory. In order to afford that restoration, the city rented out various buildings. Some of the residents had probably changed, but back in Arden's day, the main occupants had been the Webber Research Institute, a mental health clinic, physicians' offices, and a psychoanalysis wing.

"You have your initial consultation with Dr. Harris tomorrow morning at eight thirty." Victoria whipped out a photocopied map and circled one of the outer buildings with a red pen. "Go out the front doors, then take a right down Maple Lane. Webber Research Institute, located in the Mercy Unit, will be on your left, just past the power plant and black-smith shop."

Arden stared at the building labeled Cottage 25, her heart slamming. The FBI agent had said it was closed, that they were no longer using it, but it had long been rumored that a tunnel linked the Mercy Unit and Cottage 25.

"And Cottage 25?" Arden's voice echoed, and the vast space seemed to fill with bleak imprints of the past.

"Administration. But most of the building is in disuse. I think it's the next one slated for restoration."

Arden felt herself relax. "What about Harley? Harley Larson." She had to see Harley. Harley was the only one who would understand. Harley had been through what she'd been through.

Victoria frowned in thought. "Mr. Larson was here, but he didn't stay."

Arden tensed again.

"He left after a couple of hours, as I understand it."

"Why?"

Victoria shook her head. "I have no idea." She handed Arden a heavy gold key that was worn smooth.

A key. Even the Holiday in Artesia had upgraded to a card system.

"Unfortunately, the main lobby elevator is the

only one in working order right now. That is, except for service elevators."

Why had Harley left? Had coming back been too much for him? Or had he been turned down for the program? Would they turn her down?

All along she'd been thinking she would have Harley's support when she got here, that they would be a team once more, and be able to lean on each other.

Arden dragged her bag across the black-and-white-checkerboard lobby floor to the antique elevator, pushed the button, and waited.

When the brass doors finally jerked open, a shriveled old woman stood in the corner. "What are they serving?" she asked loudly. "I hope it's not turkey and mashed potatoes."

The woman shuffled off the elevator. She looked around. "Where's the lunchroom?" she asked, as if she were accusing Arden of making off with it.

Arden got herself and her bag into the elevator. The space was hot and stuffy. Taped next to the round, black basement button was a yellowed label that said LUNCHROOM.

"It's in the basement," Arden said.

"Huh?"

"You're on the wrong floor." This time she made sure she spoke with more volume.

"I am?" Panic set in. "Oh, oh."

Arden held the OPEN button while the woman got back inside.

"My daughter-in-law tricked me into coming here," the woman confided. "Told me it was just for a week, while she went on vacation. Been here six months. Don't have a car. Can't drive anyway. And where would I go? They sold my home. I don't have a home." She looked at Arden with eyes that were clear and lucid. "Is that why you're here? To visit your mother-in-law? Did you trick her into coming, too?"

"No, I'm staying in the women's wing. I don't have any relatives here."

"Good for you. My name's Vera. Vera Thompson. I suppose you think that's an old-lady name."

"I'm Arden."

Vera glanced around with that sudden, swift irritation old people often displayed. "Did you push the button, Arden?" Vera pointed. "Push the button."

Arden pushed the button. They shook and shimmied to the basement. The door opened.

"Turkey," Vera muttered as she exited the elevator for the second time, seeming to have completely forgotten Arden now that the food had presented itself. "I hate turkey." At the last minute, she turned back. "Lock your door before you go to bed. The shadow people run up and down the halls at night." She passed a tongue across dry lips. "And if somebody tells you they're taking you to stay at a rest home for a week, don't believe 'em."

The elevator door closed. Arden was happy to escape to the fourth floor.

Once there, she discovered Victoria had told her a skewed version of the truth. Arden's fourth-floor room did overlook the front drive, but the pair of six-foot-tall, wooden-framed windows hadn't been cleaned in years, and she could hardly see through the glass. There was also no chain lock or dead bolt on the door.

What was it with these people? Did they think serious crime didn't happen in small towns? Some of the bloodiest, most horrendous murders had taken place in sleepy, idyllic burgs in Middle America.

The room smelled old. Wood and plaster had absorbed and encapsulated the air of almost 150 years. No amount of paint or furniture polish or pine-scented air freshener could cover it up.

A piece of paper on a table near the bathroom listed amenities. For an additional fee, she could eat turkey downstairs. Also located at basement level were vending machines.

The room had a single bed, tidily made with a smooth, beige spread. She checked the bathroom. Claw-foot tub enclosed by a white, plastic shower curtain. Clean sink. Clean towels. New bar of wrapped soap.

Back in the sleeping area, she looked through the desk drawers. Empty except for a Gideon Bible. Those people got around.

The room was stuffy.

She undid the latch on one of the windows. It opened like a double door, swinging inward to expose wrought-iron bars.

The evening air was cool against Arden's face, but it didn't ease her claustrophobia. Outside, construction workers had gone home, and only a few cars dotted the parking lot.

Darkness was falling.

Arden needed to get away. Just for a little while, she assured herself.

She left the room, key in one pocket, cash and ID in the other. Rather than risk an encounter with the diners returning to their rooms, she took the stairs.

The lobby was deserted, the little office Victoria occupied closed.

Arden hurried out the front door and down the sweeping stairs. There was no sidewalk. She ran across a grassy area, clinging to the shadows of the buildings and evergreen trees.

I've done this before.

But not alone.

Someone had been with her. A man. A dark-haired man whose name and face she couldn't remember. Harley? Maybe it had been Harley.

They'd run down the hill, smothering their laughter, excited and thrilled to be out of the building.

It had been late summer.

Crickets had chirped and fireflies had flickered in the darker areas beneath the trees.

Years ago, patients had once farmed some of the asylum ground. They'd milked dairy cows and harvested apples from the orchard. On a slanting hillside that was much too steep to farm or graze, the dead had been buried. No real headstones. Just rows of numbers etched into four-by-six-inch granite slabs that stood upright, the numbers cross-referenced between the covers of a handwritten book.

That other night, while running down the steep slope with the dark-haired man, Arden had tripped over one of the numbers and had tumbled to the ground.

The man had plopped down beside her and they'd looked up at the stars.

Now Arden slowed, then stopped. She looked up. The sky was cloudy. No stars.

He'd kissed her. The night of their escape. Then, just as quickly, he'd jumped to his feet and given her a hand up. Together they'd run the rest of the way down the hill.

Arden thought of that night, trying to remember. . . .

They'd gone to a bar. Grumpy Steve's. Grumpy Steve's had pizza. It had darts. It had alcohol.

She needed a drink.

A drink would help. A drink always helped.

Chapter 6

Nathan Fury watched Arden disappear into Grumpy Steve's.

He waited in his rental car.

And waited.

After an hour, he gave up and went in after her, pausing just inside the door.

Grumpy's was a neighborhood bar, the kind with a pinball machine and Pac-man game in the corner. The walls were covered with old framed photos of Madeline, interspersed with the occasional mounted fish. A board on the wall advertised chili on Fridays, fried catfish on Saturdays. But their specialty was pizza.

A family with two small children sat along the far wall opposite the bar, one of the kids begging for change for the pinball machine. Two guys in dusty seed corn caps sat smoking and drinking at another table.

Arden was at the bar, dressed in jeans and a black T-shirt, navy blue jogging shoes hooked over the bar stool's footrest.

He crossed the room and slid onto the stool beside her.

She turned her head, glass in hand. Her eyebrows lifted in acknowledgment. She glanced at the suit he'd had on last time she'd seen him, then tilted her head and shook an ice cube into her mouth.

It had been cruel to bring her back here. He knew that. But her stint in New Mexico hadn't been doing her any good. Fury had been behind getting her reinvolved in the project and new investigation, and it had been a tough sell. Nobody else had thought it a good idea. And maybe it wasn't. Maybe he was just being selfish.

"Have you eaten?" he asked. "Want to split a pizza?"

She was a little drunk. Again. Her eyelids had that heavy look, and there was a slight smile at the corners of her mouth.

The old Arden hadn't been much of a drinker. He'd never seen her have more than a few glasses of wine or maybe an occasional mixed drink.

A coaster appeared in front of him. "What can I get you?" the female bartender asked. She was tall and blond, about fifty.

"Light beer. Whatever you have on draft."

Arden pushed her glass closer. "I'll have a refill."

The woman poured Arden a double shot. Bourbon on the rocks. Albert French's drink of choice.

"How about that pizza?" Fury asked again.

"Sure."

The bartender handed them both a laminated card that served as a menu.

Arden perused it quickly. "Mushroom, spinach, and pineapple."

It was what she'd ordered last time they'd been there.

"Sounds good to me. Medium should be fine." Fury grabbed his glass of beer. "Let's move to a booth."

She didn't argue, which at first surprised him. But once they were situated in a dark corner, her reason for agreeing became obvious.

"Now are you going to tell me your name?" She leaned forward, arms crossed on the varnished tabletop.

"Nathan." He waited a moment, hoping for the smallest flicker of recognition. None came. "Nathan Fury."

She extended her hand. "Nice to meet you, Nathan Fury."

They shook.

It was hard to let go of her hand, hard not to hang on longer than was appropriate, but he somehow managed.

How surreal to be sitting face-to-face in the very same booth they'd sat in before, and have her stare at him with the eyes of a stranger.

It hurt like hell.

They'd been agents together, partners. Later they'd both been in Project TAKE. TAKE had marked the beginning of the end of their personal and working relationship.

His hair had been brown then. It started to turn gray after his bout in the tank. Arden had noticed it first.

"Have you been painting?" she'd asked him one morning. "You have paint in your hair."

"Where?"

"There."

He'd looked in the mirror and had seen two patches of gray at his temples. That was the first visual indication that the tank was a bad thing. He'd already suspected it was messing up their minds.

Two days later, he announced that he'd had enough. By that time, he, Arden, and Harley Larson were the only ones left. Everybody else had bailed.

"My head is getting fucked up," Fury had told Arden. "You've changed. I've changed. We have to stop. We have to get out. Can't you see that we're taking on traits that belong to the killers?"

She'd refused to believe him. "I'm the same person I've always been. And I'm not a quitter. I've never quit anything in my life."

"This might be a good time to start."

She'd accused him of being jealous. Jealous that she was doing so well, that in the short time they'd been on the Hill she'd become a star, while Fury had complained of motion sickness and headaches that left him weak and pale.

He dropped out.

She and Harley Larson stayed.

Fury had met Larson only once at the beginning of the indoctrination. He'd seemed a nice enough guy, although a little nervous and shy.

Arden and Larson became a dream team. A dynamic duo.

"What happened to Harley?" Arden now asked

him. "He called me a few days ago. He told me he was coming back to the Hill."

She'd remembered Larson, but she'd forgotten Fury—someone she'd once professed to love.

Recent studies had proven the existence of voluntary memory repression, and Fury couldn't help but wonder if she'd erased him on purpose.

"Larson was here, but decided not to stay." Fury hadn't seen him. He hadn't wanted to see him. "Nobody is forced to stay."

Maybe she'd been right. Maybe he had been jealous.

Their pizza arrived.

"And you?" she asked once the bartender was gone. "How are you involved?"

"I guess I'm the gopher."

With the pointed spatula, he slipped a slice of pizza onto a small plate and passed it to her. "Just overseeing things for the Bureau. I don't know how much you remember about TAKE," he said, "but the FBI has a symbiotic relationship with Dr. Harris and his crew."

TAKE wasn't the only project going on in the old hospital. Private funds and grants were paying for all kinds of studies involving sleep deprivation, music therapy, and memory function.

"Dr. Harris presents the protocol for TAKE, and the FBI approves and finances it. We wanted the best research scientist to head the project, and all research scientists need cash to fund their studies. It works out well all the way around. We get Harris, and he gets the funding he needs."

"I had a vague understanding of how it worked, but I'm surprised the FBI is willing to give up that much control," Arden said.

Fury served himself a slice of pizza. "This isn't J. Edgar's FBI."

"Thank God. Are you staying at the Hill?" she asked.

"I'll be dividing my time between here and Quantico."

His job had been to get Arden to the Hill. During her time there, he was to report back to headquarters and FBI director Nelson Roberts. On a personal level, he was there to keep an eye on her. "I have some open cases needing my attention, plus I'm working on the recent Oklahoma family murder case."

She stared at him a long time. So long that for a moment he had the notion that she knew everything. Who he was. That he was stretching the truth about his presence on the Hill. But somebody had to watch out for her. *He* had to watch out for her.

Her hair was shorter than it used to be. Straight and smooth. One length, hitting at about the chin. He remembered how the strands had felt between his fingers. Soft and silky.

Her skin was pale. She had a few freckles across the bridge of her nose, light and almost invisible.

He was supposed to have met her family, but each time their plans fell through. Each time some FBI business got in the way. Then they broke up.

"Are you going to tell me how we knew each other?" she finally asked.

His heart thudded, and he suddenly wished he'd

ordered a double bourbon for himself. "We were both in the academy at the same time." He lifted the glass of beer to his mouth. His hand trembled slightly. He didn't think she noticed. "A long time ago."

She nodded, seemingly satisfied. "I thought it was something like that."

"Do you remember anything about it?"

"About the academy? A little, but I don't remember you."

She didn't seem to care. That bothered him. It shouldn't, because how could she care about someone she didn't even remember? That would be like loving somebody you never knew.

He was tempted to tell her who he was, to get it out in the open, but he worried that it would be too much for her to absorb on top of the news about French. She'd cracked once before; he didn't want it to happen again. And their personal relationship had ended before she was bleached. It would be unfair to confuse her with it. That he'd never stopped loving her had no bearing on anything. It was his private pain, not hers.

They ate the pizza. He had three pieces; she had two.

Just like old times.

She finished her drink.

He could see she was preparing to order another.

"Do you think that's wise?" he asked, placing a hand over the glass. "You have a big day tomorrow."

Wrong thing to say.

She dropped back in her seat and gave him a hard

look. She could do that. Drill a hole right through you.

Then she leaned forward and tugged a small billfold from the back pocket of her jeans. She got to her feet, dropped a ten-dollar bill on the table, and left.

Just like that.

Outside, the streets were deserted, the traffic lights obediently doing their duty, turning from green to red, directing people who weren't there. Arden looked up. The air was heavy; the sky had no visible stars. Winter was coming. It wasn't obvious, but she knew. She could feel it.

A single drop of rain hit her forehead. Arden didn't quicken her pace. Rain was something she'd grown to miss while living in New Mexico.

Trying to forget her irritation with Nathan Fury, she crossed the four-lane, feeling exposed until she ducked under the shadow of the massive evergreens lining the drive to the asylum.

The brick under her feet was slick and uneven. Abandoning the road for the grass, Arden made her way through the cemetery, her eyes straining to spot the small numbered markers.

From somewhere behind her came the sound of a vehicle.

It slowed. Headlight beams reflected off tree trunks as a car turned up the drive.

The car moved slowly, the engine working hard to make it up the steep incline. When it drew even with her, it stopped. The electric passenger window silently lowered.

"Hop in," Fury said. "I'll give you a ride."

He'd been right. She'd had enough to drink. That was what had made her mad.

She remained ten yards from the car. "I'd rather walk." To demonstrate, she began hiking up the hill, the raindrops quickly increasing in number and speed.

He drove beside her. "Come on. Get in."

The rain got louder. It came down hard and cold and stinging. Her shirt was soaked. Her hair was dripping. Rain ran in her eyes, burning, blinding.

The car was suddenly looking pretty good, but she was already wet to the skin, so what was the point?

A flash of lightning lit up the sky, followed by a crash of thunder. That was the point.

Arden jumped in and slammed the door behind her. From the driver's-door control panel, Fury raised the electric window.

Classical music played. The defroster blasted away, shooting tepid air in her face.

She didn't like classical music. It sounded frantic to her, always building, building, building. Was broken glass soothing? Were splinters soothing? Classical music was sharp and jagged and tense. It made her nervous, ready to jump out of her skin. If the present music were a soundtrack, the scene it was embellishing would be of a woman being chased through a maze by a madman with an ax.

With the flick of her wrist, she turned off the music.

"Sure," Fury said dryly. "I don't mind."

"You can't tell me you actually like that."

He stepped on the gas pedal and the car lumbered up the steep hill.

"Did you know that Mozart is the cutting edge of music therapy?" he asked conversationally. "Rats that listen to Mozart have increased brain function. And Alzheimer's patients perform better on spatial and social tasks after listening to Mozart."

"I'll keep that in mind next time I feel like getting social."

He laughed.

At the top of the hill, Fury stopped the car under the overhang next to the pillars and wide marble steps.

Home sweet home.

He pulled out a business card and handed it to her. "Here's my cell phone number. If you need anything, I'm staying around the corner, past the old blacksmith shop in one of the private doctors' cottages."

She got out of the car.

"Eight thirty tomorrow morning you meet with Dr. Harris."

"I don't need a babysitter."

"Nobody said you did."

"That's exactly what you've been saying."

She slammed the door and he drove away.

For a few hours, she'd almost been able to forget about the Hill. Forget about Cottage 25, and an inexplicable fear that kept creeping up on her, causing her stomach to plummet and her heart to pound.

She almost wished Fury hadn't left.

Chapter 7

Arden rechecked the digital clock by her bed. It seemed to be stuck on three A.M. Too bad the room didn't have a TV. You could come across some weird shit at three in the morning.

From outside in the hall came something that sounded like a light footfall—almost like running. The sound increased in volume as it approached her door, then faded into the distance.

She tossed back the covers, swung her feet to the floor, and grabbed the jeans from the nearby chair.

She always slept in a stripped-down version of whatever she'd worn that day. Now she quickly stepped into the jeans, buttoning them under the hem of the dry, white T-shirt she'd changed into when she'd gotten back to her room. She felt around the dark floor until her fingers came into contact with her sneakers, which were still wet and cold from the rain.

It was a struggle to get her bare feet into them. Once they were tied, she moved to the door and listened.

The silence and the late hour made her begin to

wonder if she'd imagined the noise. Had she actually fallen asleep and dreamed the footfalls?

Then the flurry of movement returned.

And stopped directly in front of her door.

Vera's shadow people?

There was no peephole. She swung to the side, back pressed to the wall, eyes and ears straining.

A tiny rap sounded on the door, followed by a whispered, *"Ar-den?"*

Harley?

She pivoted and opened the door.

Curly blond hair.

Eli. Backlit by wall sconces.

He looked at her clothes. "Couldn't sleep either?"

"What are you doing here?" And in pajamas? Striped pajamas.

"We're having trouble sleeping."

"We?"

"Me and my friends."

The friends he'd told her about in the car.

"We're playing cards. Wanna come up?"

Since she couldn't sleep and was curious to hear more about what they were doing on the Hill, she thought, *Why not?*

She locked her door and pocketed the heavy key. "What was that noise I heard?"

"This?"

He shot away, cantering down the hall, taking long strides while his bare feet landed softly.

Ka-thunk, ka-thunk, ka-thunk.

Then he came back, skidding to a stop in front of her.

"Yeah," she said dryly. That explained Vera Thompson's shadow people.

"Sometimes we time each other. See how long it takes to run the floors of this wing. My best time is seven minutes. But we have to do it quietly; otherwise the guard will chew us out."

They took the stairs to the fifth floor, then down a hall that hadn't yet been restored. It smelled of moldy, crumbling wallpaper.

"We asked for this room," Eli explained. "So we could hang out. So we could stay up late and play music without bothering anybody. Plus, it's just cool."

He pushed open the door.

Somewhere, Nag Champa incense burned, the overpoweringly sweet scent covering up anything that may have been unpleasant. Repetitious, hypnotic music drifted from a boom box on the floor against the wall. CD jewel cases were scattered nearby.

"I quit counting at twelve minutes," said a girl in a black tank top and gray flannel pajama bottoms. She sat cross-legged on the floor, cards fanned out in her hand. "We were about to send a search party."

She had short, unnaturally jet-black hair, choppy bangs, and a gold lip ring. "I'm out." She put down a run of face cards, then discarded.

Her playing partner, a young man with wavy, not-so-black hair, weakly dropped his cards, rolled to his back, and put an arm across his eyes. "I have a headache."

Eli introduced them as Franny Young and Noah Viola.

Franny said hi. Noah waved without lifting his head or uncovering his face.

The room had massive windows on all four sides. A cathedral ceiling stretched skyward like a bell tower. It was a nice space for the claustrophobic and light deprived. Not a nice space if you had vertigo.

Eli offered Arden something to drink. "We have Mountain Dew, Mountain Dew, or Mountain Dew."

No wonder they couldn't sleep. All that sugar and caffeine. "I'll have Mountain Dew."

He unscrewed the top of a green plastic quart bottle, splashed some yellow liquid in a blue plastic cup, and handed it to her.

The room had very little furniture. Two twin beds, neatly made up with beige spreads, and a rollaway shoved into the corner. A low, modular couch was positioned against one wall, with a plastic coffee table on a rug in front of it.

It looked thrown-together, as if the administration hadn't foreseen using the room.

Franny poured herself some soda. "Sorry we don't have any ice. There's an ice machine in the basement, but they lock it up at seven." She plopped down on the couch. "This whole place closes up when the sun goes down."

Arden took a long swallow of the tepid drink. Not as bad as she'd expected.

The windows were low and deeply set, with wide stone ledges like something in a castle. She settled herself in one, her back supported by the stone frame, knees bent.

Eli grabbed a plastic outdoor chair and pulled it close so the three of them formed the points of a triangle, Noah quiet and lying outside.

"People from town talk so much garbage about the Hill." Franny picked up a pillow in a white case and hugged it to her. "They say they used to perform lobotomies here. Not that long ago, either."

A lobotomy. Was that a twisted version of the truth? Arden wondered. Was she really a walking vegetable and nobody had told her?

"You are so full of shit," Noah mumbled from the shadows. "Who said that?"

"I don't know. I don't remember. It's just something I heard."

"What are you doing here?" Arden asked, hoping to steer the conversation away from lobotomies.

"Easy money," all three said in unison.

"We were in college," Franny explained. "And we read in a campus paper about how they were looking for study subjects. I needed some time off anyway. And my student loans were freaking me out. This will pay for almost a year of school. Seemed perfect."

Arden remembered those ads in college papers, seeking students to participate in research. She'd never known anyone who'd actually done it.

"What kind of studies?" Arden asked.

Eli glanced at Franny, then back to Arden. "Right now we're testing the Mozart effect. Doing things to see if listening to Mozart improves our memory.

Later, we're going to do some sleep-deprivation stuff."

Was everyone here listening to Mozart?

"I considered selling my eggs," Franny said, "but then I read about all the dangerous drugs you have to take, and how it can really mess you up. . . ."

"They can have my eggs," Noah piped in.

Franny tossed her pillow at him. "Easy for you to say."

"Hey, if I had something somebody wanted, I'd sell it."

"Then become a prostitute, why don't you?"

Noah sat up, legs crossed. "That's what we're doing, isn't it?" He grabbed the pillow Franny had tossed at him.

"We're participating in a scientific study," she said.

Noah fluffed up the pillow. "You are so delusional."

"You're such an elitist."

Franny looked at Arden. "Eli and I are doing this for tuition. Noah doesn't even need to be here."

"What are you talking about?" Noah asked, his voice rising.

"His parents are filthy rich," Franny explained, ignoring Noah. "They'll pay for undergraduate and graduate school."

"Only if I major in some business field. You know that."

"Your dad would cave." Franny swung around. "Just take a bunch of core stuff, then pull a switch on him."

"It's the principle of the thing."

"You just want to pretend to be like the rest of us. You want to *play* poverty. Of course, that kind of thing is more fun when you know you can go back."

Noah tossed the pillow on the couch and crawled to the boom box. He shut it off, removed the CD, and held it up. "This Boards of Canada CD? Mine." He put it in a case and stuck it in the pocket of his hooded sweatshirt. "Fuck you, Franny. I didn't ask for your psychoanalysis."

He left, slamming the door behind him.

Franny crossed her arms and sank deeper into the couch. "Baby."

"Should somebody go after him?" Arden asked. "He was pretty upset."

"He'll be back," Eli said. "Noah's always going off about something. It used to freak me out whenever he did that. I'd get all worried and concerned and replay everything in my head. Think about what I should have said, then what I'd say next time I saw him. Then he'd come strolling back, acting like nothing happened."

"Just la-la-la," Franny said. "He's such a piece of shit."

Arden had seen the dynamic before. One of those all-too-common situations of two guys liking the same girl.

Eli had been a little subdued since entering the room. Gone was the gregarious person who'd given her a ride from the airport, and the bouncing boy in the hall. This version of Eli was choosing to remain in the background while the drama played out around him.

Arden looked at Franny. "So, how long have you and Noah been dating?" she asked, vocalizing her assumption.

"Two years," Franny said. "Part of his hang-up is that I come from a poor family. We're talking plastic-bags-over-our-shoes-in-the-winter poor. Food-stamps poor and homeless-shelter poor. Noah's family is rich. Filthy rich. Which shouldn't be a problem, right? But it is. Noah's ashamed of how easy his life has been, how easy he's had it. And he doesn't completely trust me. In the back of his mind, he worries that I might be playing him for his daddy's money. That is *so gross!* And so not who I am."

"You did just tell him he could get his whole education paid for," Eli reminded her.

"Why shouldn't he? Why should he deliberately make things harder for himself just because he doesn't think it's cool to be born into money?" She jumped to her feet, putting up both hands in a double talk-to-the-hand pose. "Okay. I'm not talking about this anymore."

Arden finished her soda, unfolded herself from the window ledge, and presented her empty cup to Eli. "I'd better get back to my room, try to get some sleep."

From somewhere came muffled musical notes. Franny dug under a pile of clothes and pulled out a cell phone.

"You're where?" she asked the caller in disbelief.

She paused for a response, then relayed the information to Eli and Arden. "Noah's in Cottage 25."

Arden's heart thudded the way it always did whenever she heard or thought about Cottage 25.

"He can't find his way out," Franny told them. She got back to Noah. "Okay, okay. We're coming. Leave your cell phone on and I'll call you when we're in the building."

She disconnected, slipped on a hooded sweatshirt, and stuck the phone in her pocket. "He got in a service door with a broken window."

Eli and Franny both grabbed their shoes and put them on.

"Let's find a night watchman," Arden suggested. Adrenaline was still racing through her veins. "Hopefully he has a master key."

Two pairs of eyes locked on her. "We can't tell him Noah was roaming around, breaking into buildings."

Of course, it would be much too anticlimactic to simply alert a guard. "He didn't break in."

Arden was glad she wasn't their age anymore. Everything was such high drama, and Noah's little performance an obvious plea for attention.

Eli tugged a gray sweatshirt over his head, then produced two plastic flashlights, one red, one yellow. "He could get kicked out of the study."

He had a point. Not a very valid one, but a point.

"How old are you?" Arden asked as they headed out the door.

"Twenty-two," Eli said.

Arden wasn't so much older. Not in people years,

anyway, but in FBI-agent years it created quite a gap. Agents grew up fast. But then, if you spiced that up with months of denial and shook well, it might just even out.

"Twenty-one," Franny said.

Daniel had turned twenty-two in August. Arden had sent him a birthday card with her return address. No response. Was he okay?

The quest for Noah was nothing to do with her. A hip version of a lovers' quarrel. The practical thing would be to continue to her room and try to catch a few hours of sleep before her eight-thirty meeting.

On the other hand, she didn't feel comfortable leaving this bunch to their own devices. They were naive. Not that she thought anything would happen. It was just that they seemed capable of finding trouble without even trying.

But he's in Cottage 25. You don't want anything to do with Cottage 25, remember?

At the last minute, when she should have headed toward her room, she changed course.

Eli handed her one of the flashlights. Not wanting to attract the attention of the night watchman, they took the stairs, moving as silently as possible in shoes with soles that sometimes squeaked, using sign language instead of talking.

Shh.

This way.

Wait. I hear something.

Okay. Let's go.

The only thing missing was Scooby-Doo.

On the first floor, Arden peered through the rectangle of safety glass. She motioned that all was clear; then they slipped out the heavy, noisy door.

The rain had stopped.

Arden pulled in a deep breath. The air was spectacular. Washed clean. She could see the stars.

Not nearly as spectacular as a New Mexico sky, but the lack of pollution was quite amazing. Her lungs didn't know how to react to the absence of refinery fumes.

There was a brief flurry of conflict as Eli and Franny struggled for the leadership role. Eli relented and Franny took off, moving quickly through the wet grass, sticking to the shadows.

It was cold and damp. Arden wished she was dressed in more than a T-shirt.

As they hurried in the direction of Cottage 25, she began to recognize landmarks. The apple orchard was around a corner and down a hillside, near where Fury was staying. There would be a wide wooden bridge that led across a stream, and a circle of gravestones, broken and unreadable, covered with lichen, clustered at the bottom of a small hollow.

Like the other buildings, Cottage 25 was made of red brick. It wasn't as tall or as big as the main structure, but it was every bit as unsettling. Four stories. Rows and rows of windows, all dark.

Franny waved them to follow. Moving single-file, they circled the building, checking doors until Franny ran down a short set of cement steps and came upon a door with a broken window.

Franny turned the knob and pushed open the door. *Come on,* she rapidly motioned.

Arden froze.

It was like the time she'd called Daniel and couldn't speak. "I'll wait out here," she whispered, ashamed of the panic in her voice. She handed Eli the flashlight.

They went in without her.

Chapter 8

The heavy door closed solidly behind them.

Franny and Eli hesitated, neither wanting to move into the belly of the building, away from the exit.

"I can't believe she was afraid to come with us," Eli whispered in the dark. "I mean, she's an FBI agent."

"*Shhh.*" Franny frowned even though he couldn't see her. "She'll hear you. And she *used* to be an agent."

Eli returned to the door, his head bobbing, blocking what little light fell through the door's small window. "She's wandering around the yard," he whispered. "I can see her up there."

"I don't blame her for not wanting to come," Franny said. "I'm scared."

Eli came away from the window to pat the top of Franny's head. "Poor widdle girl."

Letting out an annoyed laugh, Franny ducked and knocked his hand away. "God, I'm surrounded by lame-asses. And I'm five-foot-eight. Hardly widdle."

"Don't harass me. You're always harassing me

about something. I was just trying to keep things light."

Franny didn't know if he was really offended, or just acting like it. With Eli, you never knew.

"Well . . ." They'd stalled about as long as possible.

This whole thing was such typical Noah melodrama crap. Staging some elaborate scene to get Franny's attention, make her feel sorry for him. Trying to project his neurotic behavior onto her, turning everything around to make her feel guilty for growing up poor.

She was one of those pathetic women who was attracted to instability. And high drama. She'd never been drawn to guys who were normal, even if they were cute and nice and smart. She had to have someone who was wounded and damaged in some way. Maybe because she'd never had much of a family. Maybe because nobody had really looked out for her. Whatever the cause, she felt a need to nurture.

She wanted Noah to be happy about who he was, but once that happened, *if* that happened, she'd probably lose interest in him. That was why the more messed up a guy was, the better.

Which was really messed up. Oh, but people were sick and twisted and weird.

"Come on." Eli reached for her, grasping her hand.

Her heart jumped and fluttered and sank as the subtext shifted.

Here she'd thought this little adventure was to find Noah, and Eli was looking on it as an opportunity to touch. To be alone with her in a dark, scary place so he could maybe even put his arm around her.

Did guys ever outgrow that opportunistic way of thinking? Or was it part of their genes?

She didn't pull her hand away. She clicked on her flashlight.

Eli did the same.

"Keep the light pointed to the floor," she whispered, "so it won't shine out any of the windows."

Together, they moved slowly and awkwardly through the dark, cavernous space until they reached a pair of heavy double doors with wire mesh set in small, face-level windows.

Franny took out her cell phone, keyed in Noah's number, and pressed DIAL.

No answer. She tried one more time before sticking the phone back in her sweatshirt pocket.

"Come on." Eli tugged at her hand.

They went through the set of double doors, then down a hall.

Franny shone her flashlight along the walls, pausing on a bulletin board with a yellowed calendar pinned to it, left over from when the hospital was a working asylum.

That made her feel weird.

She tried Noah again. Still no answer. "He's probably not getting a signal in here."

"This is creepy as hell," Eli whispered.

Was his voice kind of shaky?

She could feel his palm getting sweaty. Her own hand was freezing. Her whole body was freezing.

"You know what I think?" Eli whispered. They were standing really close. "I think he's fucking with us. I don't even think he's in here."

Why hadn't she thought of that? Of course that's what had happened. He was probably lurking in a grove of trees, watching the cottage, laughing his ass off. No, Noah wouldn't be laughing. He was too much of a masochist for that.

Franny tugged her hand free of Eli's. "Let's get the hell out of here." She turned and hurried back the way they'd come, their swiftly moving footsteps slapping the floor, echoing loudly in the emptiness.

Through the cafeteria and down the hallway, to the double doors. With Eli on her heels, she threw her weight against the door.

And hurt herself. *Owww.*

The door didn't budge.

She tried the other one, pressing down hard on the metal bar. Locked. Eli tried, with no better results.

Her heart was slamming now. "We have to find another way out."

They turned and hurried back through the cafeteria of Cottage 25. Another set of doors led to another hall, then a ramped, linoleum-covered incline.

"We're going down," Eli said. "We don't wanna go down."

They stopped to catch their breath.

"Maybe we can find an emergency exit," Franny said.

Eli checked out the surroundings, the beam of his flashlight bouncing off metal heating ducts and clusters of rusty pipes. "You've heard about that girl, haven't you?" he asked. "The mental patient? The one who died in this building years ago?"

"Stop it."

They hadn't yet thrown themselves into each other's arms. They hadn't clutched each other in fear. For Eli, this was probably like taking a girl to see a horror movie, only better.

"You know the one I'm talking about?" he asked, wandering away. "The patient who hid down here somewhere until she died?"

"They didn't find her body for six months." Franny could play this game too. "That's what I heard."

Maybe they should start shouting for help. Maybe Arden would hear them. Even if she didn't, she would surely become concerned when they didn't return.

She would find the night watchman and he would let them out.

Right now, Franny would love to see the night watchman. "I heard she was dead for so long," Franny said, "that her decomposing body left an imprint on the cement."

"Hey—a door!" Eli shouted.

Franny turned and hurried toward him, her flashlight beam bouncing.

A windowless door painted over in layers of thick black enamel.

"It's probably just a closet." A smothering sensation washed over her. "Come on. Let's go back the way we came."

"You know what I'll bet?" Eli ran his flashlight up and down the door. "I'll bet this is the old morgue."

He didn't know that.

"Stop it, Eli."

No way could he know that.

"Wait." He stepped closer. "Don't you want to see what's inside?"

A tingly feeling moved up the back of her neck and across her scalp. "We need to get out of here," she said. "We need to get out of here *now*."

How much time had passed? Arden wondered.

It seemed like a long time.

Had it been a long time?

This was stupid. She was freezing. Her skin was beginning to feel tight and dehydrated. Her eyeballs burned. Sleep suddenly seemed very desirable.

And here she was, standing outside Cottage 25 in the middle of the night, while her new buddies raided the place. What would it be next? Pranks with toilet paper and shaving cream?

Stupid, stupid, stupid.

A week ago, if someone had asked her to name the last place on earth she'd want to be, the Hill would have been her response.

But then, did you ever reach a point when things felt right? When you said, *This is where I'm supposed to be at this minute? This period in time?* Did that ever happen?

They'd been gone a long time.

She was pretty sure of it.

Two choices: Go after them, or find the night watchman.

Even though the situation had escalated into something extremely annoying, she didn't want to get anybody in trouble.

Jeesus.

No flashlight. Black as hell.

She slid her feet along the cement steps, feeling for the edges as she descended. Five steps down and a turn to the right brought her to the damaged door. Before she could change her mind, she opened it and barged through. It closed behind her with a clang. A narrow passageway took her to a room with tall windows that were a lighter shade of black, giving everything the look of a negative.

Down a wide hallway, smooth linoleum underfoot.

It smells the same.

She remembered that smell.

Like people.

Lots of people.

Almost like a grade school. A uniquely human odor of hundreds of bodies packed into a space that was too small. Of perspiring heads and stocking caps that could use a good washing.

She didn't want to be there. God, how she didn't want to be there.

A little illumination, coming from a few rooms that were apparently being used as offices where electronic equipment hadn't been completely shut down for the night. A bit of light from street lamps.

Not street lamps.

The windows faced east. The sky was beginning to lighten. Birds had started singing even though it was still dark. They knew dawn was coming.

A double door.

Had Eli and Franny come this way? How long ago?

It seemed years since she'd been at Grumpy Steve's. Years since Fury had given her a ride to Building 50.

Arden slipped through the door. With her hand on the cold, clammy metal railing, she moved slowly down the steps.

In a hole. You're a mole.

Smell was a time machine.

It hurled you back into another world with the jolt and intensity and immediacy of an electrical shock. Good or bad. You had no choice in the matter. Your olfactories never asked your opinion. It was just, *Here we are! Right in your face.*

If Arden had had a choice, she would have asked for a whiff of her grandmother's cinnamon pancakes.

Or the scent of apple wood in the fireplace. Home. Her parents' home.

A place of refuge. A place that was supposed to be safe.

Stop. Don't think. Thinking never does a damn bit of good.

She wouldn't have asked for the stench of a basement. Of damp wood and mildewed cement. The smell of the metal railing on her palm, penetrating her skin. The smell of water.

Not regular water. Salt water, with a touch of chlorine.

Her legs began to tremble and she had to stop her descent. With both hands gripping the metal railing, she waited.

The trembling continued.

As if driven by some electrical impulse, the trembling traveled through her legs, up her torso, to her arms, neck, and head.

She broke into a cold sweat.

Her legs crumpled. She sank to the step and sat there, her cheek pressed to the cement wall, her hands still gripping the railing above her.

An old fear. An irrational, reasonless fear she couldn't even name because the visual memory no longer existed. The only thing left was the feeling, the emotion.

She was a child afraid of the dark.

Her legs and arms began to ache—a reminder of the passage of time.

She stood up.

Beyond the stairwell, metal steam pipes clanged and whistled.

It's not the fear of the building. It was the irrational fear of coming face-to-face with the memories they'd taken from her here. Almost as if they'd locked them up in a jar somewhere and hidden them away for her to find upon her return.

A quart canning jar with her name on it.

ARDEN'S BAD MEMORIES.

That's what the jar would say. The words written

on some cute, homey label. The jar tucked into a cupboard next to the strawberry preserves.

Open the jar.

Stick in a knife.

Spread the jam on a piece of bread and take a bite. . . .

She gave herself a mental shake. How much time had passed?

Someone shouted her name from deep below. "Arden! Arden! Can you hear us? *Arden!*"

Franny. Calling her.

And now the voice was joined by another.

Eli.

They sounded scared.

They sounded terrified.

What did they have to be frightened of? No one had taken their memories, had they? There were no labeled jars with their names on them, were there?

In their case, Cottage 25 was just a building.

Yeah, like Hitler was just a man.

Shut up! she told herself. *Shut up! If you can't say anything helpful, then just shut the fuck up.*

Right.

So she would find those pesky kids, she told herself in a chipper voice. *Silly, silly . . . kids . . .*

She was no better off than a child who was afraid of the—

A door.

Painted black.

She'd seen that door before.

She stared at it a long time. She tested the knob.

Unlocked.

She pushed it open.

A couple of small safety lights illuminated the gray cement floor. Bulky shapes like coffins with legs were waiting.

Not coffins.

Float tanks.

The name bobbed into her head.

Some people called them isolation chambers.

Like going back to the womb.

Had Harley said that?

The smell: metal corroded by salt.

The rubber-lined tanks were filled with water and enough salt to float the occupant like a cork. No submersion. Just total darkness. With nothing but your own thoughts.

And the voice of a madman . . .

A jolt of consciousness brought her back to now, to the immediate time and place.

For a moment, she'd backtracked. For a little while, she'd forgotten the mission and why she was there. Forgotten about Franny and Eli and the kid who'd run off. What was his name? Noah. That's it. They were on a quest for Noah.

She crossed the room. She headed for the nearest tank.

They'd always reminded her of iron lungs used by TB patients. Metal, with gauges on the side. Temperature and heat gauges so the water wouldn't get cold. A timer.

That could be set for hours . . .

It wasn't so much what they looked like, but what they did.

The suffocating isolation.

Locked in a box.

In the dark.

No control, completely dependent on another person to let you out.

And then the added element of water . . .

It didn't make it any better.

She undid the latch and swung the lid open. Even though the tank was empty and dry, it still smelled like disinfectant and old rubber, and like somebody's wet, cotton swimsuit that had been left in the corner.

Her memory was fuzzy, but tactilely her fingers recalled the edge of the metal encasement. Her feet remembered the tread on the ladder. The temperature of the water. Almost as if someone had peed in it. And its buoyancy, the way the salt felt as it worked its way into every crack in your skin, every little abrasion. Burning like a vat of battery acid.

When she was done, her fingers and toes would be wrinkled, her legs white and trembling. Like some pickled old woman, she used to think as she struggled from the container with the weakness of an astronaut back from six weeks in space.

Arden slammed the lid.

Float tanks were supposed to be good things. Hippies and New Agers loved them, claiming that an hour or two in the tank every few weeks made them better able to focus. That it cleared their heads of excess garbage.

But then, most objects weren't bad until the human component came into play. A stick was just a stick unless someone picked it up and beat the shit out of you with it.

There were three tanks in the room. All identical, all industrial green.

She approached the second tank. She opened it.

Also dry.

The third one was warm to the touch.

The power of three . . .

Two hours was the maximum amount of time a person should remain inside. Arden had the feeling she'd been locked in there for much, much longer.

Somebody's words came back to her. *My head is getting fucked up.*

Was there water in the tank? They should be emptied every time they were used.

Was the tank occupied? Right now?

She wanted to run. She wanted to turn and get the hell out of there. But what if someone was trapped in the tank?

Harley. Could it be Harley? Maybe he hadn't really left. Maybe he'd been right here all along.

She unlocked the lid.

Snap. Snap. Two metal latches that reminded her of the latches on an old lunchbox you might find in a junk shop.

She swung the lunchbox open.

She recoiled. She blinked.

A body.

Nude.

Male.

Long, dark hair.

She let out a gasp, dropped the lid, and jumped away.

Her foot caught on something and she tumbled backward, everything suddenly moving too fast.

She reached out, trying to catch herself, stop herself, her hand making contact with a metal table. She pulled it down with her as she went, crashing to the floor at the same time her head struck concrete.

Chapter 9

Pain knifed through Arden's head.

"In here!" someone shouted.

She tried to get up; the movement sent a wave of dizziness washing over her.

The shout from the hallway was followed by the sound of pounding feet.

A door crashed open, slamming against a wall.

"Come on!"

Someone—Eli—grabbed Arden's arm. "We found a way out!" He pulled her up from the floor.

The pain in her head intensified. Sharp, white light strobed behind her pupils.

The scene was delivered in choppy fragments.

A dark room, with bits of gray seeping around corners and through cracks.

A girl with a name Arden couldn't remember.

Noah. Where had he come from?

An argument was going on between the girl and Noah.

"Don't make such a big deal out of this," Noah pleaded. "I thought it would be funny."

"Funny if you get us kicked out of the study?" the girl asked.

Can't remember her name. What is her name?

"It's your fault. You were tormenting me," Noah shot back.

"I can't talk about this now," the girl said.

"But I want to."

"Shut up. Just shut up."

Arden had to tell them something. Had to tell them about . . . what?

Her head.

Tell them that her head hurt.

Hurt like hell. And they weren't helping.

From the edges of her pain came Eli's impatient voice. "Hurry!" And, "Be quiet!"

In an awkward cluster, they exited the room, Arden stumbling, trying to keep up, trying to ignore the throbbing in her skull.

The girl grabbed Arden's other arm, and then they were half dragging her, running and panting.

"We have to get out of here before somebody comes," the girl said, her voice breathless.

Running is always a good choice. Can't go wrong with running.

"Left?" That was Eli.

"No, right."

Noah? Was that Noah's voice?

"Here! Turn here!"

Skid around a corner.

Jerky images, everything coming too fast.

Through a thick, institutional door, metal lock bar clanging heavily.

Another corner and up a set of stairs.

Burst outside.

"Don't stop," the girl gasped.

Everything—the brick buildings, the stand of evergreens in the distance, the grass—was washed in a predawn fog. Sharp rain pelted Arden's face.

Pasty, gaunt face framed by dark, stringy hair.

They ran for the trees. Wet grass, soaking through shoes.

Wet and cold.

What am I doing here?

She was finished. Done in. Couldn't go another inch.

Arden quit running, quit trying to keep up. "Stop."

The girl and Eli paused, still gripping her arms.

"Let go." Arden tugged her arms free. Her legs buckled, her knees sinking into the saturated ground.

The girl and Eli tried to reattach themselves.

"No." Arden shooed them away with a sloppy sweep of her hand.

Leave me alone. She'd had enough. Enough of their pulling and dragging and shouting.

Her vision was blurred. She felt queasy. Her head hurt, hurt, hurt.

Gaunt face. Stringy hair. Open eyes. Looking at her. Staring at her with accusation.

"Oh, my God!"

The girl's voice seemed to come from the other end of a long tunnel. "She's hurt! She's bleeding!"

Bleeding? Who were they talking about?

Arden felt a finger poking gingerly at the back of her head.

Her. They were talking about *her.*

She didn't know if it was the mental image of somebody sticking a finger in a cracked skull that did it, but the queasiness in Arden's stomach intensified.

She knocked the girl's hand away, crawled a few feet, and threw up. When the most severe of the nausea faded, she shoved herself to her feet and began making her way to the trees.

The ground tilted ninety degrees. She fell, her face slamming into the wet, muddy grass.

Everything was fine and dandy until a roar intruded upon her consciousness. Until she returned to the real world and panic-filled voices.

The rain was coming harder now, beating down on Arden's face, pattering against fallen leaves, the sound of a million striking drops competing for space in her throbbing head.

A fresh argument was taking place a few feet away.

"—your fault," came the girl's voice.

"Don't say that, Franny. How can you say that?"

Franny. That was her name. The name Arden hadn't been able to remember. They'd met in the tower room. Franny and Noah had been playing cards.

"My fault?" Noah asked. "How is it my fault?"

"She was looking for *you.*"

"Hey, I didn't tell her to come after me. I didn't tell her to hit her fucking head."

"Did you call 911?" Eli asked. He was crouched a few feet from Arden, staring at her, hands wrapped around his knees.

"I tried, but my phone's acting up," Noah said.

"Franny, call 911."

Arden rolled to her back, her arms outstretched. How had this happened? How had she gotten here? Yesterday life had been so much simpler. Yesterday she'd been two thousand miles away.

"Shit," Noah said, his voice tense. "Here comes a car. Should we run?"

"You are unbelievable," Eli said.

The roar of a car engine. A slamming door.

"Who is it?" Franny asked.

"Fury." Eli sounded worried. "It's Agent Fury."

Nathan Fury strode across the wet grass, a high-powered flashlight sweeping the area. Dawn had arrived, but was hiding. Rain pelted his black trench coat while birds sang hopefully from a windbreak of evergreens.

Kids.

Three, to be exact.

Fury had seen them around. He knew they'd taken some time off from college to participate in a study of Harris's.

They stood in a semicircle. As the distance between Fury and the group closed, he saw someone sprawled on the ground.

He directed his flashlight beam at the body, beginning at the feet.

Sneakers. Jeans. A T-shirt. Then the beam rested on the ashen, muddy face of Arden Davis.

A heavy stone dropped in the pit of his stomach. He started to run when the body moved, when she lifted her arm and draped it across her face to cover her eyes.

He immediately downshifted his emotions, immediately collected himself and fell back into the role of Special Agent Nathan Fury, detached, cool, and in control.

"What are you doing out here?" His voice was remarkably steady as he walked toward them, his leather shoes sinking into the soggy ground.

All three started babbling at once.

"She hit her head."

"She needs a doctor."

"She's bleeding."

He crouched beside Arden, one arm resting on a bent knee, the other reaching out to touch her cheek. "Arden?"

She pushed herself to a sitting position. "I'm okay." Her voice was weak, slightly slurred.

Had she been drinking again? What did he mean, *again?* Had she ever quit?

"We were just, you know, goofing around," the kid named Eli said. "Somehow she hit her head."

Fury wasn't interested in the details of who did what. He probably wouldn't get the truth anyway. Arden needed a hospital. "Help me get her to my car. I'll take her to the emergency room."

Arden protested, but not as much as he'd expected, which was a bad sign.

With the help of Eli, they got her to the car, packing her into the passenger seat.

"We'll be okay," Fury said when the kid started to get in the backseat.

Eli nodded. Doors slammed and then Fury and Arden were moving down the rough road.

"Do they give you morphine for a concussion?" Arden asked, head against the seat, eyes closed.

Fury tried to miss the larger dips in the cobblestone drive, but some were unavoidable. "They won't want to sedate you."

"Too bad. Morphine would be nice."

That figured.

Over the past several months, there had been a lot of talk around Quantico about how far she'd fallen. People, even FBI agents, liked to gossip and exaggerate, but he was afraid everything people had been saying about her was true.

After two hours in the emergency room, a CT scan, and tetanus shot, Arden was diagnosed with an extremely mild concussion, given something for the pain, and told to go home and rest.

"No stitches?" she asked the young ER doctor.

"I think you'll be okay without them." He left the exam room to put together a prescription and home-care information.

Arden remained where she was, her legs dangling over the end of the padded exam table.

Fury stood across the room.

He hadn't bothered to remove his soaked and wrinkled coat, which was unbuttoned and hanging limply. His short hair was rumpled. He stared out the window of the old brick building at rain that was falling harder than ever, his back to her, hands in his pockets.

"I don't mind rain," he surprised her by saying. "It's kind of peaceful. . . ."

Earlier, while the doctor had been examining her head, Arden had remembered what she'd forgotten. "I saw a body," she now blurted out.

Fury slowly turned to look at her. "What?" He glanced around the room, as if expecting to find a corpse nearby.

"A body."

"Where?"

"Cottage 25. In one of the float tanks."

He recoiled, then seemed to collect himself.

She could see him thinking things over, weighing her mental stability and injury. Organizing, reorganizing. Dismissing. "You've had a concussion. The doctor said you might be a little confused for a while."

"I saw a body in one of the float tanks."

Her voice sounded certain. She knew from experience that you had to sound certain, if you wanted results. Even if you weren't certain you had to fake it. And Fury wasn't telling her anything new. In fact, she was afraid her mental state was worse than he could possibly guess.

"Dead?" Fury asked.

"I don't know."

Fury pulled out a cell phone, punched in a number, and lifted the phone to his ear. "I need somebody to check the basement of Cottage 25. The float tank room," he told the person on the other end. "I have someone here who claims to have seen something, maybe a person, in one of the tanks. Check it out and get back to me."

He pocketed the phone. "What were you doing in Cottage 25?"

Something stupid. "Hanging out with the cool kids."

He gave her a pained look.

"I don't know. What am I doing in Madeline? What am I doing here, talking to you? Does everything have to have a reason?"

"It was a simple question."

"Your patronizing attitude is annoying."

"I don't mean to be patronizing." His expression was blank, his voice calm. FBI. He was so good at that. She used to be good at that, too.

Things changed.

"We were trying to find Noah," she told him. "He'd gotten lost inside Cottage 25. Typical kids' stuff. I went along to keep an eye on them." She shrugged. "It didn't work out very well."

Fury's phone rang.

He answered it.

A brief conversation, followed by, "Thanks." He disconnected and gave Arden a satisfied look. "All three tanks are empty."

Of course they were—*now.*

"It was probably Noah in the tank," Fury said. "The whole thing was a prank meant to scare the hell out of his girlfriend. You found him instead."

He could be right.

"Talk to Noah," Fury said. "Maybe you can get him to come clean."

"I'll do that."

Paper crinkled as she slipped off the exam table and stood up. A wave of dizziness hit her, and she had to wait a moment for it to fade.

Nothing seemed real. She felt like a bystander in her own life. Someone watching the show. But then, life was a series of parts. Some you played better than others. "Maybe I should look at the tanks myself."

She didn't want to. The thought of going back there made her feel queasy all over again. She wasn't sure she could do it, and she found herself hoping Fury would talk her out of it.

"Arden. Listen to me. You heard the doctor. You need to rest."

The mask he wore slipped a little, and his expression seemed to show real concern. Part of the act.

She imagined herself as an Olympic judge, holding up her number. She gave him a ten.

"Let it go," he said. "You've had a head injury. You're confused. It was dark. You're looking for things that aren't there. Looking for things that don't exist."

She would forget it. The choice seemed both right and wrong. It brought relief, but also a nagging unease.

The air around them smelled like the disinfectant the young doctor had used to scrub her scalp. Her arm felt tingly and hot from the tetanus shot. It would be sore as hell tomorrow.

Fury was watching her. Very closely.

Blue, blue windows behind the stars.

Who had said that? Neil Young?

Yes. Along with other things she could no longer remember.

She had the sudden, strange notion that Fury wanted to touch her. She stepped back.

She had to be careful. She had to watch what she said. And who she said it to. She even had to watch what she was thinking. Especially around Fury. He was reading her mind right now. He was in her brain, strolling around, whistling.

I should leave. I should get my stuff and get the hell out of here.

She smiled at him.

He smiled back.

Don't trust anybody.

Not even herself. Especially herself.

"Give this a little time," Fury said. "You just got here. What do you have to go back to?"

"Why do you keep saying that? I had a life."

"You were running."

"I wasn't running. I was trying to *endure.* There's a big difference." She examined his face closely. "You're afraid of them."

His brows drew together in puzzlement. "What are you talking about?"

"The tanks. I saw it in your face when I said I wanted to see them."

"That's nonsense."

But he was suddenly nervous. It wasn't blatantly obvious, but she was still good at reading people, and Fury was nervous. "You've been in one, haven't you?" she probed.

He rubbed a hand across the back of his neck. He stared down at his feet.

After a few moments his head came up and he looked directly at her. It suddenly seemed as if the doors between them had blown wide open. She could see all the way to his soul. And what she saw was fear. Raw fear.

She suddenly knew where he'd gotten the gray hair. Not from a cadaver's hand, but from an isolation tank. He'd done time just like she had.

The doors slammed shut.

"The tanks are relics of the past," he said with conviction. "They don't use them anymore. Nobody uses them."

Chapter 10

Framed covers of *Time* and *Newsweek* hung on the wall of Dr. Harris's office.

> Dr. Phillip Harris, Ph.D. and Head of Psychiatric Research at the Webber Institute, Wins Nobel Prize for Medicine.

Arden leaned close to check the dates on the magazines. Three years ago. The recognition had been for his studies in isolation therapy. Which was why the FBI had looked him up in the first place. They'd wanted the best.

But then, the guy who'd invented the lobotomy had also won a Nobel Prize.

It was a widespread belief that psychiatrists became psychiatrists because they themselves had wounded psyches in need of repair. Arden believed that to be true, but there were also the researchers, the doctors whose egos told them they were the sanest people on the planet. Those guys were after something other than an answer to their own phobias and anxieties. That's where Harris fit in. He was looking for acclaim from his peers and the world.

She'd been waiting fifteen minutes.

She sat back down in the leather chair across from a massive mahogany desk. Two minutes later she got up again to examine a photo on the wall.

The photo was of Harris's research team, dwarfed by the old hospital behind them. Most of them wore white lab coats. What looked to be Harris's wife and two daughters stood nearby.

The office door opened.

Arden's heart pounded and she swung around.

Harris entered the room in a hurry, closing the door behind him. "Arden." His voice was full of warmth, sounding like a favorite relative. "It's so nice to see you." He walked to her, pulled her into his arms, and hugged her firmly. He smelled the same—like some kind of woodsy aftershave.

He released her and motioned to the chair she'd just vacated while he took a seat behind the desk and placed a manila file in front of him.

She hadn't forgotten him.

Tall and thin, about forty-five, the hair at his temples turning gray. Not a handsome man, but a man with presence and energy.

People said he never slept. It had always been a big rumor, anyway. That and the infatuations his patients developed over him. But she'd never held it against him. Patients developed infatuations for their doctors all the time.

Her own feelings about Harris were mixed. At first she hadn't liked him. He'd seemed too cold, and much too tidy. But he'd grown on her. He still seemed too in-control and in-charge, which she found annoying, but there was also something comforting about stepping back and letting somebody else take care of things for a change.

And he probably knew her better than she knew herself. After all, he'd been in control of her very thoughts.

"How's the head? I heard you had some trouble."

"I'm fine." Had Fury blabbed to everybody?

"Running around Cottage 25 in the middle of the night. What was that all about?"

"Kids' stuff. Foolish stuff." She didn't want to talk about it. It had been a stupid thing to do.

"I'm glad to see you, but I'm going to tell you outright that I'm against your being here," he announced. "I told Agent Fury that. I want you to know it, too. You've been pushed as far as you should be pushed."

"I'll sign a waiver absolving you of all responsibility," she told him.

"It's not just myself and the project I'm concerned about, Arden. It's you. I care about my test subjects. I care about my patients."

"Don't worry about me. I'll be okay."

He shook his head and mumbled something about, "Damn FBI," then asked, "Any return of memory?"

The bleaching process had been similar to the original indoctrination, except that a recorded voice repeatedly instructed her to forget the horror she'd witnessed the day of her parents' death, while also telling her to let go of everything she'd previously learned in the tank. A posthypnotic suggestion taken to the extreme and amplified with drugs, sensory deprivation, and isolation.

"A few flashes here and there, but nothing significant."

"Which is what you wanted."

Arden leaned forward. "Dr. Harris. Did any of the previous subjects ever talk about—" She stopped. If she told him she sometimes heard Albert French in her head, he might not allow her to return.

"About what?"

She sidestepped. "The tanks . . . How much they hated the tanks."

"All of them. But we don't use the tanks anymore. Don't worry about them. Everything has been modified and streamlined."

"I don't care. I just want to catch whoever killed my parents."

He looked worried. "*You* are my main concern," he said.

She waved a hand—an air-erase of his words. "You know what I mean. Don't hold back. That's all I'm saying."

He clasped his hands over her file. "You know what I want? I want you to leave here. I want you to go back to New Mexico, where you've started a new life."

She gave him a small smile. Apparently he and Fury weren't working from the same page. That was good.

"You aren't going to go back, are you?" Harris asked.

"No."

"I can refuse to let you return to the program."

"I have to do this."

He let out a resigned sigh. "I knew I couldn't talk you out of it. We'll start slowly. Monitor you closely. I'll try not to push you harder than you should be pushed, but we've had to accelerate the pace. FBI request."

"Since I've been here before, the shorter time frame may not matter."

"I hope not, but I have reservations about it, too."

"I just want to start. I just want to get going."

"Which you'll be doing. When you leave my office today, you'll meet with my assistant. She'll give you a schedule and fill you in on the details. You'll complete some paperwork. Tomorrow you'll have routine preliminary tests. If everything checks out, we'll start you day after tomorrow. In the meantime and during the indoctrination, we want you to exercise. Eat right. Get a good eight hours of sleep each night."

"No problem," she said, even though she couldn't promise eight hours.

"We'll begin with the depatterning phase. Empty you out before we feed you new information. After that, we'll give you a refresher on French."

She swallowed.

"If someone is copying French, then it makes sense to reintroduce him to your conscious and subconscious mind," Harris continued. "After that, you'll view a videotape of the most recent copycat crime. The FBI hopes you'll be able to tie the two together and come up with a solid profile."

She nodded. She knew the drill.

He opened a desk drawer and pulled out a transparent plastic jewel case containing a DVD.

The case had her name on it.

"Your final interview." He handed it to her. "Before the bleaching."

Her mouth went dry and her heart began to slam all over again.

"It's not an assignment. Not a part of what we'll be doing here. You don't need to watch it. I just thought it was your right to have it. Never watch it if you don't want to."

Could she make herself pick it up? She wanted to knock the interview off the desk as if it were a spider. Instead, she grabbed the DVD and got to her feet.

When the alarm went off the next morning, Arden dragged herself out of bed. She dressed in gray jogging pants and a T-shirt and sweatshirt, topping them off with a soft, black stocking cap.

As if she could go more than a mile, she thought wryly.

She shuffled to the elevator.

There was a time when she would have sprinted down the stairs, bounced out the door, and hit the jogging trails. That seemed like another life. It *was* another life.

Her eyes weren't awake; she had trouble seeing

the elevator buttons. She poked and the door creaked open.

The alarm had been set for six A.M., meaning she'd gotten three hours of sleep.

Once outside, she took a few tentative steps. From old habit she brought her hands up, elbows at her side. One foot here, one foot there.

Oh yeah. Almost as natural as walking.

She could see her breath. She liked that.

The increase in oxygen cleared her head. Suddenly she was enjoying herself, enjoying the strength of her body, the movement that was *better* than walking.

Why had she quit doing this? It felt so good.

A footfall sounded behind her and Noah appeared wearing a sweat-soaked gray sweatshirt and black wind pants.

"I forgot how good this feels," she said once he was even with her. "If a person could fly, I think it might feel like this."

"Don't push yourself too much the first time."

Good advice.

Her lungs burned and sweat poured down her spine. She was tempted to keep going, to do another mile. And maybe another. Instead she slowed her pace.

Approaching the main building, they decelerated to a brisk walk.

Arden's body suddenly felt stiff and awkward, as if it were meant only to run and not walk. The sun was higher in the sky, burning off the dampness in the air. Sunlight fell on cold surfaces, causing small curls of steam to rise.

"I wanted to tell you I'm sorry about the other night," Noah said. "I don't know why I did it. It was stupid. Franny just makes me mad sometimes, talking about how I have it so easy. It drives me a little crazy."

They stopped a few yards from a set of heavy double doors.

"I have to ask you something," she said. Standing next to him, Arden realized how small and rather frail he seemed. "Were you in one of the float tanks?"

He tugged off his striped stocking cap. Dark, damp hair stuck up in every direction. Steam rose from the top of his head. "I heard you saw something in one of them." He pulled up the hem of his gray shirt to wipe his face, then let it drop. "It wasn't me. I swear. Why would I do something like that?"

"To scare us. To scare Franny."

He grinned, then shook his head. "I was too scared myself."

"Did you see anything unusual? Hear anything?"

"Nothing. Not until you fell and made a buncha noise. That's how I caught up with everybody."

Had she imagined it? Imagined that she saw someone in the tank? The more time that passed, the more she was beginning to think Fury was right. She'd been confused. Or maybe it had been a crisis apparition. It was a documented fact that under high levels of stress or agitation, people sometimes saw things that weren't there.

"We're having a picnic this afternoon," Noah said.

"Tomorrow we start on a new study, and this might be our last chance to have fun for a while. Plus, the weather's supposed to be nice for a change. You should come."

"Thanks." She gave him a smile, feeling somewhat relaxed for the first time since arriving on the Hill. "I might do that."

Arden spent the next several hours being screened for TAKE. When they were done drawing blood and testing her reflexes and mental skills, she walked across the grass toward Building 50 and her room.

Someone shouted her name, and she turned to see Noah, Eli, and Franny sitting on a blanket in the sun. Noah gave her a big wave and motioned her over.

Until that moment, she'd forgotten his earlier invitation.

Franny jumped up and spread out an extra blanket. "You have to join us."

Arden was tired. She wanted to be alone, but they were all smiling at her with expectation, and the blanket and lawn were inviting.

She joined them.

They ate bread and cheese, and strawberries dipped in chocolate. They drank champagne out of plastic cups. They laughed and drowsed in the sun until it started to get low in the sky and Vera Thompson found them.

"Did you hear them last night?" Vera gave Arden a hard stare.

Arden propped herself on her elbows. Now that the sun was down, the air was getting chilly. "Who?"

"The shadow people."

Noah made a choking sound. Franny frowned at him and he struggled to control himself.

"No, Mrs. Thompson," Arden said. "I didn't hear anything."

"You must sleep like a log then. They was running all over the place."

Arden looked from Eli to Franny to Noah. "Were you racing in the halls last night?"

They shook their heads.

"You gotta be careful." Mrs. Thompson pointed an arthritic finger at Arden. "Lock your door. Don't forget to lock your door."

"I won't."

What a cruel joke God played on old people. *Now that you've made it all these years, now that you've put up with all this shit, I'm going to hit you with one last trick: dementia.*

"I lock my door every night," Arden said.

Vera suddenly took visual note of the others. "That goes for the rest of you too." She pointed at each of them, one at a time. "Lock up tight."

"We will," Franny said.

Eli bobbed his head and smiled, while Noah stared hard at the ground, a fist pressed to his mouth.

Vera shuffled away.

Noah released the burst of laughter he'd been holding.

"Jesus," Eli said under his breath.

"Poor woman," Franny said.

Noah jumped to his feet. "Somebody should put her out of her misery."

Franny looked up sharply. "Noah!"

"I'm sorry, but I never wanna get that old and deranged." He tugged on his stocking cap. "Hey, I was gonna tell her that the shadow people could slip under the door, but I didn't."

"Gold star, buddy," Eli drawled sarcastically.

They packed up. Arden folded her blanket and handed it to Franny. Five minutes later, she told them thanks and headed to her room.

Fury caught up with her outside Building 50.

"I'm leaving for a couple of days," he said, a little out of breath. "Something's come up."

He wore jeans and a corduroy jacket, looking very un-Fury-like.

"Concerning the Oklahoma murders?"

"Mainly an unrelated case. But I have people trying to establish a solid link between the Oklahoma massacre and the deaths of your parents. So far, nothing but the MO to connect the two. There was never much in the way of solid evidence gathered from your—" He stopped.

She got it. Small-town cops were ill equipped, in more ways than one, to deal with such carnage.

"You have my cell phone number?" Fury asked.

"In my room."

"Call if you need anything. I'd hoped to be here tomorrow when you started the first phase." He seemed worried.

"No big deal."

"I'll be back in a day or two."

She nodded. "Everything will be okay." She didn't know what difference it should make to him.

The next morning, Arden got up early, jogged, showered, and headed to the Mercy Unit and Project TAKE. Even though it wasn't yet eight o'clock, the building was humming. People in lab coats rushed up and down hallways, and the energy in the structure could be felt on her skin. Doctors were being paged, and people pushed medical carts from room to room.

A busy place. She couldn't remember if it had been that busy when she'd been involved with the program before.

TAKE was located on the first floor, in a solitary wing.

They were expecting her. "We are all so excited to have you here," said a perky young blonde as she poked around at the back of Arden's hand, trying to isolate a good vein.

"Why am I getting an IV?"

"Saline solution." The girl taped the needle in place and released the rubber tubing on Arden's arm with a loud snap. She straightened and opened the flow wheel on the drip bag. "To make sure you don't get dehydrated. Do needles bother you?"

Arden glanced up at the saline bag hanging from the metal rack. "It's just that these things make me think of being sick."

From there, she was put on a gurney and wheeled into a room that appeared to have been last updated in the twenties. Green tile on the walls. Heavy porcelain, pedestal sink.

Dr. Harris stepped into the room and closed the door.

He smelled like woodsy aftershave again, but underneath that, she detected an unpleasant scent. Something she didn't like and couldn't place.

"Sorry to keep you waiting." He pulled a syringe from the deep pocket of his white lab coat, uncapped the needle, and prepared to inject the fluid into her IV.

"What's that?"

"Something to help you relax and make the time go a little faster."

"No, I mean what is it? Exactly."

"A mild sedative. It will also help to make you more susceptible to our suggestions. It's part of the protocol." He looked at her. "Would you rather I didn't use it?"

"No." They'd used drugs before, but never an IV line. Who was she to complain about a mild sedative? "Go ahead."

"Remember that you are in control. At any time during this process, you can stop everything. You can say you've had enough. Understand?"

She nodded. "Go ahead."

He injected the drug.

Within seconds, heat began to spread through her body, and her muscles grew limp.

"That's it. Don't fight it," he said. "Let us do all the work. You don't have to do anything but relax."

She drifted. Floated. Lost track of time.

Dr. Harris addressed someone else in the room. Someone Arden couldn't see.

"Take her down to the basement and through the tunnel to Cottage 25."

Arden tried to speak, tried to protest, but she couldn't move.

She finally placed the smell.

Like corroded metal. Like rubber.

Like an isolation tank.

Chapter 11

Smells.

Salt water.

Disinfectant that burned her throat.

Corrosion. Rust.

A clanging. A far-off echo of metal against metal. Like the tolling of a buoy in a heavy fog.

Arden had no body. No appendages. She'd left them somewhere. Forgotten. Discarded. Unnecessary.

The voice. That was all that mattered. Everything was the voice.

"You become who you kill," the voice said. "You can't forget that. If you look into someone's eyes as you kill him, you steal a little of his soul."

Like bad radio reception, the voice faded in and out, forcing her to strain so she could hear every word. But even if she missed something, it would come back.

It always came back. Repeating the message.

A man's voice.

"I kill people," he said. "A rage builds inside me, a deep, seething hatred for humanity. When that happens, when I'm to the point where I'm about to explode, I don't care about anything. I just want to kill. I need to kill, to take a life."

His voice was low and deep.

She liked that.

"More than one life. Several. I want to hurt. I want to inflict pain. Not only physical pain. Mental pain. I'm not talking torture. I'm not one of those kinda guys. We got some of them in here, and that's not what it's all about. That's not what I'm into."

Arden strained to hear his next words.

"Annihilation. Wiping people out. Making a huge, fucking statement about the world, about people and life in general.

"Most people are just a bunch of fucking worker bees, going about their business, not even thinking of the big picture. I want to make them see the big picture, you know. I want them to see that none of it matters. That it's all shit. All fake. People need to know that. They need to wake up. They need to be shaken out of that false reality of self-importance they've created."

True, Arden thought.

"It's not a big deal. The world created rules, but those rules aren't for me. They have nothing to do with me."

His voice faded, as if he'd moved from the microphone, or turned his head to the side.

She strained to hear. She didn't want to miss anything.

"Killing isn't a big deal. Squashing ants. That's all

I'm doing. But everybody thinks it's a big deal." He laughed.

A nice laugh. Deep. Full of sarcasm.

"But it's all a joke. That's what I'm teaching. That it's a joke. You're all too serious. Life's a joke. That's what you gotta remember. That's what you can't ever forget."

Arden had lost all sense of time and space. There was nothing but the present. Nothing but the floating and the darkness and the tolling of the bell.

And the voice.

Without the voice, existence would have been unbearable. She would have been trapped in the dark with nothing to cling to. The voice was what kept her going, kept her from losing her mind.

"I'm going to talk about the killings," he said. "I'm going to describe them in detail."

She'd already heard it several times. So many that she had it memorized, and could tell his stories along with him. At first, she just quietly mouthed the words.

I watched from a hill outside their house. It was night, and all the lights were on. They didn't even close the curtains. I could see them moving around in there. My own private show.

Arden began to whisper the words aloud. . . .

"They didn't even put up a fight. They never do. They just stand there like a buncha sheep, you know. That always makes me madder. The way they whimper and cower and beg for mercy instead of taking action. Out of all the people I killed, not one ever tried to kill me. Some fight me, but nobody's ever aggressive. Well, that's not completely true. I had one grandpa who came running in with an ax. But the guy was so old and weak he could hardly lift it."

He laughed again.

Arden laughed with him, causing the bell to clang.

"I wiped out the whole family. All of them. Grandpa. Mom and Pop. What ended up being a son and his wife, plus a coupla their brats. I swear, I felt worse when a neighbor poisoned my dog. I liked that dog."

Arden felt his sorrow.

"You wanna know why I target Middle America? White, middle-class families? Because they are the biggest frauds of all. I hate frauds. I hate phonies, and all them little towns scattered across the Midwest are as phony as they come. How do I know that? Because I grew up in one. All Mom and apple pie is what it seems like to the outside world. People look at them and wonder what's wrong with their own life."

Arden nodded and the bell clanged again.

It was true. Everything was true.

"I hate those fucks. Life is dirty. And life don't mean nearly as much as they think it does."

The voice went on to tell about another set of murders he'd committed, and another.

"But I have my apprentices," he said. "We all have to have apprentices. People to carry on our work when we're gone. People to keep the flame of anarchy alive. I agreed to this recording so the truth could be told. Not some twisted media version of the truth that's only about forty percent truth and the rest something that'll be turned into a Hollywood movie. I'm all about the truth. When they make a movie about me, I want it to be accurate." There was a slapping sound, like hands clapping. "Long live Albert French."

"Long live Albert French," Arden whispered. Her voice echoed back at her.

Chapter 12

The voice stopped.

Arden held her breath, hoping it would start again.

Silence.

Silence and darkness.

A confused awareness of immediate space slowly crept into her consciousness.

A box. A container. Something coffinlike.

Awareness of self slowly followed.

She was in the box. In the darkness.

Floating.

Arden heard the sound of clanging metal. Of locks being undone.

The lid to the box lifted and bright light blinded her. She tried to raise her hand to shield her eyes, but her arms wouldn't move.

"Turn off the overhead light," said a voice that was so muffled Arden couldn't tell if it belonged to a man or a woman. "It's hurting her eyes."

The brightness faded.

Two people, male and female, leaning over her,

doing something to her wrists and ankles. Had she been restrained?

"Got the IV?" the woman asked.

"Out," replied the man.

"Here's a Band-Aid."

Tearing paper, then something being taped to the back of her hand.

"Can you sit up?"

The woman was talking to her. To Arden.

Hands gripped her elbows and shoulders. They pulled her forward. Water gushed with the movement, following her, trying to cling but having to finally give up and settle about her waist.

"There you go," the woman said happily.

One ear popped, and suddenly Arden could hear the hum of the room, hear the room breathing.

Cold air hit her chest. A shiver went through her.

"The sooner we get you outta here, the sooner you can have a warm shower," the woman said.

Grasping her by both arms, they pulled her to her feet, water sloshing.

Naked.

In some far-off part of her mind, she knew her nudity was something she should care about—but she didn't. Did a baby feel self-conscious when it was born?

They wrapped her in a blanket. It didn't help. She was so cold. Freezing.

"Step out of the tank," the guy told her.

She looked down.

Even though they'd dimmed the lights, Arden's vision was all screwed up. There was a film over her eyes, and a shifting, reddish aura around everything. As if she'd been pressing her hands to her eyelids.

But she could make out a pair of pale legs that must be hers. She could feel them trembling violently.

Would they ask a newborn to stand?

"Come on," the woman encouraged. Fingertips moved across her shoulder, pressing through the blanket.

Arden liked the woman. She had a coaxing, motherly voice. The guy, on the other hand, seemed hard. Impatient.

Like the male nurse in *Harvey*. Yeah. She loved that movie. And hadn't Jimmy Stewart been great? They wouldn't dare make a movie like that now. A comedy about a guy who was really nothing more than a raging alcoholic. Not PC at all.

"Come on," the woman repeated.

I aim to please.

Arden concentrated on one leg. On lifting that leg. Getting it over the side of the tank. Her foot finally made contact with the grid of the metal platform. One more step and she was out.

They whisked her off, and suddenly the movie changed from *Harvey* to *Silkwood*. Suddenly she was Meryl Streep getting mercilessly scrubbed down by mean hands. Water poured over Arden's face, with no concern for her eyes or nose or the fact that she might be trying to breathe.

I'm not radioactive.

She meant to speak the words out loud, but that didn't happen.

Was she radioactive?

After the shower, they dried her with rough towels, helped her into a hospital gown, then pushed her into a chair in order to wrap a blood pressure cuff around her arm. When they'd finished taking her vitals, a tray of food appeared: turkey and mashed potatoes.

The canned, clinical smell made her gag.

"Not hungry?" Mom asked.

Arden gagged again.

The tray disappeared.

A small box was stuck in her hand.

"Juice," Mom said. "You'd at least like some juice, wouldn't you?"

She helped Arden lift it to her face, guiding the tiny bent straw to her mouth. Apple. Not bad. Good, actually.

"I'll try to find something else for you to eat," the woman said when Arden finished off the juice.

It didn't seem that she'd even been gone when she was back with a container of yogurt.

Lemon.

Arden took three bites before her stomach cramped.

"It's the meds," the nurse said.

Arden's vision was still fuzzy, but clearer than it had been. She could now see that the woman was dressed in white pants and a pale-green nurse's smock. She was about fifty-five. A little on the heavy side.

The woman took the container from Arden. "We'll just take it slow."

Suddenly Arden began to move and she realized she was in a wheelchair. She was being pushed from the shower room, down a long hallway to a new destination. A small room with chairs on one side and a retractable movie screen on the other.

"Sleep." Arden's throat was raw, and the word came out a croak. She could hardly keep her eyes open. She felt like shit. She didn't want to watch any damn movie.

"The doctor has some things he wants you to view," the nurse said.

"Too tired. I need to sleep."

"I'm sorry." The woman looked as if she meant it. Head tipped to the side, an apologetic expression on her face. "I have to follow the doctor's orders. He doesn't want you to sleep yet. It's part of the protocol."

"I can't give anything my full attention when I'm so tired." Arden looked down at the floor.

Wood. Hard. But maybe not *that* hard.

"When it's over, I'll come back and get you."

The nurse clicked a few keys on a laptop computer, turned off the light, and left the room.

Arden took the opportunity to slip from the wheelchair to the floor. She dropped to her knees, then melted the rest of the way until she was lying on her side, her face against the floor.

It felt pretty damn good.

The stomach cramps had stopped. She was dry

except for her wet hair. Somewhat dressed. Amazing how luxurious a few simple things could be.

Her eyes began to drift closed as she glanced at the screen above her.

A robin's-egg-blue, Colonial-style farmhouse.

Her breath caught. She was suddenly transfixed.

Car doors slammed. Voices could be heard in the distance. People conversing in low tones.

The camera moved toward the house, a single pair of footsteps crunching across gravel.

The video was in color and amateur; the sudden camera movements made her feel motion-sick.

It wasn't until she spotted the yellow crime-scene tape wrapped around the massive trunks of the trees in the front yard that she realized she was watching a crime-scene video.

The recording had a weird, almost 3-D appearance that digital often had. Objects seemed to have an outline, as if someone had drawn around them with a black felt pen. It also had a voyeuristic quality that went along with handheld cameras.

It was late summer or early fall.

Trees were thick with leaves, the leaves casting deep, contrasting shadows on the grass. Along the house, thick clusters of flowers bloomed, and a trumpet vine curled up thick creosote poles and crept along wires leading to upstairs windows where young children and babies slept in what they thought was a bucolic, idyllic slumber.

The camera's depth of field was amazing. In the far distance, fences could be seen, along with a pasture dotted with black-and-white cattle. Nearby, round, giant hay bales waited to be moved from the field.

Grant Wood, eat your heart out.

Eat your heart out.

Why did people say that?

What did it really mean?

Eat your heart out.

The eye of the camera moved up the wooden front steps across the gray porch. A hand reached past the lens and the screen door creaked open.

A cluster of uniformed officers and a couple of detectives looked up and moved aside.

One of the officers, a female with blond hair, detached herself from the cluster. "I'll give you the tour."

"Did anybody feed the dog?" asked an off-camera voice.

"Dog?"

"There was a dog here earlier."

The camera followed the blond officer through a dining room to the kitchen.

It had probably been updated twenty years ago. Fake butcher-block countertops. Double sink. Double refrigerator, the doors covered with magnets and photos. Family shots. Some of those awful school photos. A couple standing under a palm tree, wearing big straw hats and holding drinks with umbrellas. Smiling.

It was almost impossible to leave a farm for more than a couple of hours at a time. There were so many responsibilities. So many animals that required constant, vigilant care. It was probably the only vacation they'd ever taken. On a farm, you had to try to find some small measure of comfort in the day-to-day existence. Maybe the song of a bird, or the sight of a herd of deer. Because there wasn't anything beyond those four hundred acres. Nothing anybody there would see until they reached retirement.

If they reached retirement.

Lying on the floor in a pool of blood that had hardened and turned black was a woman dressed in jeans and a green 4-H T-shirt. Her throat had been slit from ear to ear.

On the floor near the small kitchen table with a laminated top was a smaller body, this of a child of maybe eight or nine, lying facedown.

"Same MO," their hostess said, pointing. The hair was matted with blood that looked like black tar.

It was easy to mentally re-create the domestic scene. Mom had been cooking supper while the child sat at the table doing his homework.

People can be so predictable to the point of being boring, Albert French's voice seemed to whisper in her ear.

The officer lifted her hand and motioned with a crook of one finger.

Follow me.

The camera followed.

Arden followed.

They went back through the dining room and living room, up the stairs.

The first floor had been bad enough, with green shag carpet and loud floral wallpaper, but the second floor was even more tasteless.

Same horrid carpet. More wallpaper. Everywhere.

Every single surface shouted at you. Floral stripes of mauve and hunter green. Another room with about ten shades of pink.

Executed for bad taste.

It made perfect sense.

Avocado-green fixtures in the bathroom. It could have been a cool retro look if not for the fact that this wasn't retro and had been done in total seriousness. A teenage girl had been taking a shower at the time of the slaughter, and had grabbed the shower curtain as she went down.

The plastic curtain was gold.

"The shower ran so long that the well went dry," the tour guide said. "Just a trickle by the time police arrived on the scene approximately twelve hours after the murders."

They left the bathroom.

"The nearest neighbors realized something was wrong when the cattle got hungry and started bawling and raising a ruckus."

The blond officer paused in front of another door. "This is the saddest one."

The camera turned.

A nursery.

Finally a room that had a bit of taste. Recently redecorated with Peter Rabbit décor. In the white crib lay a dead infant.

"A girl," the guide said, her voice suddenly tight. "Throat slit. You'd think he could have . . . I don't know, smothered her instead."

She broke down.

The person operating the camera made some kind

of noise, some sound of sympathy, but that only made her cry harder.

The screen turned black. Two seconds later the tour guide was back. She'd recovered from her crying fit. In fact, they weren't even in the house anymore; they were in a barn.

"The father had been out in the field," the woman explained. "He'd parked the tractor and was heading inside for supper when he was killed."

A man's body hung upside down from a rope and pulley.

"We're going to get the bastard who did this," the officer said. "Get him and make sure he fries."

Why was she taking it so personally? Arden wondered. Didn't she know it was all a game?

The video ended. The screen went blank.

Arden pushed herself up off the floor and was back in the wheelchair just as light flooded the room.

"How are you feeling?" the nurse asked from the doorway, her hand on the switch.

"Better." Arden smiled. "Much better." The video had cheered her up. Was that wrong? It didn't seem wrong.

Chapter 13

Nathan Fury stood to the side of the one-way glass, hands in his pockets, waiting in semidarkness. The glass was his window to a small, sterile room with bright overhead fluorescent lighting, industrial gray carpet, and white walls.

As he watched, the door opened and a nurse entered pushing a wheelchair with Arden Davis slumped in the seat.

"She looks bad," Fury told Harris, who stood nearby, arms crossed at his chest. To Harris's right, seated at a control panel, was a technician who was there to record and document Arden's postdepatterning and indoctrination responses.

Arden's hair was stringy. Uncombed. Her eyes were dark pits. Someone had dressed her in a hospital gown, a lightweight green robe, and blue slippers.

It didn't seem to be enough clothing.

"She looks pretty good, all things considered," Harris said. He wore a white lab coat with his name embroidered above the pocket. Beneath the hem of the coat was a pair of razor-creased dress pants and shiny leather shoes.

Was she cold? Fury wondered. She looked cold.

He could barely recall his own "awakening" from isolation. And of course he'd been in the tank. Different situation. New protocol dictated that the subjects experience isolation and deprivation in the comfort of a small Mercy Unit room.

The nurse pushed the wheelchair to the center of the room. She locked the wheels, then leaned forward and patted Arden on the shoulder. "Someone will be in shortly." Her voice was piped from the microphoned room. "Are you comfortable?"

Arden didn't respond.

The nurse straightened, glanced up at the glass, turned, and left the room, closing the door behind her.

"Is she okay?" Fury asked.

"We're watching her vitals. They're fine. She's healthy. Strong."

Fury wasn't talking about her vitals.

"Her present condition is the result of drugs, stress, deprogramming, and sleep deprivation," Dr. Harris said. "She'll come around fairly quickly once the drugs are out of her system. You'll see."

Harris motioned to Arden behind the glass. "There you go. She's all yours. Remember that she'll be confused. She may not recall certain recent events, but most of that memory loss should be temporary."

Fury left the control room and entered the follow-up room. Three metal chairs with plastic seats were lined up against one wall. He grabbed a chair and placed it in front of Arden, sitting so they were face-to-face.

"Hi, Arden." He spoke quietly.

She didn't react.

He reached for one of her hands. It was like ice. He picked up her other hand and rubbed them between both of his.

She tugged her hands away. "What are you doing?" Her voice was a harsh, annoyed whisper.

"Do you remember me?" He hadn't meant to word it quite like that.

She had to give it some thought. "The FBI agent?"

"That's right. Nathan Fury."

"Fury."

"How are you feeling?"

"Tired." Her voice came out a whisper. "I want to sleep."

"As soon as we're done here, you can go to bed. I just need to ask you a few questions." Fury rubbed a hand across his face. "You just saw a film, remember?"

She nodded.

"About a murder."

Again the nod.

"I want you to tell me what you know about the perpetrator. About the person who committed the crimes."

She ran a tongue across her lips and stared into space. "A man. A man who's intelligent." Her tone was worshiping. "More intelligent than most men."

Fury tried not to let her unnerving attitude toward the murderer shake him. "Did you notice anything peculiar about the crime scene? Anything that may have clued you in, that may have given you information about the killer?"

She sat there awhile, head down, face hidden by her hair, seemingly staring at the floor. Had she fallen asleep?

"Was it real?" she asked. "Or a movie?"

"It was real." She'd probably told herself it was a movie just to get through it. Some people did that.

"Okay." She was silent a moment. "It was Albert French."

Fury knew they'd fed her fresh information on French—the personal interview done a few days before his execution.

"He would have left there on a blood high," she said without emotion. "He'll probably take a few days off. A week, maybe two; then he'll strike again."

Unlike serial killers, who sometimes disappeared for months, even years at a time, spree killers, mass murderers, could never get enough. As soon as the blood high wore off, they were at it again.

"It wasn't French," Fury said.

"What do you mean?" Her voice rose.

"French is dead. He was executed. The murders you saw on film occurred after his death."

She raised her head to look directly at Fury. Her eyes narrowed. "I was just talking to him."

"That was a recording. Made before his execution."

"You're lying. He's not dead," she insisted. "I can feel him. I'd know if he was dead."

Her response wasn't a surprise. The idea of indoctrination was to make the subject feel one with the killer. How else could she get into his head? But it was still unnerving as hell to see her choosing sides. *French's* side.

She thought the recording had been live. That was understandable, given the circumstances and the fragility of her mind.

Arden stared at him with bruised, intense, burning, fanatical eyes. "Albert French was talking to me in the tank."

Fury's stomach dropped. "Wh-what?"

"He was talking to me in the tank."

"You haven't been in the tank."

She was mixing up her most recent visit with that of several months ago. He leaned closer. "You're confused, Arden." He spoke softly. "We don't use the tanks anymore."

She frowned and seemed to be focusing on something inside her head. "Are you sure?"

"Positive."

"Why should I believe you? Why should I trust you?"

Because I love you, he thought. "Because I have your best interest in mind," he said.

Chapter 14

The shadow people were running again.

Vera felt the vibration as they raced down the hall.

Her room was dark.

She fumbled on the bedside table, her stiff fingers coming in contact with one of her hearing aids. Lying on her back in bed, she worked the small, awkward piece into her ear.

Footfalls; then she heard the shadow people sniffing at the crack under her door.

Vera wanted to turn on a lamp, but she was afraid the light and noise would attract the intruders, draw them to her. Then they would know she was inside the room and they'd come after her.

If she held very still, maybe they'd move on to another door, another part of the building.

What they wanted with an old hen like her, she didn't know. What they would want with any of the dried-up residents was a puzzle.

Maybe it was the building that attracted them.

A lot of bad things had gone on inside these walls. A lot of horrible, horrible things.

Bad things left an imprint on a place. The kind of imprint shadow people could sense.

No matter how still Vera remained, she couldn't keep her heart from racing, from pumping so frantically that anybody would have been able to hear it a block away. And the fear. She was sure she smelled like fear.

The sniffing stopped.

Whatever was out there continued on down the hall.

She forced herself to move, to get out of bed and hurry to the drawer where she kept the knives and scissors.

Residents were discouraged from having sharp things, but to hell with that, Vera had always said.

With a knife in her hand, she stood there breathing hard, barely able to make out vague shapes.

A table.

An overstuffed chair.

The door to her studio apartment was secured with a gadget she'd ordered off the TV. One end went against the door, the other end against the floor. You had to pull a lever to set the whole thing. The lever was hard to pull, and Vera was always afraid she hadn't gotten it tight enough.

They were coming back.

She could hear them.

Running in a pack.

Mob mentality.

They paused outside her door, all slobbering and out of breath from their mad run.

The doorknob rattled.

Oh, my God.

The knob turned.

The door shuddered, as if something heavy had thrown itself against it.

The shadow people are coming.

Vera backed toward the bathroom. With a jerk, she stepped inside the small space, slamming the door behind her.

No lock.

A safety feature, so employees could get to you if you needed help. Or if you decided to drown yourself, which she'd considered a time or two. Who wouldn't, in a place like this? But what about the shadow people? Hadn't anybody thought about them? About keeping them out?

Vera wore thin cotton pajamas. Her feet were bare and the tile floor was cold.

Times like these, she missed her husband.

Simon had been fearless. He'd watched out for her. He would have been able to fight the shadow people.

But Vera was old. Her bones were fragile and her ropy blue veins were close to the surface, just hiding under rice-paper skin. You wouldn't know it now, but when she was young she'd been quite a looker. She used to swim. Hours a day sometimes, so her body had been hard and strong.

Not anymore.

The door to her apartment crashed open.

She imagined the shadow people searching the room, finding her empty bed.

Footsteps sounded on the wooden floor outside the bathroom.

Since when did shadows wear shoes?

The world was such a strange place, so different from when she was young. When she was a kid, shadows were just shadows. They didn't move and sound like people.

She'd deliberately left off the light. But that had probably been a bad idea. Shadows were nocturnal. They could see at night, but she couldn't. A most unlevel playing field.

For some reason, she was no longer afraid.

She'd been staring at death a long time.

Her husband was gone. Her friends were gone. The only people left were ones she could do without, like the daughter-in-law who'd tricked her into coming here.

Bitch.

Oh, she'd much rather have died peacefully in her sleep, but how many people got that lucky?

Very few.

But that knowledge didn't keep her from putting up a fight. She tried to hold the bathroom door closed, but the shadow was much stronger.

The door flew open.

That's when everything sped up and slowed down.

The shadow walked upright like a human. It was wearing something——a hooded sweatshirt.

It could have very well been a man. Any man. For a moment she wondered if it *was* a man, if she was confused the way she got confused sometimes.

It grabbed for her and she sidestepped, lifting the knife, plunging it at the dark shape above her, striking nothing but air. Something struck her once, twice, in the chest. The knife slipped from her fingers and clattered to the floor.

She felt cold steel against her neck, against her throat. With one swift slicing movement, her jugular was cut.

Air hissed and blood bubbled, erupting and spilling hotly down the front of her pajama top.

So hard to get out blood . . . When she had that miscarriage and Simon had wrapped her in a sheet and hurried her to the hospital, she thought she'd never get the blood out.

The floor was slick.

She lost her balance; her feet went out from under her.

Oopsie-daisy.

That was okay, because she was sinking fast anyway.

She fell over backward, her legs striking the edge of the claw-foot tub. She grabbed at the plastic shower curtain as she went down.

The world was so much meaner now, so much more disturbing.

She was tired of this life. Ready to leave.

She'd had enough.

Life was crazy; then you got killed by shadow people.

Chapter 15

The soles of Arden's shoes slapped rhythmically on the asphalt as she took the final curve of the jogging path and headed for Building 50 and her room. It had been two days since her stint in isolation, and her brain was beginning to feel less foggy, her thinking less muddled.

Yesterday, Harris had mentioned the possibility of one—or even two—more sessions.

Arden didn't want to go back.

You have to.

There had been times when she could have sworn she'd been in the tank, even though she knew she must be confusing this visit with the previous one.

Same place.

Same drugs.

"And a similar technique," Dr. Harris had told her, "which brings about a conditioned reaction. It explains why patients who've been treated with painkillers for serious injuries experience the same pain years later when given the same drug. Conditioned reflex. It makes sense when you understand that information associated with physical or mental trauma is encoded at the cellular level."

At least the day was beautiful, Arden thought. Crisp, but not too frigid. Sun shining. A chill wind occasionally caused fallen maple leaves to scurry across her path and march in a row like little soldiers. Shadows were long and dark, almost black, the way they were in early winter when the air was dry and the sun was low in the sky.

She kept finding herself transfixed by the shifting pattern the few remaining dead leaves made on the sidewalk.

Upon entering the building, Arden headed across the lobby toward the stairs, passing an old woman with an aluminum cane waiting for the elevator.

"Arden?" the woman called after her in a hesitant voice.

Arden paused.

"I've seen you talking to my friend, Vera," the woman said. "She didn't come down for breakfast, and I'm going up to check on her. We always eat breakfast together."

Vera's friend didn't come right out and ask for company in her mission, but the subtext was obvious.

Arden backed up. "I'll come with you."

"I'm Betty Stewart."

The elevator shimmied to the fifth floor as Arden and Betty stood side by side, facing the door. "Told Vera it was a bad idea to have a room all the way up here, but she said she wanted a view and to be as far away from everybody else as possible." Betty laughed. Her stooped shoulders, draped in a thick sweater, shook.

The elevator stopped and the door clanged open.

"Her daughter-in-law tricked her into coming here, you know," Betty said, stepping into the hallway.

"That's what I heard." Apparently everybody knew the story.

"I wanted to come," Betty told her. "I like it here. It's nice having people around all the time. I used to live alone and hated it." She paused, raising a long-nailed finger to her lips. "I always get mixed up. Only been up here a few times. Here it is. This way." She pointed. "I remember seeing that fire extinguisher."

Arden was once again struck by the magnificence of Building 50's architecture. From where they stood, the detailed arched doorways repeated themselves, leading off into infinity.

"It's spooky up here," Betty whispered loudly, jolting Arden out of her admiration for the way sunlight fell through a tall window, making a contrast of light and shadow on a particularly lovely stretch of molding.

You knew when your mind was beginning to slip, she thought, because you paid special attention to insignificant details. To the way light fell, the way doorways were outlined by shadow upon shadow upon shadow, and leaves left a pattern on the walk.

Something nagged at her brain. A smell. A memory . . .

Arden put out her hand, stopping the woman.

Her other hand automatically reached for the gun she used to wear at her waist.

It wasn't there, of course. When would she quit reaching for something that wasn't there?

Death had a smell.

Not always of rot, which a novice might think, but of other things. And blood had a distinctive, recognizable odor. Metallic, combined with something heavy and sweet.

"Stay here," Arden said.

Betty lifted a large-knuckled hand to her throat. Her mouth dropped open and her eyes grew large. "That's Vera's room. Should we call somebody? Should we go back downstairs and find somebody?"

Arden didn't take her eyes off the door. "No need to get ahead of ourselves."

It could just be the smell of age. Or an imprint left behind by someone who'd lived there decades ago.

Arden approached the room, stopping in front of a door someone had painted in several layers of thick black enamel in an unsuccessful attempt to cover up the years.

The door was ajar, looking as if it hadn't quite latched. Arden reached for the ornate knob—and saw that the catch plate had been ripped from the wooden frame.

She pushed the door open further.

She paused to listen, then stepped inside.

A single bed. Unmade. No signs of struggle.

"Vera?"

Her voice came out too loud in the small space. Arden crossed to the bathroom door, which was also painted black, also ajar. With her fingertips, she gave the door a slight push. It swung open practically by itself.

Draped over the claw-foot tub, her body tangled in a transparent shower curtain, was Vera. The woman's throat had been sliced from ear to ear and she was very, very dead.

Nathan Fury was walking toward the Mercy Unit and the Webber Institute when his cell phone rang.

Arden.

"You might want to come to Building 50," she told him. "Fifth floor."

He was about to ask why when he heard the sound of a far-off siren, followed by another and another.

"We have a dead body," Arden said.

He disconnected and headed for Building 50 while the sun shone brilliantly and blindingly in the sky and the sound of sirens drew nearer.

Inside, people had gathered in the lobby, looking nervously at the elevator, stairs, and ceiling as if they could see through all the layers to the horror above.

Fury slipped through the crowd and took the stairs. He was slightly out of breath when he reached the fifth floor.

He found a young policeman hovering just inside the door to the crime scene. Fury flashed his badge and the cop relaxed in relief, then quickly stiffened again as he obviously recalled what was waiting for them inside.

"Where's Arden Davis?" Fury asked. At the blank

look his question received, he elaborated. "The woman who found the body."

"Oh. Her. She and the old lady went down the hall and around the corner. I told them someone would be there soon to talk to them."

Fury nodded, then did a quick visual perusal of the room.

"In there." The officer pointed.

He was about twenty-five, light haired, a few freckles on his face. Most likely his first homicide, from the way he was acting.

Fury crossed the room and sidestepped into the bathroom, careful not to touch anything. The old woman was tangled in a clear shower curtain, her throat sliced.

It was a chillingly familiar MO.

He stared at the woman's chalky face and blue lips.

What kind of monster murdered a helpless old woman?

The same kind of person who murdered schoolchildren and infants.

Directly behind him, the officer made a choked sound, then scrambled from the room.

Fury looked down. They were in luck—if you could call it that. The perpetrator had left a fairly well defined bloody shoe print on the white tile floor.

Didn't clean up his mess. Amateur, or blatant.

Five minutes later the place was thick with cops and detectives. Fury answered a few questions, left his cell number, then went in search of Arden. On the way, he passed the young officer who was now sitting on the floor, his back against the wall, eyes closed, sweat pouring down his face.

The guy should stick to traffic tickets. Some cops just weren't meant for homicide.

Fury found Arden in a suite down the hall that had been designated for interviews. She sat in a metal folding chair, her arm around an elderly woman wearing a bulky sweater and white Velcro-fastened walking shoes, whom she introduced as Betty Stewart.

"Have you been down there?" Arden was dressed in black sweatpants and a navy-blue sweatshirt. Her hair was pulled into a short ponytail, her face pale and free of makeup.

He nodded.

"We're waiting for somebody to take our statements," Arden said.

"It's awful." The old woman fingered a cotton handkerchief with pink embroidered flowers and looked up at him with red-rimmed eyes. "I was afraid something was wrong when she didn't come down to breakfast, but I never dreamed it would be anything like this."

Arden patted the woman's hand, then got to her feet. She grabbed Fury by the arm and steered him away. "Do they have any idea who did it?"

"Not yet."

"Motive?" she asked.

"Nothing stolen. No obvious signs of rape. They found a knife, but it's not the murder weapon. Too small and dull."

"Used for defense?"

"Most likely. We're hoping she got in a pass or two. Police are keeping their eyes open for someone with defensive wounds. They'll also be testing blood samples."

"Think it could be a resident?" Arden asked. The ease with which she dropped into her old FBI role didn't escape him.

"You saw the crime scene. What do you think?"

"Had to be someone strong. That gash in her throat had a lot of strength and anger behind it. It couldn't have been made by some weak eighty-year-old."

"Not all of the residents here are necessarily weak. Many are part of the independent living program."

"When I was little, we raised sheep. The wolves and coyotes killed the sheep and ate them. They had a reason. But domestic dogs . . . that was another thing. They played with the sheep. They tortured them. But they never ate them. In one night, we lost twelve sheep. None of them were dead when my dad found them, but they were all so severely injured that they had to be put down."

"Did you ever find the dogs that did it?"

"That was even more disturbing. Two were some kind of mixed breeds, but one of them ended up being this fluffy little poodle. We actually found sheep wool in its teeth."

"So you're saying this was done for fun. For pleasure."

"Blood sport."

He thought so too.

"Security here is a joke," she said. "Anybody could have gotten in. Plenty of places to hide."

"The killer could be someone from town." Fury frowned in thought. "Someone from out of town. Somebody just passing through."

"It was the shadow people," Mrs. Stewart said loudly from her seat under the window.

Fury looked from her to Arden, his eyebrows raised in question. *What's she talking about?*

"Vera said shadow people were after her," Arden explained. "She said she could hear them running up and down the hall."

"Did you ever hear anything?"

"I heard running. But it wasn't shadow people. It was Noah, Eli, and Franny. They get bored and run around at night. Harmless stuff."

"Let's go talk to them," he said.

They left Mrs. Stewart in the care of a staff nurse, told the detectives they would be back, and headed off to find Noah, Eli, and Franny.

They found them lying on the floor in the semi-darkness of a murky, incense-thick room, groggy music playing, the lamps dimmed with red scarves. Nobody got up to answer the door. Franny just weakly shouted for them to come in.

"What was all the noise out there?" Franny asked. She was lying on her back, eyes closed, hands on her stomach. "Somebody die?"

Fury crossed the room and turned off the CD player.

The bottom seemed to fall out of the room.

"Hey," Noah complained weakly.

"Are you all high?" Arden asked.

"High?" Franny giggled and folded herself into a sitting position, legs crossed. "You think we're high?"

"Just chillin'," Eli said.

He and Noah sat up. Eli stretched and got to his feet. Noah rubbed his head and sleepily eyed the pillow beside him. "What happened to the tunes, man?"

Arden pulled a scarf from the nearest lamp. The bulb was weak and didn't cast much light. All three blinked as if it were the sun.

"There's been a murder," Arden announced.

They took it in slowly.

"No," Eli said. "When? Where?"

"Last night. One of the elderly residents."

"Oh, man," Noah said. "That sucks. Who would kill an old person?"

"And why?" Franny added. She got to her feet and wrapped her arms around herself, shivering.

"Were any of you out last night?" Fury asked.

The three looked at one another.

"We'd just finished a session at Mercy," Noah said. "After that, we got something to eat in the cafeteria, then came back here and crashed."

"*Really* crashed," Eli said. "It was like, seven or seven thirty."

"You didn't go out after that?" Arden asked.

They shook their heads, appearing baffled by the questions.

"Are you thinking one of us did it?" Eli asked incredulously.

"We just wanted to know where you were," Fury said. "And if you saw or heard anything. Routine questions. Everyone in the building will be interviewed. In the entire complex."

Eli relaxed a little. "Okay. That's cool."

Once Arden and Fury stepped outside the room, Fury zoomed in on her.

"And what about you?" he asked as they walked down the long hall. "Where were you last night?"

She stopped.

He stopped.

"In my room," she said slowly.

"All night?"

"Yes, all night."

He stared at her. She refused to break eye contact. Staring, staring.

A blink from him.

Flash.

Something in his eyes, happening so quickly that it was gone before she could get an accurate reading. But it had looked uncomfortably like suspicion.

Chapter 16

Noah sat on the windowsill of the room he shared with Eli and Franny. Arden and Fury had just left, and his roommates were debating the situation.

"What should we do?" Franny asked. "Leave? I don't want to leave."

A rage builds inside me, a deep, seething hatred for humanity. I don't care about anything. I don't care if I get caught. I just want to kill. I need to kill, to take a life.

Noah watched Eli rub his head, stirring up his bushy hair. It was a mess. He probably hadn't washed it in days.

None of them had gotten much sleep lately. Or at least Noah hadn't, and he didn't think Franny and Eli had either. He couldn't remember much about the procedures they'd endured, but he knew they'd been rotated in and out of the isolation tanks, then watched closely for a period of time before being turned loose. When they'd headed for their room last night, none of them had spoken. They'd walked across the dark grounds like three zombies, gotten some food in the cafeteria that they couldn't eat, returned to the tower, and crashed. Hadn't even stripped down to their underwear. Just crashed.

Killing isn't a big deal. Squashing ants. That's all I'm doing.

"She was old," Eli said. He picked up the spiral notebook he always carried with him.

He thought of himself as a writer. What kind? Noah wasn't sure. Eli didn't write stories; he just wrote about himself. What he thought about people. His reaction to different situations. Descriptions.

Noah had once told Eli that if he was going to be a writer, he had to do more. He had to tell a story.

Eli just threw him the finger.

"Do you think the killer's still here?" Franny rubbed her arms. She sounded scared again. "I think he—or she—could still be in the building. That's what I think. This is a big place. A maze. A killer could hide anywhere."

Noah got up from the stone window seat.

It had been nice there, with the sun on his back. Down on the ground, police were everywhere. Poking around, probably looking for the murder weapon.

He went over to the CD player and started stacking his CDs. He loved music more than anything in the world. More than Franny, and that was saying a lot.

After a while, he abandoned the plastic jewel cases. He unzipped his duffel bag and dug inside, looking for some clean clothes.

He spotted the shirt he'd worn last night. Quickly,

he grabbed the canvas handles of the bag and walked across the room.

"Where are you going?" Eli asked.

"To take a shower."

"I'll take one when you're done. Then maybe we can go into town and get a pizza. I gotta get outta here for a while."

"Yeah." Noah nodded. "That sounds good."

"Chicken and pineapple!" Franny said. "And darts. They have darts at Grumpy Steve's."

The mood was lifting. Even though someone was dead, they were moving on. That's what you did. Moved on.

People are resilient, Noah's shrink always told him. *They can handle a lot of things you wouldn't think they'd be able to handle.*

Noah had been through some weird stuff in his life. He'd been alone with his grandfather when he'd died. The old guy had sprawled out on the couch. Said he was going to shut his eyes for a minute. He never opened them again.

Noah was eight.

He remembered shaking him, trying to get him to wake up. He spent the whole day there, waiting. Getting hungry. Bored. Then his mom came to pick him up and all hell broke loose.

The bathrooms in the asylum were cool. Pale green tile on the floor. Smaller green squares of one-inch tile on the walls. Black trim. Porcelain sinks like they used to have in old schools. Unlike some of the other rooms, this one had a regular stand-up shower. No claw-foot tub.

And huge windows. Some with original, poured glass. The kind that was hard to see through.

Windows were a big thing here. An important part of the Kirkbride design. Even in the 1800s, they'd understood the importance of sunlight. They'd understood how a person could come unglued without it.

Light.

Touch.

Sensory deprivation.

Noah had read a lot about it before coming to the Hill. He knew that people—perfectly sane people in similar situations—had lost it in less than twenty-four hours. Funny that being alone like that could cause a person to lose his mind.

Years ago, they'd done experiments with babies and found that the ones who were touched and held and talked to learned much faster.

He reached behind the curtain and turned on the shower.

He pulled off his dark green, long-sleeved cotton shirt. He loved that shirt. Had had it for three years. Wore it all the time.

He stripped the rest of the way, then stepped into the shower.

Water beat against his chest. It ran in rivulets down his legs and swirled around his feet before disappearing into the drain.

What Franny and Eli didn't know was that Noah had gone out last night. On a run, as they called it.

He didn't remember the actual act of stabbing Vera Thompson, but he remembered the way her blood smelled. He remembered her dead eyes, and the gash in her throat that had almost severed her spine.

He remembered wiping her blood on his face.

He remembered tasting it while Albert French whispered in his ear.

We all have to have apprentices. People to carry on our work when we're gone.

Noah washed his hair.

Then, slowly and methodically, he washed his body using the liquid soap Franny had gotten from the health food store. She said it was biodegradable and wouldn't harm the environment. He liked that about her. Her concern over things she could do nothing about.

He would miss her.

He shut off the shower and dried himself. He combed his hair. He shaved. When he was done, he stepped back and regarded his reflection in the mirror.

A fragile, sad, sensitive person looked back.

A tragic figure.

Now he finally understood that he'd been too unstable for the project. What he hadn't wanted Franny to know was that his old man had bought his way in with a big fucking donation. The Hill had sounded exciting, even romantic, certainly something to do; plus Noah hadn't wanted Franny to leave him behind. He certainly hadn't wanted her to take off by herself with Eli, who'd liked her for a long, long time.

Noah removed his sneakers from the duffel bag.

He put them neatly side by side on the floor. On top of that, he placed the folded, bloodstained shirt he'd worn last night.

Naked, he climbed onto the stone window ledge, undid the metal hook latch, and shoved the window open.

Fresh air hit him in the face.

The sun was brilliant, almost blinding. Off in the distance, in a grove of nearby trees, birds were singing like crazy.

There was nothing else to do. No other solution. He couldn't face Franny. No way could he face Franny.

No way could he face his dad.

Or himself for one more second.

And music. How could he ever listen to music with the same innocence?

He couldn't.

Long live Albert French.

He pulled in a deep breath.

And jumped.

Chapter 17

Someone screamed.

Franny looked at Eli to gauge his reaction; then they both scrambled to the nearest window.

A crowd was gathering below.

Someone was lying on the ground. Naked. Face-down.

Dark hair. A circular tattoo on the shoulder. A tattoo Franny recognized.

No!

She ran to the bathroom and burst inside, her eyes rapidly scanning the small space.

The empty shower stall. The empty room. The open window.

"No!"

She ran from the bathroom, out into the hall, down the stairs, flying over them three and four at a time. Footsteps behind her: Eli's.

Out the door and into the blinding sunlight.

Sobbing loudly, she shoved people aside until she broke the circle, until she was on her knees on the ground next to Noah.

"No, no, no." She shook her head, tears streaming down her face, into her mouth.

Someone turned him onto his back.

Someone threw a coat over him.

Blood pooled in his mouth and ran down the side of his face. He pulled in a sucking breath and lifted a hand to her. The suffering in his eyes squeezed her heart.

She had the most inane thought: He should have picked a taller building. Now he was suffering horribly, with shattered bones and pierced lungs.

But maybe he would live. Maybe he wasn't dying.

"He's in pain!" she shouted to anybody who would listen. "Help him!" she implored. "Make him stop hurting! Make the pain stop!"

Time was weird. Stopping. Starting. Voices fading in and out.

Millions of voices. A soup of conversation, nothing distinguishable, women and their high *sshhh, sshh, sshhh* the only sound to pop out.

At some point in that wall of noise, Noah's body relaxed.

The pain—for him, at least—ended.

Franny looked up, searching for a familiar face, spotting Eli, his eyes glistening. "He's dead, Eli!" she shouted. "He's dead!"

Earlier, they had made light of another death. Someone old. Someone half senile. But this was Noah. This loss touched her personally, and the pain was intolerable. She thought she'd die from it.

Throughout most of Franny's life, she'd never missed having a mother. It had never mattered. Now she needed one. At times like these, a girl needed a fucking mother.

Paramedics appeared out of a sea of faces. They put Noah on a gurney and covered him.

Wait till I tell Noah, Franny caught herself thinking. *He's not going to believe this.*

Arden moved through the crowded lobby. People were looking outside, craning their necks to see what had happened.

"What's going on?" she asked, her heart pounding with a sense of foreboding and urgency.

"Somebody jumped from the roof."

"Not the roof," another person added. "It was the tower room. Someone jumped from the tower room."

Arden edged her way through the crowd and out the main door. She walked rapidly down the worn marble steps, past the passive white pillars and across the grass. She spotted Eli's curly hair. She spotted Franny—Franny's anguished face.

Oh, my God.

Arden started running before her brain issued the command. She was swept along by a reaction that seemed to come from somewhere else, someone else.

"What happened?" she heard herself shout to both Eli and Franny.

Their responses came in slow motion. They looked at her, recognition finally registering.

Relief to see her. Then pain. Horror.

Eye contact was broken. They turned their heads toward the body lying under the white sheet.

Arden understood, but she didn't want to believe and had to make sure. "Where's Noah?"

No. Not Noah. It couldn't be Noah.

Franny put a violently trembling hand to her mouth. Her face crumpled in a wave of agony.

Arden had to see for herself. She pushed her way through the throng of bystanders. "I need to see him," she told two men getting ready to heave the gurney into the back of the ambulance.

"And you are?"

With one smooth movement, she unzipped her sweatshirt, quickly flashed it open, then let it drop before anyone could see that she didn't have a badge. "FBI."

People murmured, looked down at their feet, dropped back, and let her through.

Before she lost her nerve, without a pause, she lifted the sheet.

Noah.

Skin the shade of paste. Lips already blue.

She'd liked that kid. He'd been a good kid. Annoying, but a good kid.

The blood on his face was already turning dark.

No. She couldn't accept it. What was going on? This was all wrong. All screwed up.

She dropped the sheet, turned and moved blindly through the crowd.

Death was all around her. Breathing down her neck.

Hot breath.

Cold breath.

No breath.

Her dead father.

Her dead mother.

Run! It's here! In the house! Death is in the house!

She'd run that day—outside. Six inches of snow on the ground, and she was wearing nothing but a pair of socks because she'd kicked off her boots at the door. But she had to get away. Away from death. Away from the images death had left behind.

She ran through a field to the barn, out the other side and into the corncrib.

Is he coming? Is he back there?

Up she climbed.

You'll be trapped. Once you get up there, you'll be trapped.

But she could climb like hell. When she was younger, her dad had always called her his little monkey. He'd send her up to the top of places he and the hired hands were afraid to go. Nobody had been to the top of the corncrib, the cupola, for years and years. Nobody but her and the rats . . .

She used to climb up there to get away from her parents because nobody had the guts to come after her. She used to climb up there on Fourth of July to watch the fireworks being set off in the nearest town fifteen miles away.

Nobody else.

The killer didn't come after her either. He didn't have the guts.

On the Hill, the ambulance gave a couple blasts of its siren, then drove off.

Arden almost bumped into someone.

She sidestepped.

So did he.

She sidestepped again.

So did he.

She looked up.

Fury.

Images collided in her head, and for a moment she was back in the corncrib, and Fury was looking up at her, begging her to come down.

She'd run that day.

Her mother and father were dead. There had been nothing she could do but save herself.

You could have killed him. You could have killed the man who murdered your parents.

Instead she'd hidden. She'd never even gotten a look at his face. . . .

"It's Noah," she heard herself telling Fury.

"I know."

For a while now she'd thought of Fury as her friend. But a face she'd thought of as occasionally kind now seemed threatening. Eyes that had seemed sympathetic now appeared harsh and cold.

Funny how lighting changed everything.

"He jumped," she told him in a voice devoid of emotion.

Fury's gaze moved past her.

She turned to see Harris standing in the distance, hands in the pockets of his white lab coat as some silent form of communication passed between the two men. She looked for Eli and Franny. They were gone.

What was going on?

Franny, Eli, and Noah had all been weird and

lethargic when she and Fury had gone to their room. She may have had a dislike of classical music, but since when did listening to Mozart make you crazy? Since when did listening to Mozart make you jump from a window?

Dr. Harris was a research scientist, and some research scientists felt justified in pushing their patients to the edge and beyond. Was he doing that with Eli and Franny? Had he done that with Noah? Did the study they were involved in have anything to do with Noah's death?

Eli burst through the crowd. "I was just up in our room." He was out of breath, his eyes big, his chest rising and falling. "Noah left a bloody shirt and bloody shoes in the bathroom."

Chapter 18

At three A.M., the morning after Noah plunged to his death, Arden slipped silently from her room. Dressed in dark jeans and her navy-blue hooded sweatshirt, she walked down the hall. Dim lights illuminated the way, casting shadows on the coved plaster ceiling.

Trust your gut.

She'd learned that as a kid, as a woman, as an agent. But there had been a few times in her life when her gut had lied, when it told her someone good was really bad, and the other way around. At least now she knew what was what. Well, not *exactly*, but she knew she had to get out of there if she wanted to discover who'd killed her parents. The answer to that question wasn't on the Hill. The only thing she would find on the Hill was death and confusion.

The bloody shoe print had been a positive match, tagging Noah as the likeliest murderer of poor Vera Thompson. DNA testing would take longer, but given the circumstances, Arden didn't hold out much hope for an alternative conclusion.

Before leaving, she had one last thing to check off her list. Two things, if she counted the heart-to-heart she planned on having with Eli and Franny.

First she had to prove to herself that what she'd seen that night in Cottage 25 had been nothing more than a crisis apparition.

She took the stairs, the soles of her running shoes letting out a squeak against the marble surface. When she reached the first floor, she paused to listen.

After the recent "events," as Fury had called them, they'd hired more guards. Police patrolled the grounds.

If anybody stopped her, Arden would say she was going for a walk. No law against that, even at three A.M. But it would look damn suspicious.

Clear skies had once again given way to gloom, obliterating the moon and stars. Lampposts lined the cobblestone streets. The light they gave off was fuzzy, with undertones of orange, almost as if the light were being projected from the past.

Arden clung to the shadows and walls. The leaves under her feet were wet from dew; they hardly made a sound. Along the way she spotted the occasional policeman or guard. Her FBI training in stealth procedures clicked in, keeping panic to a minimum.

Cool logic. Hyperawareness.

She went directly to the back entrance of Cottage 25, the entrance Noah had used on a day that now seemed years ago.

Down steep cement steps surrounded by cement walls, turn right to a door hidden from view.

The broken glass had been temporarily replaced by a thin piece of plywood. Finding a loose corner, she bent and splintered the wood, stuck her hand and arm through the hole in the glass, and unlocked the door from the inside.

There had been talk of putting in an alarm system, but that kind of thing took time, and apparently the work hadn't yet been accomplished, because nothing announced her invasion.

The only thing different between this visit and the last was that this time there were more lights. No blinding overhead lights, but small, low-watt bulbs partially illuminating areas above dark doors set in little square dead ends with high ceilings.

It was unnerving visiting a building that had once housed so many patients. She could still feel them. Their imprint was there. Clinging to the air, gathering in black corners. Civil War veterans with slippered feet and minds confused by death and blood and killing.

Arden moved through them, through the ghosts. Through the empty cafeteria that had been abandoned one fine day, never to be revisited.

Oops. Forgot to tell you we were leaving. Forgot to let you know we weren't coming back.

And so the building had waited. Days, months, years . . .

Arden found the stairs where she'd collapsed that night. She steeled herself, braced herself against the feeling that had hit her before.

Things were different now. She was tougher. Noah's death had given her resolve, a purpose that went beyond her own fear of the dark and things she couldn't remember.

She made it down the stairs to the tank room door, with its thick, black paint and wire mesh window that was too high to see through.

From a room down the hall came the muffled sound of a television. An alien glow poured from a doorway.

Someone—a security guard?—was watching an old sitcom.

Arden slowly opened the tank room door.

There they were. The tanks. Green. Metal.

A light that glowed orange.

In use.

Fear filled her throat. It crept up her spine and the back of her neck.

She'd expected to find the tanks empty. The purpose of this final visit was strictly to reassure herself.

She crossed the room. An IV rack with a half-empty glucose bag stood next to one of the tanks, the tube feeding into the tank through a small access hole.

She unfastened the locks, hearing yet not hearing the sound of metal hitting metal. Caring yet not caring about the person down the hall.

With both hands, she pushed up the heavy lid.

A body. Floating like a cork on a bed of salt water.

This was the man she'd seen before. The man everyone had told her didn't exist. This was a man she knew and recognized.

Harley.

Chapter 19

Harley's eyes were closed, his skin the color of chalk, his lips blue. He hadn't shaved in what looked like weeks.

Arden put a hand to his cheek, above the growth of heavy beard.

His skin was cold. She felt for his carotid artery—and detected a weak, steady pulse.

His wrists were attached to the sides of the tank with straps similar to the wide restraints on an electric chair.

She unfastened them.

Someone could walk in at any second.

She leaned closer, and whispered, "Harley. Harley, it's me, Arden. You have to wake up now. It's time to wake up."

She turned her ear to the door and listened intently.

Footsteps.

Slow and shuffling—coming down the hall.

She closed the lid, fastened the latches, then slipped behind one of the other tanks.

A switch was flipped, washing the room in glaring fluorescent light. Above her head, tubes hummed. Someone entered, the hydraulic cylinder on the door making a hissing sound as it closed.

Footsteps and soft-soled shoes.

"Howdy, Mr. Larson. How are we doing?" A woman's voice. The same nurse Arden had had.

"Heat gauges fine. Don't want you to get cold, but we don't want to cook you either." She chuckled. That was followed by the sound of beeps as the woman checked the IV pump.

Would she look in the tank? Would she see that someone had released the straps?

Two metal pops as the woman undid the catches. A creak as the lid was raised.

"Can you pee for me, Mr. Larson? Come on. You can do it."

That was followed by the sound of urine spraying forcefully into a container. Then, "That's my boy. Much better than having a catheter, now, isn't it?"

Another creak as the lid was lowered. Metal snapped; then the nurse walked briskly from the room, turning off the light behind her.

Arden's rigid muscles released and she dropped the rest of the way to the floor. She sat there a moment, letting relief wash over her while her eyes readjusted to the dark.

It had been tense, but the timing couldn't have been more opportune. The nurse shouldn't be back for another hour at least. Maybe two hours if they were lucky.

Arden got to her feet and quickly checked the other two tanks.

Empty.

Dry.

She hurried back to Harley. She shut off the IV pump, then reopened the tank lid. "Harley. Wake up, Harley."

His eyes sprang open.

She jumped, hesitated, then stepped forward again.

"Harley?"

"Arden . . . ?"

"What have they done to you?"

This wasn't happening. It wasn't real.

"You came."

"Yes." Tears stung her eyes. "We can't talk now." She pulled herself together. "We have to get you out of here."

"Tired."

"No excuses. You have to move. You have to help me."

His eyes drifted closed.

She placed his hands on the tank sides. "Hang on here," she commanded quietly and earnestly. "Hang on here and pull yourself up."

With her help, he managed to get himself to a sitting position, water sloshing from the tank, soaking Arden's pants and shoes.

"Sit there a minute. Catch your breath."

She didn't want him passing out when he tried to stand.

He held up his hands and examined them as if surprised to find them there, looking at them as if they belonged to someone else.

He ripped out the IV needle and tossed it over the side.

Okay. He was bleeding now. She would have handled that differently, but okay.

While he stabilized, she searched the room and found a cupboard containing towels, hospital gowns, and pants.

She towel-dried his hair and back, then wrapped the towel around his shoulders and checked the IV puncture. The bleeding had almost stopped.

"Stand up. Put your hands there." She made sure he had a grip on the sides of the tank. "Push yourself to your feet." With her hands under his armpits, she lifted.

He came up with a gush of water—until he stood naked and trembling. She draped his arm across her shoulders while she gripped his waist. "Turn around. That's it," she coaxed. "Down the steps. One at a time. There you go. That's good."

At the bottom of the steps, Arden aimed him toward a chair.

He dove for it, collapsing heavily in the seat.

Arden quickly and efficiently finished drying him off. She tugged a hospital shirt over his head and stuck his feet into a pair of hospital pants, pulling them to his knees. Slippers on his feet.

"Stand up."

He stood. Wobbling, but upright.

She finished pulling up his pants while he leaned heavily on her, his hands on her shoulders. Like dressing a giant baby. Harley was tall, at least six feet, but no longer big. At one time he'd probably weighed over two hundred pounds. Now she would guess he was closer to 180.

Gripping his hand, she looped his arm over her shoulder once more. With her other hand at his waist, they walked.

Or rather, Arden walked. Harley shuffled. The soles of the slippers were soft, and didn't make much noise.

She opened the door a crack and listened.

The TV was still on. It would mute the sounds of their departure.

They made it through the door, then up the cement incline to the true basement level.

Then the stairs . . .

She glanced around the hall, hoping a wheelchair would materialize. But then they would need an elevator, and that might attract attention.

"Grab the railing."

She placed his hand on the metal rail.

With each step, it felt as if he were pushing her through the floor. With each step, he seemed to get heavier.

Halfway up, he paused, breathing hard. He pressed his face against the wall, mouth open. "What are we doing . . . ?" he gasped. "Why are we doing this? I'm so tired. Just gonna rest my eyes a minute. . . ."

"We have to leave." She leaned hard into him as she tried to brace him against the wall to keep him from slipping any further.

"I don't want to."

"You have to."

"Why?"

They didn't have time for this. In his drug-laden state, he wouldn't grasp what she was telling him anyway. "I'm rescuing you," she said. "Don't you want to be rescued?"

A few beats went by. "Sure." He attempted a shrug. "Yeah, okay."

She'd hoped for a more enthusiastic response, but coming from a guy who was practically comatose, she'd have to take what she could get. "You have to help me. We have to get up the stairs."

He began moving again. She shoved from below and behind until they finally made it to the first floor, through a set of fire doors.

She spotted a wheelchair, looking as if some ghost had just walked away from it.

She grabbed the chair, locked the wheels, and helped him into the seat. Then they were moving down the hall into the deserted and unused part of the building. Through the old cafeteria to the hidden stairs.

By the time they abandoned the chair, Harley seemed a little less groggy. A little stronger.

Together they climbed the cement steps.

Outdoors.

How much time had passed? Arden wondered. How long until daylight? How long until the nurse discovered he was gone?

And what now? What do I do now? With a man who can hardly walk?

They needed wheels, and she didn't have as much as a bicycle.

"Ah." Harley gave a drugged, visual sweep of the area. He pulled in a deep breath while he stood, legs braced apart, struggling for balance.

Arden grabbed his elbow and helped him toward the thick stand of trees that marked the boundary of the asylum grounds. It wasn't until they reached deep cover that she let him stop, one hand braced against the trunk of a tree, the other on one knee.

He was shaking.

Like a leaf, her grandmother would have said.

Arden unzipped her sweatshirt and peeled it off. "Here."

It was too small, but she stuffed his arms in the sleeves, then tugged it together in front, just managing to zip the zipper. "I want you to stay here. I'm going to get a car," she told him. "Won't that be nice? To get in a warm car? But you have to stay here. If anybody shouts for you, don't answer. Okay? Understand?"

He didn't.

He let out a heavy sigh and sank, his back to the tree trunk. He just kept going . . . until he was lying on the ground, curled into a fetal position.

"Sleep." She rubbed his back the way you might a fussy baby. "You can sleep now. Just go to sleep."

It was too dark to see his face.

He didn't answer. A moment later his breathing changed, becoming deep and rhythmic.

She straightened and began to run, moving swiftly through the trees, a bed of silent pine needles under her feet.

Chapter 20

Arden rapped softly on Eli and Franny's door. When no one answered, she pounded.

From inside came a rattle, then the sound of something being knocked over. The door opened and Eli stood there, bleary eyed and blinking like an owl.

Arden barged in and closed the door. "You and Franny have to get out of here. *Now.*"

Clothes and other belongings were scattered everywhere.

"We can't leave," Eli said.

"What are you talking about?" Franny was in bed, a box of tissues on her stomach, more used tissues on the floor.

"No time to explain, but we have to go. We have to get out of here."

"We're seeing Dr. Harris tomorrow morning," Eli said. "He's putting us through some tests. He wants to make sure that what happened to Noah had nothing to do with the study we're involved in."

Arden forced herself to slow down and take a couple of deep breaths. "I didn't want to get into this now, but you've been in the tanks, haven't you? All three of you."

Franny looked from Eli to Arden. "How did you—"

Eli jumped forward. "Shhh!"

"I knew it!" Arden dropped her hands and shook her head in disbelief. "Jesus!" They were using naive kids as test subjects. Scuttling them through the underground tunnel that joined the Mercy Unit to Cottage 25.

"We can't talk about it," Eli said. "We signed papers. We've been sworn to secrecy."

"Bullshit! You don't owe anybody anything," Arden said in frustration. "Look what happened to Noah."

"Noah didn't kill that old woman," Franny said. "That's what everyone is saying, but Noah couldn't—*wouldn't* do anything like that."

"He might if he'd been listening to madmen like Albert French whispering in his ear for days on end." Arden waved her arms in frustration. "Is that what they did? Is that what Harris fed you in the tanks instead of Mozart? Were you listening to tales of murder instead of *The Magic Flute*?"

"He just told us we'd be in the tanks. That's all I know!" Franny grabbed her head and started sobbing. "I don't remember! We can't talk about it! Don't ask us to talk about it!"

"Okay, just come with me." Arden tried to calm down while she lowered her voice. "At least give me a ride to Charleston. If I can't convince you to con-

tinue on, then you can leave me there and come
back. No big deal."

"I'll give you a ride," Eli said. "No problem. Why
didn't you say that to begin with?"

"Pack a few things—in case you decide not to return. We have to hurry."

Franny was already on her feet, reaching for a
backpack.

Eli swung around. "You're going?" he asked in
disbelief.

Arden picked up a black duffel bag. "This yours?"
she asked him.

"Yeah, but—"

"These your pants?"

"Yeah, but—"

She stuffed them in the bag. "This?" A shirt.

"That's Noah's."

"This?"

A pair of corduroy pants.

"Noah's." Franny took both articles of clothing
and held them close.

Once Arden was sure they were adequately moti-
vated, she ran through the building to her room,
grabbed her backpack, stuffed as much as she could
inside, then returned to Eli and Franny's room before they changed their minds.

They were ready.

Franny scanned the room. "I know I'm forgetting
something important."

"It doesn't matter," Eli said. "I don't know about
you, but I'm coming back."

The building had so many entrances that it was easy to slip out without being seen.

"Don't exit through the main gate," Arden said once they were in the car with the engine running. "Go out past the evergreens."

"Why don't you just wait and leave in the morning?" Eli put the car in gear. "Why all the secrecy?"

"Watch for a dirt road somewhere on the right." From the backseat, Arden leaned forward and pointed across Eli's shoulder. "There it is. Turn there."

Eli turned.

The headlights illuminated the thick grove of trees, the glare bouncing off tree trunks. Everything looked the same as Arden scanned the area for something familiar. "Stop."

He stopped.

"Cut the headlights, but not the parking lights."

She jumped out, leaving the door open.

From the passenger seat, Franny watched Arden move through the orange glow of parking lights to disappear into the darkness.

Eli nervously drummed his fingers against the steering wheel. "What's she doing?"

"I don't know."

"Maybe we should get out of here before she comes back."

"What are you talking about?"

"Maybe she's hidden a weapon out here and she's going to kill us."

"*What?*"

"Well, somebody around here is killing people,

and it isn't me. Maybe Arden framed Noah. Planted the bloody shirt and shoes. Maybe she killed the old lady."

"Arden didn't do it," Franny said.

"You don't know that."

"I trust her."

"You aren't going with her, are you?"

"Maybe. I haven't decided."

"We'll look guilty if we leave."

"But we're innocent. What do we have to worry about? There is nothing to tie us to that old woman."

"What about Noah? We were with him. They'll try to connect us to his death. They'll think one of us pushed him from the window."

She hadn't thought of that. She'd been too wrapped up in the loss, the pain of Noah being there one minute, gone the next. "Why would we do such a thing?"

"We wouldn't need a reason. Nobody will care if we have a reason."

But maybe Eli *had* a reason, Franny thought. Eli had always been jealous of her relationship with Noah.

"Arden's bossy," Eli said. "Did you notice how bossy she is?"

"I thought you said you liked her."

"I did. At first. Before she got so bossy."

"She's older than we are. She knows more."

He let out a snort. "She doesn't know anything. She's a mess. She's been *bleached*. How could she know anything? I'm not saying she's a bad person. That's not what I mean. I'm just saying she's not somebody you can put your faith in. Her sense of reality is skewed."

"Are we so different?" Franny asked. She wasn't sure what had happened to her in the tank. Afterward, her head had been fuzzy. Even now, she was having trouble putting events together. Sorting them out. Harris had told them the confusion would pass. Was it true? Or had her brain been fried? Had she and Eli been bleached too?

"Look at Noah," she said. "Look what happened to him. She may be right. They may be doing more to us than we know. If we stay, I'm afraid I'll let Harris talk me into something. You know how he is." He'd convinced them to be part of his secret, accelerated TAKE study, hadn't he?

Eli straightened. "Here she comes."

"She has somebody with her." Franny strained to see.

It didn't help. Dark was dark.

"Oh, my God," Eli said in disbelief. "I think it's that guy."

Franny tried to think of the guys they knew. Fury. Harris. The night watchman, who sometimes let them into the vending area and didn't squeal if he caught them running up and down the halls. "What guy?"

"That guy. That Harley dude."

"I thought he was gone."

"I thought he was dead."

Arden was half dragging, half carrying him.

"He *looks* dead," Franny said.

They opened their doors and jumped out to help.

Together, all three managed to get Harley in the backseat and close the door solidly behind him.

Harley was trembling violently, and through the thin layer of clothes, his skin was ice cold.

They dove back in the car.

"Go!" Arden shouted.

Eli reversed.

"Straight. Straight! No headlights. This road takes you out by the old cemetery and dairy barn."

He slammed the vehicle into forward gear; then they were bouncing over the dirt road.

The car bottomed out.

"Sorry." Eli slowed. "That's that Harley dude, isn't it?" He gripped the steering wheel.

"They had him restrained in a float tank," Arden said. "He's probably been at Cottage 25 all this time. All the while they were telling me he'd left. That's what they'll do to us too. They'll tell everybody we quit and left."

Franny couldn't shut off her head. Shut off her paranoia. Was this real? Was this really happening? Or was *she* in the float tank, being fed a fake reality?

From the backseat, Harley let out a moan and began rocking back and forth, his head in his hands. "Two times two is three. Two times two is three. Brigitte Bardot and Marilyn Monroe. Killed JFK. Killed Chauncey Gardiner. Killed Roosevelt. Killed Howard Hughes. Howard Hughes was a very big man, and a very big man he was. Bleached and restored. Bleached and restored. Amen to that. Amen to that." He paused. For a moment Franny thought he was done. It turned out he was just catching his breath.

"Gotta find my groove," he mumbled. "I lost my groove."

He raised his head and caught Franny staring. She wanted to look away, but couldn't risk upsetting him any more than he already was. One thing she knew for sure: She wasn't returning to the Hill. Not if a fried mess like Harley was the outcome.

Chapter 21

RN Pauline Welsh woke up with a sudden jolt, almost tumbling to the floor, her heart pounding the way it did whenever she had a falling dream. She wiped the drool from her face with the back of her hand. On TV, someone was selling a new diet supplement. She looked at the luminous dial of her wristwatch.

She'd missed her four A.M. patient check.

No big deal, she thought as she pushed herself from her stuffed, vinyl-covered chair. Unless he'd peed in the tank. Then she'd have to drain it and start over.

That was the one good thing about working nights. Nobody around to squeal on you when you made a mistake.

Pauline never got in a hurry. Hurrying didn't help when you were a nurse. Hurrying got you into trouble.

She wasn't crazy about the night shift. Some people loved it, but they were introverts. Took a special kind of person to work nights.

Pauline opened the heavy tank room door, and flipped on the overhead lights.

Her feet hurt. Her back hurt. At her age, a body couldn't recharge when it worked nights and slept days. People weren't meant to be awake at night.

She reached for the locks.

They weren't latched. *Did I forget . . . ?*

That's when she noticed the IV drip—shut off, the needle on the floor.

Water. Pooled around her feet. Squishing under the soles of her shoes.

Her heart began to hammer, and the heartburn and indigestion that had been dogging her for the last several hours intensified.

She lifted the tank lid.

Empty.

He was gone.

Pauline had never lost a patient. Well, she'd had patients *die*, but she'd never *lost* one.

She looked frantically around the room, and checked the adjoining bathroom. Then she hurried up the hall.

He couldn't have gone far. He had to be nearby. Had to be in the building. If not, she was in deep poop, as her dead honey used to say.

Dr. Phillip Harris's phone rang, waking him from a restless sleep.

It was one of his assistants, his voice frantic. "Harley Larson is gone."

Harris pushed himself up in bed. "What do you mean, gone?" Beside him, his wife stirred and turned on the bedside lamp, her face sleepy and concerned.

"The night nurse went to check on him, and he wasn't in the tank."

Harris's first thought was to call the police to report Larson missing, but how did you report someone missing who wasn't supposed to be there in the first place?

He could figure this out. He always figured it out.

"It doesn't look as if he got loose by himself," the assistant said. "The service door was broken into."

Harris had heard that MO before, and he had a good idea who was behind the break-in and Larson's disappearance.

"I want you to check on Arden Davis," Harris said. "Also the student test subjects. Report back to me as soon as you know anything."

He hung up.

Breaking and entering. Possible kidnapping. That would work, but did he want to involve the police?

"What is it, honey?" his wife asked.

"Just some inept people making stupid mistakes."

"Are you sure he's really asleep?" Eli asked over his shoulder. "Are you sure he's not dead? I mean, the guy hasn't moved."

They were heading north, with no immediate plan other than to put distance between themselves and the Hill.

Arden reached over the seat to the back of the station wagon, where Harley was curled up in Eli's sleeping bag. She put a hand close to his nose and mouth. "He's breathing."

There was a weird feeling in the car. A tension full of questions that couldn't be answered. Since leaving the Hill, no one had offered any theories. They hadn't talked about what had possibly been going on with Harley, and what had happened to Noah. They focused on the road. But now that the sun was up, marking the start of a new day, the mood inside the car was becoming restless.

"We're going to have to get gas," Eli said.

Arden looked over the seat. "You have plenty."

"Gauge doesn't work." He tapped the glass. "It always says half a tank."

"I need a bathroom," Franny said. "And a map. We need a map."

They stopped in the next town—a sleepy little burg with three gas stations clustered on the perimeter, competing for business.

Harley slept through the gassing up.

They took turns staying with him while the bathroom was hit, a key attached to a hubcap passed among them. Eli squeegeed the front window; Franny purchased water and a few snacks. Arden paid at the counter.

Heading out of town, they spotted a farm store with a high percentage of trucks in the parking lot. Which meant that even though it was early morning, the place was open for business.

Everyone waited in the car while Arden hurried inside to buy clothes for Harley.

Jeans. Underwear. Long-sleeved T-shirt. Sneakers. Sweatshirt.

She paid in cash, the purchase seriously depleting what little money she had.

Back in the car, Harley stirred. His eyes were still closed, but he was letting out deep sighs and struggling to turn over in a space that wasn't big enough. Suddenly, he sat up, head and shoulders hunched in the cramped space. He unzipped the sleeping bag, kicking and worming his way free. "I gotta piss."

Eli drove behind the store to an area littered with fence panels and farm equipment like bale feeders. He pulled to a stop, jumped out, and opened the back door, which was hinged on the top, affording easy access.

Harley staggered out and without pause began peeing on a metal calf feeder. While he was occupied, Arden opened the packet of boxer shorts and removed the labels from the jeans.

"Put these on," she told him when he swung around to get back in the car.

He dropped his hospital pants.

Franny let out a choked laugh and covered her mouth.

Harley was still unsteady on his feet. With Eli's help, he got into the boxer shorts and jeans. That was followed by the long-sleeved T-shirt, then the sweatshirt.

She'd forgotten socks.

The shoes were a little snug, but he managed to stuff his bare feet into them.

"I'm starving," he announced once the change of clothing was complete. "Anybody else hungry?"

Eli, Arden, and Franny looked at each other in relief. He was speaking in complete sentences. He was making sense.

"I have some granola bars." Franny held up three different packages, fanning them out like cards. "And water."

"I want real food. Bacon. Eggs. Coffee." Harley rubbed his hands together. "Doesn't that sound good? Man, that sounds good."

They decided to wait until the next town before stopping. Just in case anyone had witnessed Harley's public urination and striptease.

There were times when the anonymity of a chain restaurant—a chain anything—was best. People came. People went. Nobody noticed as employees and customers moved through the drudgery of a sameness that never changed.

Harley was too hungry to hold out for that kind of place.

They stopped at a little restaurant a few miles off Highway 77 north, in the middle of nowhere. Ten miles to the nearest town in every direction. The building was square, and constructed of cement block. The way it sat right on the two-lane gave you the impression it had once been a gas station.

"Let's try to keep a low profile," Arden said.

A bell above the door jingled, announcing their arrival.

They didn't need a bell. All eyes were on them before the bell ever made a sound. Everybody had watched from the window as they'd gotten out of the car. As they'd made their way across the gravel parking lot, past the semis loaded with cattle, and the flatbeds with hay.

The coffee shop was hardly bigger than a large living room, with windows on three sides, kitchen in the back, tables shoved close together.

As soon as they stepped in, Arden knew it was a mistake. She opened her mouth to say something about this not being a gas station and they'd better leave, when Harley plopped into the first empty seat he came to.

The rest of them followed with less enthusiasm.

The place had an uncomfortable vibe. Not threatening. The people now trying *not* to stare were curious about strangers because they saw so few. Stepping into the breakfast grill was similar to walking into a stranger's kitchen and sitting down.

What are you doing here? You don't belong here.

A waitress brought them plastic-covered menus and water in scratched and chipped plastic cups. Harley downed his glass of water.

The waitress was young, probably in high school, wearing a lot of makeup, tight pants, bare abdomen, and a tiny shirt. She was nervous. She seemed afraid of them and resentful of their presence.

No school today? Arden wondered. Was it Saturday? Sunday? She had no idea. No idea at all.

Harley looked rough. His hair was tangled and clumped, his beard dusted with salt residue.

Eli and Franny would have come across better, except their eyes were bloodshot, their hair unkempt, their clothes wrinkled from spending time on the Hill in backpacks and duffel bags. Arden was sure she looked just as bad.

She felt like a fugitive. But they hadn't done anything wrong. They weren't doing anything wrong.

Conversation had stopped when they'd stepped through the door. Now it gradually picked up, with talk of livestock and corn prices drifting their way.

They ordered.

After the waitress retrieved the menus, Harley stared across the table at Arden. He had a weird expression on his face. Kind of a bemused pride.

She gave him an encouraging smile.

He was getting stronger by the second. She didn't want to push him, but she had a lot of questions to ask.

"I knew you'd come," Harley said. His voice was deep and sounded like sandpaper. He probably hadn't spoken in days.

Maybe longer.

The meal arrived and he dove in. He practically inhaled the eggs, bacon, and toast. Guzzled the orange juice.

"Would you like a pancake?" Franny offered. "I can't eat all of these."

He forked a pancake off her plate, then drowned it in maple syrup. By the time he was finished, he had egg yolk and syrup stuck to his beard.

Arden dipped her napkin into the water glass, squeezed out the excess, and offered the napkin to Harley.

Everyone was watching them again.

Now that he'd been fed, Harley could feel their eyes on him. "What are they looking at?"

Arden ignored his question, hoping to redirect his attention with the wet napkin she was still offering.

Harley looked at Eli, who shrugged. He looked at Franny, who quickly lowered her gaze. He looked at the group of men seated at a nearby table. "What?" he demanded, half rising from his seat.

You didn't threaten people in their own home.

The four gentlemen at the table bristled, and the room fell silent. The waitress froze with a tray of food. The cook appeared in the kitchen doorway, drying his hands on a white towel.

"Don't you have any manners?" Harley asked, his voice rising. "Didn't your mama teach you not to stare?"

The four men got to their feet, chairs scraping.

They were hardworking farmers. They weren't inviting a fight, but if one came their way they wouldn't back down. And they could probably kick some ass if they had to.

Arden reached across the table and grabbed Harley's arm. He turned his angry glare on her and shook off her hand.

"You'd better leave," the cook said. "Tracy, where's their bill?"

Harley crumpled. "I'm sorry."

It was like watching someone with multiple personality disorder transform into an alter ego right before their eyes. He buried his face in his hands and began to sob, his shoulders shaking.

"I'll pay," Eli said. "You can take him outside."

Arden put her arm around Harley. "Come on. Let's go."

He got up, keeping his face covered.

"My friend hasn't been well," Arden explained as they walked toward the door.

The group of men suddenly looked embarrassed and ashamed. Mental illness made people uncomfortable.

"Oh, hey." One of the men waved a hand at her. "That's okay. We got one of them in my family too. Goes off for no reason."

He blushed, realizing the words he'd meant as comfort hadn't been all that appropriate.

"We didn't mean to stare," said another man in brown canvas Carhartt overalls.

They were dressed for winter, and it dawned on Arden that the temperature had been dropping steadily.

"It's just that we aren't used to seeing somebody . . ." With one finger, he made a motion around his face.

Arden frowned in question.

"Food all over his face."

Arden gave him a tight smile and pushed Harley through the door.

So much for keeping a low profile.

Fury was shaving when his cell phone rang.

"They're gone," the caller said.

It took Fury a moment to identify the owner of the strained voice as Harris. He set the disposable razor down on the edge of the sink. "Who's gone?"

"Your ex-partner. I told you I didn't want her brought back here. I told you she was too unstable."

Fury grabbed a hand towel and wiped the remaining shaving cream from his face.

"Not only is Davis gone," Harris said, "but she's taken my student test subjects with her."

Fury wasn't all that surprised to find that Arden had taken off. She'd been ready to run ever since getting there. But on top of the recent murder, her disappearance looked bad. "We'll find her. We'll bring them back."

Harris wasn't finished. "One other thing," he said. "They kidnapped a patient."

That wasn't something Fury had expected to hear. "Who?"

"Harley Larson."

Chapter 22

Eli paid the pizza delivery guy and closed the motel room door with his elbow. He turned the lock and slid the chain into place. "One large sausage, four sodas." He put their order in the middle of the nearest bed, the smell wafting in Arden's direction. "That's the end of my money."

Exhaustion had hit them and they'd decided to stop midafternoon. A motel gave them a private place to take Harley so they could avoid a repeat of the coffee shop scene, plus he could have the shower he'd been begging for since dawn.

"I gotta get this salt off me," he'd told them. "It's making my skin crawl."

The room had been cheap. Forty-five dollars, plus tax. Two queen beds. Mirrors along one wall. A TV. Clock radio.

The musty smell that went along with old motels was free.

At the moment, the shower was running and had been running for the last fifteen minutes. Arden had begun to wonder if Harley was ever coming out.

Franny perched on the edge of the bed and grabbed a diet Coke. "Should we wait?"

"I can't." Eli opened the cardboard container. "I'm getting the hypoglycemic shakes." He held out a trembling hand, then dragged a slice of limp, gooey pizza from the box. "And I don't know if that dude's ever gonna be done."

Arden rapped on the bathroom door. "You okay in there?"

A muffled reply came back. Something that sounded like, "Fine."

Etiquette broken, Harley still alive, Franny and Arden dove into the pizza.

"What are we doing?" Franny asked after she'd taken a few bites and satisfied her initial pangs of hunger. "What's the plan? Do we have a plan?"

"Our priority was to put some distance between ourselves and the Hill," Arden said.

"We don't even know if anybody's after us," Eli pointed out. "Or even looking for us." He wiped a napkin across his mouth. "I'll bet they aren't. We're runnin' around like a bunch of kids playing hide-'n'-seek, except nobody's it."

"I think we need to go to the police," Franny said.

Arden took a swallow of soda. She wasn't used to drinking the stuff and recoiled at the carbonation. "Tell them what? It's just going to be our word against theirs. And, of course, Harley's. We have Harley."

Franny reached for a second slice of pizza. "Maybe we should tell a paper. A big paper. Like the *New York Times*."

Eli nodded, excited by the idea. "Or *Rolling Stone.* How about *Rolling Stone*?"

Franny shoved his shoulder. "*Rolling Stone*? What are you talking about?"

"In *Firestarter*, they told *Rolling Stone*."

"Maybe in the book, but not in the movie," Franny said. "Why? Because by that time *Rolling Stone* was no longer the radical voice of anarchy, it was one big voice for consumer culture and logo recognition."

Eli looked hurt, but Arden was glad to see some animation in Franny. It was the first strong reaction she'd shown since Noah's death.

The shower stopped.

"About time," Eli said. "That water tower we saw on the edge of town is probably empty."

Five minutes later, the door opened and a cloud of steam escaped. "I ran outta hot water," Harley complained.

Eli snorted.

"I was only in there a couple of minutes."

"Really?" Arden asked.

"Yeah. I just got lathered up and bang. No hot water."

He was losing track of time.

How long had he been in the float tank? She could ask him, but he probably wouldn't know the answer. He might say minutes, when it could have been hours. Even days. And where had he been when he wasn't in the tank?

She wished she'd had time to go through Harris's records. But all she'd been thinking about was getting Harley out of Cottage 25. And there was a good chance Harley's file was locked up tight.

Eli picked up the remote control and turned on the TV. He flipped through stations while Harley attacked the pizza. Franny sat in the corner of the room, turning pages in a spiral notebook. Occasionally, Arden heard a sniffle. Suddenly, Franny tossed the notebook aside and ran to the bathroom, slamming the door and locking it behind her.

Harley looked up, a slice of pizza in his hand. "What's her deal?"

How much was he ready to hear? Arden wondered. How much could he absorb right now? "Her boyfriend just died." She would leave out the part about the murder for now. "He committed suicide. We think it was directly related to Project TAKE."

Poor Franny.

With no time to grieve, she'd been thrown from one surreal situation into another. "We need to know what happened to you, Harley. We need to know everything you can remember. Maybe not right now, but when you're ready."

He nodded, reaching for another slice of pizza. "That's cool."

Behind them, Eli made a strange, strangling sound.

Harley and Arden looked up.

Eli was staring at the TV, his mouth open. Arden slowly turned her head in the direction of his gaze.

The reporter, a man wearing too much makeup, was on location in front of Building 50.

"The idyllic town of Madeline, West Virginia,

hasn't seen a murder in three years," the newsman said into the camera. "And never does anyone here recall a homicide with this level of brutality."

The camera cut to the town's chief of police. "At this time, we're still gathering evidence."

"What about the apparent suicide?" asked a female reporter. "Is there a connection between the two tragedies?"

"I don't want to comment on that until we've put together all the information. Right now we're hoping witnesses will step forward."

The camera cut back to the newsman and Building 50. "Some of those witnesses wanted for questioning are three people who disappeared from the Hill in the early hours of November sixteenth. The police department claims they aren't suspects, but rather people of interest. If you see any of these individuals, do not approach them. Contact your local law enforcement office."

That was followed by a description of the car and the license plate number. "Again, if you see this vehicle, do not approach it. The occupants could be dangerous."

"Dangerous? Me?" Eli laughed and bounced up and down on the bed, hitting the mattress with both fists.

The reporter wasn't finished. "It seems the three participants aren't the only people who've vanished. Earlier today, we caught up with Dr. Phillip Harris, head of psychiatric research at the Webber Research Institute in Madeline."

They cut to recorded footage of Dr. Harris in his office.

"Even more alarming is that a patient of mine is now missing," Dr. Harris said, standing in front of his desk, arms crossed over his lab coat.

"And you think the disappearance is in some way connected to the sudden departure of the study subjects?" the reporter asked.

"We have no proof, but it seems highly suspicious."

Arden had wondered how Harris would handle the subject of Harley. No real surprise that he'd chosen to admit to his existence, since the truth would come out eventually.

The reporter continued. "Are you suggesting the patient was kidnapped?"

"It's highly possible."

"Oh, man!" Eli said. "This is friggin' hilarious!"

Inside the bathroom, Franny heard Eli's burst of laughter. Why was he laughing? He shouldn't be laughing.

She hooked her thumb in the hem of her long-sleeved shirt, stretching the fabric over her hand in order to clean a circle of steam from the glass.

Dark, swollen eyes. No makeup. Hair not styled. She liked the messy look, but it had to be deliberately messy. This was real.

She didn't care how bad she looked. Noah was dead. Not only dead, but he'd killed himself. She should have seen it coming. She should have been able to stop him. It was her fault.

Another burst of laughter.

Franny blew her nose, grabbed the cheap box of tissues from the corner of the sink, and shoved open the door. "What's so funny?"

Sitting cross-legged on the bed, Eli pointed to the TV.

All three of their photos were on the screen, with their names below. Franny dropped down on the bed, tissues in her hand.

At times like these, it was a good thing she didn't have parents. They would have died.

"Look." Eli pointed at the television again.

A reporter stood in front of Building 50. It was a dramatic low shot, probably executed by some film grad who'd been forced to take a local TV news gig, but was still trying to be creative. Franny didn't hear what the reporter was saying because Eli kept interrupting, giddily bragging about how they were fugitives.

When the piece ended, Eli borrowed Franny's cell phone to call his grandmother in Omaha, then his parents in Chicago.

"I'm okay," he told them, laughing. "It's just a big mix-up. I'll get it straightened out. Don't worry. I'm fine. Tell Sis hi. Love you, too."

"That was short," Franny said as he disconnected and handed the phone back.

"Can't have them tracing the call. They're probably snooping through your phone records right now. Checking every call you've made in the last month."

"I think we should go to Lake County, Ohio," Arden announced.

Eli looked up in surprise. "Where you used to live?"

"We're broke," she explained. Eli and Franny would know what had happened in Ohio. It had been national news for about five minutes, until it was replaced with another horrific piece of murder or mayhem. "We have nowhere to go," she continued. "I'm only talking about a day or two. Long enough for us to collect ourselves."

It was something she'd been thinking about for a while. Would a return jar her memory and fill in some blanks? Would she recall a clue that might help solve her parents' case? Were their deaths in any way connected to Project TAKE?

And Daniel was there. . . .

Franny shivered and hugged herself. "How can you talk about going back to that place?"

"Because nobody will be expecting it," Arden said. "At least not right away. Harris is trying to blame us for Noah's and Vera's deaths. He's accusing us of kidnapping. Is he trying to cover up a research project gone awry? If so, Harley could be the best witness we have. But we need to buy ourselves a little time. We need to give Harley some space."

Upon hearing his name, Harley perked up and seemed to take a sudden, curious interest in the situation. "You kidnapped me?" he asked.

Chapter 23

At four thirty A.M., Arden was at the wheel of Eli's station wagon. The other occupants of the car were asleep, lulled by the sound of tires moving over pavement and the voice of night radio. Between weather reports of a far-off winter storm possibly moving in from Canada came the ramblings of a guy with a deep, soft, hypnotic voice that made you feel as if he were speaking just to you. As if he were visiting in your living room, sitting in front of the fireplace, everyone all tucked under comforters.

Going home . . .

It seemed the logical solution.

The only answer, really.

Yet Arden couldn't get over a sense of fate. The feeling that she'd been moving toward this point, this place, for many, many months. Ever since her parents' murders. Even when she was in New Mexico mixing drinks, she'd subconsciously known this time was coming.

A return to her roots.

A return to the past, to Lake County, Ohio.

Unanswered questions and home always called you back.

Trepidation had been hammering deep in her belly for a long time now. If she were to unzip her sweatshirt she felt sure she'd be able to see the outline of her heart, thudding away.

She hadn't seen another car for thirty minutes.

When she was young, she never noticed how claustrophobic the landscape was. How the hills and trees seemed to cave in on you, push you down, how they hid so much of the sky. When she was a child, they'd felt sheltering.

Now, as she moved down the highway, passing familiar signposts, the dark shadows that lined the road seemed threatening. Seemed to be hiding something from her rather than protecting her. From the corner of her eye, the shadows assumed familiar shapes.

Of people.

Faces. Arms. Hands. Fingers.

Suddenly, there was the McRainy farm on the left. Carson's on the right. A white cross with plastic flowers where three high school kids had stepped from this life into the next.

It made her think about church and vacation Bible school. Sitting in a pew as a kid, hair wet from her morning bath, singing hymns.

Was life just one giant brainwash? From the cradle to the grave? One giant magician's trick of illusions and delusions? With a reality that was always shifting depending on the light and your mood and what you'd eaten for breakfast that day? Were the dark shapes at the side of the road something sinister that came out only at night? When the sun rose, would they shift, change, become acceptable and non-threatening?

Did every human being have the capacity to be a monster?

Quit thinking. Just quit thinking.

But the feeling of despair that was wrapping around her chest kept swelling until it was almost too big for her body.

She wanted to wake somebody up.

Who?

Eli?

And tell him what?

Franny?

She needed to sleep.

Harley?

Harley's reality was so skewed right now that he probably thought they were on a field trip.

Night was sad.

Just past midnight wasn't bad, because it was almost the old day. One A.M. and even two A.M. weren't bad, because the bars were still open. People were still out, imitating the celebration of life.

But the hour that hit somewhere around four A.M. . . . That hour was brutal. That was when the world shut down and people went into a twisted, troubled realm of sleep. That was when your soul seemed to drown and despair became something you could taste. . . .

No wonder children were so afraid of sleep, of dreams. Because dreams could be so much more solid, so much more vivid than real life. How did you explain that to a child? Explain that a world you'd just left, the one you could taste and feel, the one with emotions bigger than you could ever possibly experience in waking life . . . how could you explain to a small child that that wasn't the real world? That *this* world, the world of softer edges and guarded emotions, was the real one? How could anyone accept that kind of logic?

Go back to bed. It's only a dream.

Right. File that along with the things your parents tell you and expect you to believe. File that with the tooth fairy and Santa Claus and the Easter Bunny.

Go back to sleep. It's only a dream.

Headlights. Far ahead of her, on top of a hill. They disappeared as the vehicle dipped into a valley, then reappeared.

At first Arden found the light reassuring. Someone else was awake in the middle of the night. Someone else was alive.

But then, as the car drew near and the bright lights weren't dimmed, the comfort changed to a threat, to a stranger behind the wheel. Maybe drunk. Maybe crazy as hell. Because you never knew. You never knew who was coming at you in the dark.

She flashed her lights.

No response.

She tried to focus on the side of the road, but her gaze kept going back to the car, to the blinding beams heading in her direction.

And then the car flew past, quickly becoming tail-lights in the rearview mirror.

An asshole in the night.

The darkest hour is just before the dawn.

She'd always taken that aphorism literally. Now she understood it meant sorrow, grief, and loneliness were most intense in those last few minutes before sunrise.

Maybe constant darkness would be best. So you never had to deal with the reminder of time, of the death of the night.

Suddenly she was there. At the one-room schoolhouse that marked where she turned south onto the hard road.

Hard road was what they called the country roads that weren't gravel or pavement. Hard roads fell apart in the spring. If the ground froze especially deep, they got soft spots in them that could swallow a tractor.

Arden used to imagine a world underneath the black surface. Everything hollow, like a shell, with tracks that led from building to building.

Maybe the idea wasn't so far-fetched. A hidden world like that.

She kept the little hatchback wagon going at about thirty-five miles per hour. You never knew when you might come over a hill and see a deer in the middle of the road. Or turn a corner to find that someone's cows had gotten out during the night.

Cattle could see at night. A lot of people didn't know that.

When she was little, she used to ride in the pasture with her dad, making one final late-night check on the calving heifers before her father would turn in for a few hours of sleep until the next round.

At first you wouldn't see anything, because the cows were black. Then, suddenly, the headlights would hit their pupils just right, and it would look as if they had no eyes, just these pits that seemed to swallow the light.

"Why do their eyes look like that, Daddy?" she would ask.

"So they can see at night."

"They can see us, but we can't see them?" she asked.

"That's the ticket."

"I don't like that."

He'd laughed at her fear.

As she slowed the car, she peered hard, trying to see into the darkness, watching for the gravel lane that led to the house.

Something moved in front of her. She slowed the car to a crawl. A possum, waddling across the road. Another nocturnal creature.

The gravel road appeared.

She turned. The car bounced down a steep hill, then leveled out. Her passengers groaned and shifted uncomfortably, but didn't wake.

The lane was in bad shape. There was only one house on it, and nobody had paid for fresh grading or gravel after the last spring thaw and rains. Tree branches and brush had grown in from both sides, making the narrow road much narrower. Plants had sprouted from the roadbed. Trumpet vine and milkweed, winter-killed but still nasty. To the car's left, she spotted a cluster of thistle that had gone to seed. It gave her a sick feeling in her stomach.

Thistle could take over an entire pasture in no time, leaving nothing for the cattle to eat. Her dad had fought it most of his life, using a spade to attack each individual plant. Of course, that didn't do much good when your neighbor sat on his porch, playing his guitar, letting his damn thistle take over the countryside while his cattle stood gaunt and waterless in feedlots with no shade.

People are stupid. People deserve to die.

Not her voice. Somebody else's.

Albert French.

The neighbor's dead-pile could get ten feet high at lambing time. Her dad had called the Humane Society on him several times, but he'd never been charged with anything. He poisoned the streams and killed the fish with his hog confinement runoff, but all he ever got was a warning.

There was a brotherhood in the country, and neighbors tended to look the other way when they saw signs of animal cruelty and neglect. And who cared about the pesticides? It was the nation's best-kept secret that Midwest farm country was one huge toxic waste dump.

The man on the radio was still talking, now about the moon and the tides and how humans were made up of sixty percent water. How the brain was seventy percent, and the lungs were ninety.

"Did you ever think about that?" he asked seductively. "What effect the moon has on your body? Because it has to have a powerful effect. Consider the woman's body. Consider her monthly cycle. It's the moon. Way up there, doing things to you way down here."

She believed him, because he had the kind of voice that made you believe.

Like Albert French made you believe.

She spotted the rusty wire fence that marked the boundary of the farm.

The mailbox was still there, with the name DAVIS in rough black letters. She could make out the faint, backward *S* her brother had painted when he was six or seven.

She turned, guiding the car between the corner posts covered with bare vines. Poison ivy, which choked everything and could get as big as a tree. You'd spray it and chop it and think you were rid of it, but it never went away. The roots just hid deep in the ground, spreading out for thirty yards, right under your feet.

The two-story farmhouse stood in the glow of the twin headlight beams. Like everything else, the house seemed to be sprouting out of the ground, the crumbling chimney giving the structure a cartoony list, like a plant in heavy bloom.

There was the massive oak in the front yard, complete with tire swing that would fill with water when it rained. Sometimes snakes liked to curl up in the cool darkness of the tire.

Oh, the illusion of the bucolic.

They'd all bought into it. The idea that a farm could be a special place, an oasis from the rest of the world where bad things didn't happen.

But she'd brought the bad things with her.

Who had said that? Who had told her that?

Who had blamed her for everything that had happened there, when she was already blaming herself?

Her brother. Daniel.

Daniel, who had painted the backward *S*.

The house stared back at her with black, empty eyes.

Focus. Just think about the now and what you have to do. Don't think about those other things.

The farm lane led forward to the garage, or left, down the steep slope to a barn that was half stone, half wood, built into the hillside.

She drove down the hill and pulled to a stop, headlights illuminating the wooden door that hung from wheels on a track.

She got out of the car, approached the door, and grabbed the metal handle. Her tactile memory awakened, she leaned back heavily while she pulled. Wheels creaked, and finally the giant door began to move, began to roll on the track.

She'd half expected to see farm machinery parked inside, but the space was empty except for tools and coiled hoses hanging on a far wall.

Back in the car, the occupants coming awake, she drove forward.

"Are we there yet?" Eli mumbled sleepily.

Arden was glad they were awake. Glad Eli was there for the comic relief she so desperately needed right now. Another minute with nothing but her own thoughts and her mind might have turned a corner and slipped away completely.

Chapter 24

Arden's parents and most of their friends hardly ever locked their doors, a few of the rare times being when they went to a funeral or to church on Sunday. That went back to the idea that nobody in the area would steal, but outsiders might come on a Sunday, when they knew the good people were at church.

The doors were locked now.

No good people left.

In the garage, Arden stood on her toes and felt along a narrow ledge to the right of the door—until her fingers came in contact with a small metal box. She got it down, slid the lid open, and pulled out a key. Put there by her father, for emergencies. Not this one. He could never have foreseen this emergency.

The garage was empty, their car gone. Daniel was probably using it. Or maybe he'd sold it. She'd left him to deal with too many things.

The door opened behind her and she jumped.

"Find it?"

Eli.

Find what?

Oh, the key. The key in her hand.

How long had she been standing there? "Right where I thought it would be."

The sun was coming up. Too bright in the sky, lodged between the garage and house, past a pasture and a field that had been fall-plowed.

Her dad had never fall-plowed. Daniel wouldn't fall-plow. Someone else must be renting the crop and grazing ground.

She felt a sudden surge of anger. Who was fall-plowing her dad's ground after the years of care he'd given it?

It doesn't matter. Not anymore.

Don't look at it. Don't think about it.

Go inside.

They walked past the slaughterhouse.

It was a building she'd avoided ever since a young farmhand had introduced her to the captive bolt gun. He'd pulled it from a drawer in the butcher table. "You put it against the animal's temple," the teenage boy had told her, holding the heavy device in the palm of his hand. "Then you press the trigger."

"Does it shoot a bullet?" Arden had asked.

"No bullets. The bolt goes through the steer's skull, then pops back out. You use it over and over."

After that, she'd had bad dreams for a long time.

It was the right key. She hadn't been sure. The only time she remembered using it had been one afternoon when she'd come home from school and the house had been locked. Not for a funeral. Someone in the nearby town of Derbyshire had been murdered and robbed, and the killer was still on the loose.

Arden's mom had been sure it must have been someone from far away, but it turned out to be the victim's nephew who'd been in need of a fix.

The heavy kitchen door swung open.

With the others behind her, Arden paused to check the floor.

A fine layer of dust.

She moved forward, doing a quick scan of the house, walking through the rooms on autopilot, not allowing herself even a flicker of emotion that the visuals might evoke.

Clearly nobody was living there. Apparently not her brother. Nobody would be coming, at least not soon.

The electricity had been left on—probably for lot illumination and cattle waterers.

"Don't turn on any lights," she said. "Someone might see."

The propane furnace was running, set on fifty degrees to keep the water pipes from freezing.

In the basement, the pantry shelves were still full of canned food. Left by her mom.

Seeing the jars hurt.

A lot of farmers had the misplaced notion that when the United States government failed and the country's infrastructure collapsed, people would flee the big cities like lemmings. Where would they go? Why, to the Midwest. They'd invade the farms, where people still had food. Where they were self-sufficient and didn't depend on semis loaded with staples from California and Texas to sustain them.

Arden had always tried to tell her mother that nobody was coming. That nobody even *knew* about them. But her mother would can her fruit and vegetables, preparing for the end of the world as they knew it. At least her family would have food. And when the city people came, she would stand at the door with a shotgun if she had to.

"You'd feed them," Arden always said with a laugh. "If starving people came to your door, you'd feed them."

Her mother would laugh, agree, and keep canning.

Armageddon had come.

Her mother was dead. And Arden and her friends were the lemmings.

They took armloads of food up the bowed wooden steps, depositing everything on the kitchen counter. They popped open preserved apples and peaches. With forks, they ate them right from the jars.

"What's your name?"

Arden looked up to see Harley staring intently at Franny, a fork in his hand, apple juice dripping down his beard. It was the second time he'd asked the question.

"Franny."

She probably would have looked scared, at least intimidated by him, if she hadn't been so tired.

He nodded. "Oh, yeah. That's right."

He was suffering short-term memory loss. He was

confused. Arden was confused. They were all confused.

And in need of sleep.

They'd left the motel room in the middle of the night, no one but Harley having gotten any sleep while there. After that, there had been catnaps in the car, but nothing substantial. Now, standing around in a stupor, staring blankly at nothing, they were almost too tired to understand that they needed to go to bed.

The farmhouse had four bedrooms. Three up, one down. The structure of the house was solid. Repairs and paint had been kept up, but nothing had been remodeled in years. On a farm, the inside of the house wasn't as important as what was outside, beyond the house. You didn't waste money on your sleeping and eating spaces.

"This is okay with me," Eli said, looking into the first-floor bedroom.

The guestroom, or spare room, her mother had called it.

Arden wasn't sure if she could ever remember anybody actually using it, which meant it was the least imprinted room in the house.

"I'll sleep here too." Franny tossed her bag on the bed. "I don't want to be by myself."

Arden and Harley went upstairs.

Harley immediately fell across the double bed in the room that had belonged to Arden's brother. The old wallpaper was still there. A cream-colored background with a repeating pattern of cowboy boots.

She remembered sitting on the floor playing with

little plastic toy cowboys and Indians that had originally been their father's. The room had been carpeted then, with some kind of brown, multipurpose stuff.

She dug blankets out of the closet, covering Harley.

He was already asleep.

She left the room and walked down the hall, her footsteps echoing.

The house smelled of dust and mold. Stale air. And that lingering, sweet-rotten scent of dead mice.

Rodents would flee the fields when the corn was being picked, running for warmth and shelter, only to end up dying inside the walls, stinking up the house for months. Sometimes the stench was so bad it made Arden's eyes water, and gave her a pounding headache. She always figured her clothes smelled like dead things when she went to school.

The hall ended.

To the left was the library, full of her father's books. Mostly nonfiction. History and geography, books about places he'd hoped to one day visit.

Unlike a lot of farmers, Arden's parents had never been the kind to expect their kids to remain on the farm and carry on somebody else's dream. Both had been well educated. Her mother was a grade-school teacher. Her dad, although he hadn't gone to college, had been self-taught and could hold his own in any discussion of politics, history, or science.

That was the mind-set of many farmers. If you didn't know it, you got the information. You figured it out.

To the right of the library was her mother and father's room.

She didn't want to go in there.

Arden forced herself to turn and step inside.

Except for a missing mattress gone from the bed's box springs, everything appeared the same. The long, low dresser on the right. Her mother's jewelry case, covered with dust. In the corner, a rack with her dad's ties. The place where the sloped floor creaked when you stepped on it. The door to the walk-in closet was open. On the inside of the door hung a long, gray wool skirt with red trim that her mother often wore to church.

Arden turned away.

This was where it had happened.

This was where her mother had been murdered.

Don't think about the mattress and why it is gone. Plenty of time for that later.

Arden had no memory of finding her mother, but she knew the details.

She didn't want to think about that day, didn't want to try to remember. Not now. She wasn't ready. Wasn't mentally prepared. She would try to remember later.

The room smelled like lingering hints of her mother's perfume, mixed with her dad's aftershave.

She missed them.

She missed them so much.

Chapter 25

Daniel Davis flew down the road in his blue Dodge Dakota. He was going too fast, and the truck's shocks were bad.

He hoped the muffler didn't fall off.

He'd gotten a phone call from Donna Glancy, one of his nosy neighbors. But then, everybody in the country was nosy. What went on down the road was much more entertaining than what you could see on channel four.

In this case, Daniel had been glad to get the report.

Someone in a small station wagon had turned in the direction of the old place. Donna had watched and waited, but never saw the car come back. And there was only one way out. Well, not exactly. If the weather had been dry or the ground was frozen, you could cross the pastures and end up on Roller Coaster Road, but it was a rough ride. And the only person capable of finding his way out would be someone familiar with the farm.

Like Arden.

That was his first thought when he'd answered the phone and Donna had told him what she'd seen.

He'd expected his sister back long before this—at least to settle the estate. But as time had passed, as weeks had turned into months and crops had been planted and harvested, he'd begun to think she'd never return.

He turned left off the hard road, down the hill. Once the land leveled out, he took a right, passing the mailbox with the sloppy letters, up the curved drive.

No car in the driveway.

The ground was frozen; there were no tracks.

Daniel circled around to the other side of the barn, stopped, and set the emergency brake. He jumped from the truck and slid the barn door open a crack. In the hazy darkness, he spotted the car. A little hatchback station wagon.

Shit.

Back at the truck, he turned off the ignition, grabbed his rifle, and headed up the hill to the house.

He entered through the back door, quietly slipping into the kitchen. Once inside, he paused to listen.

A clock ticked above the sink. The furnace was running. The counter was littered with empty jars of his mother's canned fruit. Unrinsed. Forks sticking out.

He hadn't stepped inside the house in months. And he hadn't been upstairs since the funeral. Now, the sight of his childhood home made him feel sick to his stomach, made his heart pound with the terror of memory.

When the murders first happened, he'd been numb. He'd been able to come in. Walk around. Move through the house. Talk to the cops. The detectives. Make the funeral arrangements.

Just do it.

He'd been in his first year of community college. After two years, he'd planned to go off to a university to get a degree in veterinary science.

He had a couple of friends who'd died in a car wreck, and he'd always wondered how their parents had dealt with the tragedy so calmly. How they'd planned the funeral, and welcomed people to their home, sitting around chatting as if it were just some normal day. Maybe even a fucking holiday. Now he knew that the body—the brain—did something, went through some chemical change or something that made it all pretty easy.

Autopilot plus.

Except for the little episode with Arden when he'd let his buried emotions spill out and had blamed her for everything. She'd known it was true. He'd seen it in her face.

Weeks passed, and the numbness wore off. Things got worse because you felt the pain.

He'd been staying at the house of a family friend and knew it was time to move back to the old place. But he couldn't do it. Not anymore.

A sick horror welled up in him whenever he'd confronted the idea.

He was just a kid. A kid! He shouldn't have to feel

these emotions. He shouldn't have to deal with this kind of shit. His friends—his old friends—were going to college, doing things college kids did. Drinking too much. Listening to bands. Meeting girls.

Not fair.

He'd tried to hang out with some of them last summer, but they seemed so much younger, so immature and shallow. He was only twenty-two, but he felt at least forty. Not that forty was ancient, but you weren't a kid anymore; that was for damn sure.

He still wanted to laugh at stupid things. He still wanted to enjoy a party with a bonfire and beer.

But he couldn't. That part of life was over for him. He'd passed Go and gone directly to hell.

And one person was responsible for it all. For the death of his parents, and the loss of his youth. If he were lucky, he would find her here. She should have died with them. She was supposed to have died with them.

Chapter 26

Daniel crossed through the kitchen to the dining room, the rifle butt pressed painfully into his shoulder, the barrel shaking like hell. The floor under his boots creaked; he flinched at the sound.

To the left were the curved stairs that led to the second floor.

He glanced out the front porch window, then moved forward to the guest bedroom.

The door was open. He cocked the .22, then swung into the room.

Two people. Sleeping. A curly-haired guy and a girl with short, jet-black hair. She was clutching a small stuffed animal under her chin.

Light, smooth skin. Pale mouth, with a gold ring on her bottom lip. Normally he hated those damn things, but this one was thin and delicate. Nice.

She let out a heavy sigh.

He jerked—and immediately realized he was aiming the gun at her head. He lowered the barrel, confused.

Did they have anything to do with his sister? Or were they just moochers traveling through, looking for an empty house where they could get some food and crash?

He backed silently from the room.

He went upstairs, keeping to the right, close to the wall.

In high school, he'd sneaked in late a lot of nights, and he knew how to avoid making the steps creak.

The place smelled stale and musty. Like death. Rodent death.

Shortly after the funeral and Arden's bleaching, Daniel had closed up the house and walked away. The more time that passed, the harder it got to go back. Until he'd decided maybe he could never do it. Maybe it would hurt too much.

He approached Arden's room. If she was around, he had the feeling that's where she'd be.

Empty.

On the narrow twin bed, tossed to one side, were blankets. The pillow held the imprint of someone's head.

He moved down the hall, to the room he really didn't want to see.

The gun barrel entered first. He followed it around.

Someone sat on a little stool in front of his mother's dresser with the big round mirror.

Arden, he realized with a shock.

She looked up at him, not appearing surprised. Even less surprised that he was pointing a rifle at her.

It was light outside, but the room was dark because the curtains and shades were pulled. It also faced west and wouldn't get the good sun till afternoon.

The bed had been stripped and the mattress removed. He vaguely remembered the crime-scene investigators taking it. But there was still a stain on the box springs. The blood had soaked through the layers to puddle on the floor under the bed.

He could see it in his head. How the blood had looked. Like chocolate pudding.

On a farm, you saw a lot of disturbing life-and-death events—and you got used to them. But nothing he'd ever seen had prepared him for the day he had to look at his parents' dead bodies.

"She wore this all the time," Arden said.

Wore what? What was she talking about?

Then he noticed she was holding something in her hand.

A perfume bottle.

"We'd get her different scents. New scents for Mother's Day and her birthday. She'd use them once or twice—just to make us feel good. Then she always went back to the violet perfume." She lifted the bottle. The lid was off. "Want to smell it?"

She was crazy.

All along, he'd been blaming her for not being there for him. Blaming her for not being the big sister and taking care of her little brother. But she was the one who needed help.

"I was in bed and thought about her perfume."

She had dark circles under her eyes. Her straight, red hair was stringy, parted in the middle, chin-length.

Her face was thin. Really thin.

"I smelled her perfume." She thought a moment. "Suddenly I could remember being five years old, gripping her skirt and trying to hide when she introduced me to people. And later, riding in the car, windows down, the breeze carrying the flowery scent to every corner. We were going to a party. Some kind of mother-daughter thing."

He was still holding the gun. He was still shaking. It pissed him off that she was trying to reminisce.

"But I can't remember it all. . . . I can't remember *exactly* where we were going."

"Maybe you should drink it." A childish thing to say, spoken in a childish tone of voice. How easy it was to fall into old roles. "Maybe it will unbleach you and you'll remember."

Her eyes narrowed in puzzlement.

He'd gotten her attention.

"The perfume." He waved the gun barrel at the bottle. "Maybe you should drink it."

They were all sick. All fucked up.

She lifted the bottle. She eyed the pale-lavender contents through the clear container. "You think?" She raised it to her mouth.

What was she doing? What was she trying to prove?

He lunged, tossing the gun across the bed, slapping the bottle from her hand. It crashed to the wall, shattering.

The air was instantly saturated with the scent of their dead mother.

He let out a sob.

Don't let her see you break.

Emotions he'd kept in check for so long came tumbling out. Rage and grief. But mostly rage. "Do you remember *me?*" he shouted, pounding at his chest with an open hand. "Do you remember anything about me? Your brother? The one you deserted?"

"I'm sorry, Daniel."

She did look sorry. Sorry and sad and sick and messed up. He felt himself begin to weaken and fought it.

She'd brought a storm down on their family, on their lives. And then she'd run away.

"You're a coward," he said, his voice rough, his lips trembling. "A weak coward."

She tipped her head, and her expression became even more sorrowful. "I know."

He wanted her to fight. He wanted her to argue, to try to justify herself. How could he fight someone who wouldn't fight back?

He heard shuffling behind him. Before he could turn, someone grabbed him, twisting one arm behind his back. A hand encircled his throat and squeezed, cutting off his air.

The room turned black and Arden disappeared.

Someone screamed.

That was followed by the sound of things falling over. An impact from the side sent him tumbling, crashing to the wall.

Chapter 27

Franny woke up with a jolt.

Plummeting from dream to consciousness, she let out a gasp. Her muscles spasmed violently, shaking the bed. It felt as if she'd been dropped from the sky.

From somewhere above her head came the sound of scuffling. Like shoes against a wooden floor. Rattling and banging, and things hitting a wall so hard the house shuddered.

Next to her, Eli shot out of bed.

Later she might think about that. About how funny he looked, bleary eyed and half-asleep, yet moving at the speed of light.

"No!" someone shouted from above their heads.

A female voice.

Arden's? It hadn't sounded like Arden, who was always pretty laid-back.

In dirty white socks, Eli ran from the room. He grabbed the wide wooden railing, taking the stairs three at a time. Franny tried to keep up.

They followed the shouting into a large, dark bedroom.

At first it was hard to decipher what was happening. At first it just seemed a tangle of people, rolling around on the floor, all arms and legs and backs.

Arden was slapping Harley in the face, screaming at him.

Kill her, said a man's voice in Franny's head.

Franny blinked.

Kill her.

She imagined a knife slicing across a throat. Hot blood spilling over her own hands. And the smell . . . Metallic and bitter. She could taste it on her tongue.

Franny had demonstrated in peace rallies. She'd been arrested for chaining herself to the front door of a university veterinary building to protest the experiments they were doing on rats.

But for one brief second, she'd transformed into something else. Someone else. For one brief second, she'd wanted to see blood. She'd wanted to see a life snuffed out.

She'd been here before. In this room. In this house.

Suddenly she vaguely recalled watching a video about the Davis murders. And what about the voice? Who did the voice belong to? A murderer Dr. Harris had introduced her to in the tank? Had Noah heard the same voice? Had it gotten into his head?

Eli joined in the fight.

Was he helping? Franny couldn't see.

He fell back, bringing Harley with him. They crashed to the floor; a chair skittered into the wall.

The room reeked of perfume. Something Franny had smelled before. Something floral. Something one of her foster mothers may have worn.

There was someone else in the room. A man. Lying on his back on the floor, Arden bending over him.

Harley and Eli scrambled to their feet. Eli kept a hand on Harley's chest, as if expecting him to attack again.

Franny was surprised and rather impressed that Eli had been able to overpower Harley. Under normal conditions, if Harley hadn't been weakened from the tank, the outcome probably would have been different.

"Oh, my God, oh, my God," Arden kept saying over and over.

It seemed weird to see her so upset.

Nothing seemed real, and for a moment Franny wondered if maybe she was still asleep. If maybe she'd been asleep for a long time, maybe ever since Noah had died.

The man on the floor let out a gasp. Then another.

She couldn't see his face. He was wearing jeans, faded, dirty jeans, and brown leather work boots.

"He was hurting her," Harley said in that monotone voice that gave her the creeps. "He was yelling at her and hurting her." He pointed to the bed. "And he had a gun."

Lying across the box springs was a rifle.

It was the bed where Arden's mother had died.

Franny thought about Noah.

Even though she hadn't witnessed it, she could picture him tumbling from the window. Falling gently and beautifully and gracefully to the ground.

In her mind, he always got up. Always jumped to his feet and brushed himself off, a smile on his face. *Just kidding!*

She remembered how she'd taunted him about his family. She thought about how they'd argued.

None of that should have mattered. Not the stuff about his family. None of it should have meant anything or had anything to do with their relationship.

The man on the floor was sitting up now, breathing hard, a hand to his throat. He raised his head, confusion in his face.

He's young, she thought with a jolt. *Hardly more than a boy.*

His gaze went from Arden, to Harley, to Eli, to Franny. Then hesitation before he looked at the gun on the bed.

She was much closer to it than anyone else in the room. Suddenly mobilized, she pounced, grabbed the rifle, and swung the barrel at the boy-man.

Arden put out a hand. "Franny—"

The barrel swung to Arden.

Arden froze.

"That thing's loaded," the boy on the floor croaked.

"No more fighting," Franny said calmly. "I don't want any more fighting."

"The fight is over," Arden said. "Over."

In a split second, the focus of the room had changed. Franny was the star. Franny was in charge.

She'd been invisible since Noah had died. Nobody had asked her what she thought. What she wanted to eat. Where she wanted to stop. What radio station she wanted to listen to. It was just, "We're doing this. We're doing that."

"I'm not invisible," she said, her voice trembling.

Arden gave her a pleading look. "I know. We were giving you space. We didn't want you to be more burdened than you already were."

"That thing's cocked," the kid on the floor said, the words a whisper directed at Arden.

"Nobody has even mentioned his name. In the past two days, nobody even said, 'I miss Noah.'" A shuddering, trembling sob escaped Franny. She sniffed and wiped her nose with her upper sleeve. "Don't you care? Don't you even care? What are we doing here? We should be at Noah's funeral, not rolling around in some awful house in the middle of nowhere. I didn't do anything wrong. I don't even know why I'm here."

She had the butt of the gun against her shoulder, her left hand supporting the barrel, her right moving for the trigger.

She didn't like it here. It was wrong. An ugly place. A bad place. And it was Arden's fault. "You talked us into coming, but it's none of our business. It's not about us."

"I'm sorry," Arden said.

She seemed to mean it. And she didn't seem scared. Why wasn't she scared? A gun was pointed at her. The kid said it was loaded.

She feels it too. The despair. The hollowness. The loss of self, of who she used to be.

"We're ghosts," Franny whispered.

The gun was incredibly heavy. The muscles in her

arms began to twitch. "That's what we are, isn't it?" Franny asked. "Ghosts."

Arden's eyes glistened with tears, and Franny could see she understood, that she agreed even though she didn't want to give validation to such a heartbreaking verdict.

The distance between Franny and the room seemed to grow and expand, the edges blurred.

She felt someone remove the rifle from her hands. It was the boy. The boy-man.

For a second, his eyes came into sharp focus. Brown. A very dark brown. Direct. Not a boy's eyes. Not a boy's eyes at all.

Her hands dropped like deadweights to her sides. Then Arden was there, wrapping her arms around her, rubbing her back. "Not ghosts," Arden whispered. "We're just resting. Just sleeping."

Chapter 28

"This is my brother, Daniel."

They all stood in the master bedroom. Eli had released Harley. Daniel stood to one side, the rifle pointed to the floor. Arden had her arm around Franny, who had quit crying and was sniffling and wiping her nose with the sleeve of her sweater that she'd stretched over her hand.

Had she spoken Daniel's name aloud since the day he'd accused her of being responsible for the murders that had taken place in that very room? Arden wondered.

They hadn't been able to erase that painful memory.

Franny looked up from her sweatered hand, eyes red-rimmed. "Are you okay?"

The truth was that none of them were okay, but they all knew it. Why state the obvious? "Tired. We're all tired," Arden said.

Daniel stared at her.

He was her brother. She should know him well, but he'd always been hard to read. He had a way of shutting off his expression while at the same time remaining still and watchful. You knew his brain was humming along, but you had no idea what he was thinking until he spoke.

"What are you doing here?" Daniel asked.

The hostility in his voice caused Harley to look up sharply.

"What do you want?" Daniel asked.

This was hard for Arden. His hatred hurt. It was a pain in her chest that was sharp and dull at the same time.

In her mind, she saw the isolation tank. All along, she'd been terrified of it. Suddenly she craved it. Longed for the sanctuary and the security. The bleaching that was the only thing beyond death that could stop the pain.

Franny had been right. They were ghosts.

What did she want? Daniel had asked. She wanted things to be the way they'd been before. She wanted to turn back time. She wanted her parents to still be alive.

She didn't want her brother to hate her.

She wanted to quit hating herself.

But none of those things would happen.

"We needed a place to stay," she said. "Just for a while."

He looked from her to the others, then back. "I have to talk to you in private." He took a couple of steps toward the door, then hesitated. Now there was finally something to read, as indecision flitted across his face. "Down the hall. My room, I guess."

He moved away and she followed. In his old bedroom, she shut the door as he turned to face her. "I don't want you here," he said.

She'd expected something like that. But it wasn't for him to say. The place was just as much hers as his. "You obviously aren't using the house, so what difference does it make?"

"What *difference*?"

The rifle had belonged to their dad. It was a semi-automatic. Arden had fired it several times when she was growing up.

Daniel removed the clip and jammed it into the front pocket of his jeans. Then he removed the remaining bullet from the gun's chamber, pocketing that too. He leaned the gun against the wall and turned to her.

"Do you think I don't watch the news?" he asked. "People are looking for you." He motioned toward the closed door. "And looking for them."

"We haven't done anything wrong."

"Why are you running then?"

"We need some time." She wasn't ready to give him the full story. She wasn't even sure what the full story was. "Just a little time. They want us for questioning. That's all."

"They are calling you 'persons of interest.' That's like putting the word *alleged* in front of *killer* when you saw the guy blow somebody's brains out."

"A couple of days," Arden said. "That's all."

He let out a snort of disbelief and braced his hands on his waist, elbows out. "And then what? You'll take off again?" He was wearing a heavy brown canvas Carhartt jacket that hit him at midthigh. "Haven't you stopped to think about how your running away has fucked everything up?"

"I know that."

She could make excuses. She could say the bleaching had erased more than she'd planned. She could say she couldn't face his hatred. But she wouldn't say those things, because in the end he was right. She should have stayed.

His jaw was dark; he needed to shave.

She didn't remember ever seeing him with a shadow. It made her feel weird, as if he weren't really her brother at all, but some impostor. Somebody who'd been trained to act and sound like Daniel, but didn't have the role down quite right.

"I watched the execution." His voice was quiet. "I had to. I'd been waiting for a long time."

She swallowed.

"I can't say I enjoyed it, but . . . it's a relief, you know?"

Tell him. You have to tell him.

He swung away and dragged his finger through a layer of heavy dust on the painted windowsill. He brushed the dust on his jeans. "I said too much that day."

"It was the truth."

Tell him.

How would he react when he found out that the person who'd killed their parents was very possibly still running loose? Would he hate her all over again?

"It wasn't like you killed them yourself," he said. "It wasn't like they died by your hand."

She frowned. In her mind, she imagined a knife blade slicing across skin. Flesh parting. A layer of fat, muscle, bone. She thought about Noah and what he'd done. She thought about poor Vera Thompson.

The shadow people are coming.

Whatever you most fear will eventually find you.

Daniel swung back around, head down, not making eye contact. "I have to go to work." He grabbed the gun.

"Work?" Wasn't he in school? College? "Where?"

"The grain elevator in town. In Grove."

Grain elevator? "Why?"

"Let's just say I took some time off too."

If you didn't get out of Lake County immediately, you never got out. High school graduates always said they were just going to stick around a year. Get a job. Make a little money. Save for college. But they never left. Because after a while, things started to seem . . . well, if not okay, then easy. Laziness set in, and you began to think, *This isn't bad. What's so bad about it?* And it wouldn't *be* bad. Not at the time.

But when you got older, when you looked back and tried to think about what you'd done with your life . . . that's when it hit you. That's when it suddenly became important. When you were too trapped or too sick or too old to do anything about it.

She hadn't wanted anything in a long time, but suddenly she wanted Daniel to have more than he would have here. She was eight years older. She'd looked out for him, taken care of him.

Not that it was much better out there, but he had

to at least see what life could be like beyond Lake County. For a while. And then if he wanted to come back he could. Then he would know if it was right or not.

"You should put some ice on your neck," she told him.

His skin was already turning black and blue. She could make out a couple of fingerprints. Good thing Harley was still weak from his ordeal on the Hill.

Daniel ignored her the way he used to ignore their mother when she told him to take care of himself. "I'll come back when I get off work." He pushed past her and jerked open the door. It stuck at the top, the way it always had, making a shimmying sound as it broke loose. "I'll stop at the Quick Mart and get a few groceries."

She would tell Daniel about Albert French when he returned.

His feet pounded in the hall, down the steps, and across the living room to make contact with the vinyl floor in the kitchen.

A door slammed.

Arden walked to the window and saw Daniel running across the yard, past the tire swing and down the hill to the barn. Running as if the devil were chasing him.

Daniel rounded the corner of the barn, slipping in loose gravel. He threw his body forward to regain his footing. Now that he could no longer see the house, he slowed to a walk.

On the driver's side of the truck, he hooked his

fingers under the latch, but didn't open the door. Instead, he leaned against the truck, pressing his head to his bent forearm.

When Arden was about twelve, she'd scratched her name in the moss that grew on the cement wall on the south side of the barn. The letters had been huge, maybe four feet high. They were still there.

He'd asked her why she'd done it, and she'd smiled and said, "So the farm doesn't forget me."

"You aren't leaving, are you?" he'd asked.

"I will someday. So will you."

"No, I won't."

He'd been too young to understand that for his generation staying had become an exercise in clinging to the past for the sake of his grandparents and parents. If he left, if he turned his back on them, he somehow invalidated their lives and his own. It was a no-win situation.

He always felt he had to stay. That he didn't have a choice.

But now they were gone.

A loud, harsh sob escaped him. He swallowed and straightened away from the truck, sniffling and wiping his nose and cheeks with the sleeve of his jacket.

He opened the door, wedging the rifle behind the seat. Then he slid behind the wheel and turned the ignition key, the engine rumbling to life.

He told her he'd be back, but he wasn't sure he could do it.

Chapter 29

Harley slid down in the porcelain tub, knees sharply bent. He heard water lapping, and felt it channel into his ears.

Deeper.

He needed to go deeper.

He held his breath as the water covered his face.

Eyes wide open, he could see the square of light that was the bathroom window. He could see the white, ruffled curtains and the round bulb above the sink. A sink that was full of hair he'd cut from his head with a pair of scissors. Full of hair he'd removed from his face with the razor he'd found in the cupboard.

He wanted to submerge his entire body, but the tub was too small.

He craved water, loved water, felt safe in water.

Water told him things. Kept him updated. Water remembered all the things he'd forgotten. It was an extension of himself, of who he was. It moved through him, around him.

I need a swimming pool. That's what I need.

But pool water would be cold. He needed warm water.

He lifted his head enough to exhale and take a new breath before going back down.

Rapture of the deep.

Nitrogen narcosis.

Beautiful, beautiful . . .

A sound disturbed his communion.

A muffled voice, followed by a knock on the door. "Harley? Are you okay?"

It was Arden.

Go away.

She could be such a nag.

Had she really kidnapped him? She claimed to have *rescued* him, but he wasn't sure. It felt like a kidnapping. Because he'd been someplace he loved, someplace he wanted to be. If you took somebody away from that place . . . If you broke into a building and sneaked away at night . . . If you *hid*, wasn't that kidnapping?

Confusing, very confusing . . .

He'd been trying to figure it out for quite some time. But then his head would start hurting, and he would just let it go.

Was there a ransom? he wondered. Was she asking somebody for money?

Who? Who would pay for his release? He didn't know of anybody who would pay. Harris? Yeah. Harris might. Harris would want him back.

Harris was a good guy. Not somebody you'd want to hang out with, but a kind person. You could go a long way with kindness.

"Harley?"

Damn. There she was again. This time her voice was louder.

She'd opened the door. He could see it, all fuzzy, open about a foot, a blurred head poking through.

She'd seen him naked. He didn't care about that. He had the memory of Arden's own naked body curled next to his. Or was that just a dream? Wishful thinking?

"Harley!" She shot into the room, alarmed and panicky.

Oh, yeah. I'm underwater. I forgot I'm underwater.

Meditation destroyed, he surfaced, gasping, surprised to find that his lungs were on fire. Mouth open wide, he sucked in air like a dying man.

Arden ran to the tub and grabbed him by the upper arms. "Harley! Jesus! What are you doing?"

The look on her face was priceless. Mad and worried and horrified all at once. He started laughing. That didn't help the breathing situation.

She rubbed his back. "Relax," she told him. "Relax and take easy breaths. There you go. That's the way."

She was right. It worked.

In another minute he was breathing normally.

He looked at her and smiled.

She smiled back. "You shaved." She ran a hand across his jaw. A tender, stroking motion. She touched his hair. "And you cut your hair."

She was looking at him strangely, almost as if she'd never seen him before. As if trying to figure out who he was.

Did she have memories of the two of them? Together? Or had she left them in the water somewhere? For the water to hold and store and keep safe until she was ready to find them again? Because water remembered.

He wanted her in the water with him. If she could join him there, then they would somehow make a whole person and he would be able to understand and figure out what was going on.

Don't let them see that you don't know anything. Never let them see that you're confused.

"I remember you," he said.

Her eyebrows drew together. "Of course you do."

He reached up and touched her hair, rubbing it between his fingers. The red strands made a crunchy sound that was at odds with how soft it felt. He wanted to smell it, but she was too far away.

"Do you remember me?" he asked. "Really remember?"

The puzzled look in her eyes intensified. "I'm not sure I remember everything."

"The cemetery at the Hill?" he ventured.

Her face cleared. "Yes."

"A kiss?"

"Yes."

He let go of her hair and grabbed her by the arm. He gently tugged her closer. "And more," he whispered, looking at her mouth. "I remember something else."

"Harley, I—"

She was really close now. So close that he was able to touch his mouth to hers. Just a little at first. A small, timid brush that slowly turned into more. Into open mouths and soft, warm breath.

They were soul mates.

That's what the contact told him. They'd done this before, and they knew each other. Not just as pals who'd been in an experiment together, but as something more.

He didn't know if love was part of the equation. Because what he was sensing was something different. Something symbiotic and cerebral. They were chained in a way you couldn't see. Connected beyond the mere physical.

And what if you added water to a kiss? What if they could go back to the womb together? How strong would they be then? If they became one?

He tried to pull her into the tub with him, but she broke away. Moving her hands nervously. A hand at her waist, another in her hair. Turning away from him. No eye contact.

"I'm sorry," he said, hoping to make her feel less uncomfortable.

"That's okay." Her voice was tight.

The water was getting cold.

He pulled the rubber plug attached to a small chain, then pushed himself to his feet, leaving the water behind him. "Remember that time we were in France?"

She turned back around. "What?"

He picked up a towel and began drying off. "When we went to France? We stayed at some kind of château where we drank wine on a terrace overlooking a vineyard. Oh, and we rode bikes." He pointed at her. "Do you remember that? Do you remember how it started to rain?"

He continued to dry himself as he talked. "We rode the bikes back to the château in the pouring rain? It rained all night, but we didn't care. We stayed inside. We stayed in our room."

She shook her head, the puzzlement back in her face. "I don't think I've ever been to France."

"Yes, you have. With me. You just don't remember."

"Harley, I don't think so."

"It'll come back to you. It just came back to me. Right here. Kind of a déjà vu feeling."

Now that he was dry, he reached for her again. She moved toward the door. "I have to go."

She left, closing the door behind her.

Harley smiled to himself.

She would remember him.

Chapter 30

Nathan Fury looked across the autopsy table at FBI medical examiner Jason Devore. "Thanks for coming," Fury said.

Devore wore a yellow disposable Tyvek suit, a heavy vinyl apron, latex gloves, and a face shield pulled back and resting on the top of his head. "This isn't an easy place to get to."

Devore was a busy man and in high demand. He'd been brought in by FBI helicopter, which was waiting in a nearby field to scoop him away once he was finished.

Devore looked tired, and ten years older than his thirty-seven years. The FBI did that to a person. When you were good at your job, you put in a lot of overtime.

"I've heard a lot about the Hill." Devore glanced at the dark, sweating stone walls of the Hill's Mercy Unit basement and morgue. "Always wanted to see it. Now that I have, I can say it would have been better if we'd brought the bodies to the facilities in Virginia." He shook his head. "Didn't know this place was such a dump."

It had been tough convincing the local police department to allow them to conduct the autopsies on asylum grounds.

"They don't usually have murders in Madeline," Fury said. "And when they do, bodies normally get shipped upstate. Considering the circumstances and the controversial nature of the program, we thought it better to involve as few people as possible. The town is already talking about kicking us out." But Devore's outstanding credentials should make everybody happy.

"Putting together a lynch mob?" Devore asked with a wry smile.

He was kidding, of course, but Fury had been down off the Hill a few times since the homicide and suicide, and a mob mentality was definitely brewing in town. Fury rarely displayed his ID in public, but residents seemed to know he was FBI. There were no smiles, and he was a little afraid to order food anywhere. Not that he thought someone would try to poison him, but spitting in his tea would probably be good for some giggles.

Outside, the sun was shining. In the morgue, you wouldn't know what time of day it was, or even what month. But the cooler was adequate, keeping the waiting bodies at a nice, even thirty-eight degrees. The first one they wheeled out was Vera Thompson.

"I haven't worked without assistants in years," Devore said, uncovering the body.

Fury didn't know if Devore was griping or bragging. "It'll be okay." Fury adjusted the sleeves of his disposable suit. "I've been in on a lot of autopsies."

"Not complaining," Devore said. "In fact, this is kinda fun." He looked up. "Reminds me of the old medical school days when things were a little more relaxed."

"Not sure *relaxed* is a word I've used around here lately, but . . . okay."

Devore turned on a small digital recorder and documented the time, location, victim's name, date. That was followed by approximate weight and height of the body on the table. He then did a cursory external exam, beginning at the top of her head.

The autopsy table wasn't equipped with a downdraft; the fumes were drawn from the room by an antiquated system that didn't seem much more powerful than a residential exhaust fan.

Fury's eyes and throat burned.

Devore, on the other hand, was chatting as if the stench didn't register. But then, Fury had known a coroner who would sometimes munch on snacks while perusing a cadaver. Or had that been Devore? God, it *had* been Devore.

Devore focused his attention on the body. "These . . ." With the scalpel, he lifted the edges of the stab wounds. "Weapon was a knife, which the police already determined. Anybody find it yet?"

"No."

It would make things much easier if they had. Lack of a murder weapon was one of the most frustrating stumbling blocks to any case.

"The attack came in from a high angle, with quite

a bit of force," Devore said. "Made by a fairly tall person."

"How tall?"

"Close to six feet. Maybe taller." Devore picked up one of the woman's hands, then the other. "Nails are clean." He slipped a block under her neck, dropped his face shield, readied the scalpel, and made an incision from the sternum to the pelvic bone.

The internal exam took forty-five minutes.

When it was over, they covered Vera Thompson, wheeled her back into the cooler, and retrieved the body of Noah Viola.

"What a shame," Devore said, shaking his head. "Nice-looking kid."

Noah was small and on the frail side.

Devore measured his height and looked up at Fury. "Five feet, five inches."

Not tall enough to have stabbed Mrs. Thompson, Fury thought, unless he'd attacked from a high vantage point. . . .

When the autopsy was complete, Fury walked Devore to the waiting helicopter. "Thanks for coming." He offered his hand and Devore shook it.

"I'll get a full report to you in a few days." The ME ducked and ran beneath the swirling blades, disappearing through the open door. A minute later, the craft lifted away in a swirl of leaves and violent wind.

*   *   *

That evening, in his room on the Hill, ears still ringing from the sound of the helicopter, Fury sat at a scratched and varnished desk, crime-scene photos spread in front of him.

He pored over the Thompson photos again, paying particular attention to the close-ups of spatter on the bathroom walls.

There could be no doubt that the crime had been committed in the bathroom. When Devore had first mentioned that the killer had been tall, Fury had considered different scenarios, but the spatter proved otherwise.

The blood on Noah's shoes and shirt had turned out to be A-negative, same as Vera Thompson's. The bloody footprint of Noah's shoe proved he'd been in the room.

Had there been two people involved in the murder? And was the kid's death really a suicide? Or had someone—the person who'd actually slit Thompson's throat—pushed Noah from the window?

A witness claimed she'd heard Noah say the old woman needed to be put out of her misery, but if Noah hadn't murdered Thompson, then who had? And what was the motive?

Fury's cell phone rang.

It was one of the local detectives.

"We got the credit card records for Eli Norton, Franny Young, and Arden Davis," he said. "They all drew cash from the same ATM machine near the town of Parkersburg, West Virginia. Since then, no more withdrawals."

Arden would know better than to leave a paper trail, Fury thought. She would get as much cash as possible at the beginning.

"Then we got lucky and came up with one charge to Norton's credit card. The Coffee Cup Café in Cambridge, Ohio."

Fury thanked him and disconnected.

He got out an atlas and turned to Ohio.

They were heading north on Highway 77, toward Cleveland. Arden's family farm was northeast of Cleveland, in Lake County.

Up until that point, Fury had felt Lake County, Ohio, was the last place Arden would go. Now he thought different.

Chapter 31

Eli turned off the TV, tossed the remote on the couch beside him, and sat staring at the blank screen.

The news had been full of weather.

Eli had grown up in Tucson, Arizona. He usually didn't pay much attention to weather—it bored him—but on television they'd been talking about a storm. A big storm. That made him nervous.

Franny was sleeping. Arden was upstairs. Harley was puttering around in the kitchen, banging pans and running water.

The air in the house had finally warmed up, but anything you touched was cold. The cushions under his ass were still putting off a deep chill.

He'd been having fun until they got there. He wasn't having fun anymore.

He should pack up Franny and they should get the hell out of there. That's what his gut was telling him. But he didn't want to leave Arden alone with Harley. The guy was a mess. Completely unpredictable. And violent. Now they knew he was violent.

Eli got up from the couch and walked quietly into the bedroom.

Franny was asleep, curled on her side, clutching the ragged teddy bear she said she'd had since she was three. He sank down on the bed.

"Franny?" he whispered, gently shaking her by the shoulder.

She made a small sound of protest, followed by a smacking of her lips. Her shook her again. This time she woke up.

It was getting dark, and he could barely make out her features.

"Eli?" she muttered.

"Sorry to wake you."

"That's okay."

Her words were a little slurred and groggy. He knew how it was, waking up from a long daytime nap. It really drained you. Really fucked you up.

He scooted closer, an elbow on the mattress, his head resting in his palm. "I'm thinking about leaving," he whispered.

She was silent, and he had the feeling she was trying to read his expression in the dark.

"This place is creepy," he said. That sounded childish. Dumb. "I'm getting a bad vibe." That sounded even dumber. "I know this is where Arden's parents were killed, but it's more than that. I mean, I'm not afraid of ghosts or anything."

He felt her warm fingers curl around his cold hand. "What about Arden?" she whispered back. "And Harley? I don't think Arden will want to leave."

"I don't think either of them will leave, but that doesn't mean we have to stay."

"What about going to the newspaper?"

"We can still do that. We can still get everything together and meet someplace when we're ready. Or you and I can go by ourselves."

She dropped back on the mattress, her hand still holding his. "I can't think. My brain is mush."

He loved Franny.

Now that Noah was gone, he could tell her that. Not now. Now would be a bad time. But later. When they were away from there.

"On TV, they keep talking about a storm," Eli said. "Some big-ass thing. Supposed to hit in a day or two. I think we should get out of here before that. I mean, we're in the boonies as it is. I can't imagine what it will be like if it snows two feet. I don't want to be trapped here." He leaned closer. "With that guy." *Harley.* He didn't want to say his name, just in case he heard. In case he was nearby.

"I'm not sure I want to leave Arden," Franny said. "Maybe she'll come. Maybe we can all leave."

That wasn't going to happen. Eli was sure of it.

"Spaghetti will be ready in five minutes!" Harley shouted from the kitchen.

Eli didn't want to let go of Franny's hand. Things would be okay once they got away. Just the two of them.

"I'm going to find Arden." He made himself release her. He started to get up from the bed, then paused. "Stay here until I get back, will you? I mean, don't go in the kitchen."

"Harley's okay," she whispered.

"He almost killed Arden's brother."

"He was defending her."

"Stay here. *Please*."

She laughed. "Okay."

It was the first time he'd heard her laugh since Noah died. He wanted to kiss her, but he didn't dare. Instead, he got to his feet and went upstairs to find Arden.

Her bedroom door was shut. He knocked. There was no reply, but he could hear her moving around inside. Not any big sound, but something like a footfall, or like something being set down on the floor.

"Arden?"

A louder sound. Like a scramble. Then the door opened a couple of inches. A lamp with a crooked shade sat on the floor. It backlit her, casting her face in shadow. Apparently lights were no longer an issue.

"What are you doing?" he asked.

"Nothing."

She sounded guilty. Sneaky. Little-kid sneaky.

He pushed on the door; she held it where it was.

"Can I come in?"

Giving up, she released her grip and stepped back.

The floor was strewn with papers, books, photos, and photo albums. In the center of it all was a bottle of vodka.

"I've been looking for something."

She tugged the hair back from her forehead and stared at the mess around her feet. "A passport. I used to have a passport; I'm sure of it. I wanna check the stamps. See how many I have. See where I've been."

She dropped to the floor, legs crossed.

Her ankles were bare. She was wearing a pair of old Nike sneakers she must have found somewhere.

He joined her so they both sat cross-legged, face-to-face.

"And yes, I've been drinking." She offered the bottle to him.

He shook his head. "Maybe later."

"Straight vodka's nasty. Especially the cheap stuff." She took a long swallow, as if she didn't think it was nasty at all. "There's probably some tomato juice around, but tomatoes give me hives."

"Don't wanna get hives."

"Nope."

Eli tried to think back on how all of this had happened, how Arden had convinced them that they needed to run away from the Hill.

She'd seemed coherent. Logical. Automatically falling into the role of leader. But she'd been losing her grip ever since they'd arrived at the house. She'd been acting almost as weird as Harley.

Not good. Not good at all.

"Harley says the spaghetti is almost ready."

"I'm not hungry. And there's the whole hives thing."

"It might be a good idea to eat something."

"And kill the buzz?"

She had more than a buzz going on.

"Lookie here." She held up a photo.

He took it and leaned closer to the light. A color three-by-five of a little girl dressed like a pirate. Her arms were around the neck of a dog that looked like some kind of black Lab cross.

"This you?" He pointed.

"Cute kid, wasn't I?"

He nodded and passed the photo back. "Franny and I . . . we've been talking about maybe heading out. Going to my folks' for a while." Franny didn't have any family. Hopefully she would come home with him. "Stabilize. And with the holidays not that far off . . ."

She held up a newspaper clipping. "I must have cut it out of the local paper shortly before their funeral."

Yellow, even though it wasn't all that old. The headline read, IN COLD BLOOD, REDUX? It was the story of the murder of Arden's parents.

"I don't remember it," she stated matter-of-factly. "I was hoping this"—she swept her hand across the memorabilia—"would help me remember."

"You were bleached."

"But they caught the guy," she said with a strange, sarcastic laugh. "The killer."

"Albert French."

"He got the death sentence and was executed not long ago."

"Yeah, I heard about that."

"But he claimed he was innocent. Oh, he confessed to the other killings, but not this one."

"So . . . the killer hasn't been caught?" Was that what she was saying? They were in the house where the murders had taken place, and the killer was still out there somewhere? What other secrets was she keeping from them?

"Nothing is over. Nothing is solved."

He swallowed hard. "Does anyone have any theories?"

"I do. More than one, actually."

"Yeah?" He had the urge to look over his shoulder, but restrained himself.

She took another long swallow of vodka. The bottle was over half-empty. Had it been full when she'd started? He'd be laid out flat if he'd drunk that much.

She looked up at him and shrugged. "That's all they are. Theories with nothing to substantiate them." She leaned back and hooked one hand under her crossed ankles.

Lamplight fell across the side of her face, creating a shadow on the wall.

The shadow looked like a person. Looked like a man with a long nose, large teeth, and a protruding forehead. It bore absolutely no resemblance to Arden.

Was she one of the shadow people?

Eli unfolded himself and jumped to his feet.

"Do you remember being in the float tank?" Arden asked.

"Vaguely."

"Do you remember what they did to you there?"

"No."

She nodded. "That's because Harris didn't want you to. It's because they pumped you full of drugs so you wouldn't remember. So you wouldn't argue and tell somebody. Once they put you in there, they piped a killer's words and beliefs in your ear for hours at a time. So now the thoughts you have aren't completely your own."

She got to her feet.

A small cardboard box of photos and things girls collected slipped off the bed and crashed to the floor. She waded through the mess to stand two feet from him. She tapped his forehead.

He slapped her hand away and took a step back.

"Eli is in there, but he's not alone. Somebody else is in there with him. Could be Albert French. Could be Jeffrey Dahmer."

She was paranoid. And delusional. Why hadn't he seen that before?

"What about you?" he asked.

Ten minutes ago, he'd been ready to get the hell out of there without her. But now, seeing her like this, he was more worried about her than ever. It was this place. This place was doing weird things to her head. "Maybe you should go somewhere else too."

"No place to go."

"What about wherever you were before you came to the Hill?"

"I can't go back there. I was hiding there. No, this is where I need to be right now." She dug into her pocket. "Here." She slapped his car keys into his hand. "No more hiding for me. No more running away."

He bent his head and examined the keys, running a finger along the cut edge.

Suddenly, he imagined a knife slicing into flesh. A gaping wound across the throat. Hitting the jugular. Blood not only running over his hands, but also pumping. Splashing in his face.

He shook himself and jammed the keys in his pocket.

They needed help. All of them. Arden might be right about Harris being the one who'd fucked them up, but Eli was beginning to think he might also be the only one who could fix them.

"We need to go back," he said quietly.

She looked up at him in horror. "To the Hill?"

Her reaction was no surprise. She wouldn't go back. Eli didn't know how Harley stood on the issue, but the guy sure as hell wasn't coming with them. No, it would be him and Franny.

He needed to get Franny out of there. He'd seen the way Arden's brother had looked at her.

For a year, Eli had watched Franny in the arms of Noah. And Noah had been so *wrong* for her. Why were women attracted to men who were so wrong for them? That's what he wanted to know.

Arden glanced up at the dark window. "We aren't homing pigeons." She looked back at him, and her eyes narrowed. "You have to fight the urge to return."

What was she talking about?

"You know what I think?" she asked. "I think they programmed you to return. I think they programmed you to go back to the Hill."

He shook his head. That was insane. *She* was insane.

"Once you realize that, you can fight it," she said.

"Like realizing when to stop drinking?"

Oops. He shouldn't have said that. *Don't piss her off.*

She laughed. Thank God, she laughed. Because his heart was beating fast. His hands were sweating and he didn't know why. It wasn't like she was going to kill him or anything.

She jammed her hands deep into the pockets of the navy blue hooded sweatshirt she always wore. It was unzipped. Underneath was a black T-shirt.

"Go ahead," she said. "Get the hell out of here. But don't go back to the Hill. Go home to your family. Get the Hill out of your blood."

"Spaghetti's getting cold!" Harley shouted from downstairs.

Eli mentally embraced the normalcy of those words. One big happy family, ready to sit down to a meal together. It made him want to cry.

For years, he couldn't wait to get away from his family. Be on his own. Now he'd give anything to have them around him at this very moment.

"Maybe you should wait until morning," Arden said. "It'll be hard to see the signs in the dark. You might get lost."

She was concerned about him. That made him feel like crying too.

"They were talking about a big storm on the news," he said.

Cyclone is coming! What was that from? *The Wizard of Oz?* Yeah, that was it.

Funny how many times something in his life had

referenced that movie. Was it like that for every-body?

"I'll be down in a minute," Arden said.

Eli scooped up the vodka bottle.

Somebody had to cut her off.

Eli wasn't a confrontational person, but he'd al-ways had a talent for stating his position, then get-ting the hell out of there. The present moment couldn't have been more opportune. "You know damn well I wouldn't have come here if I'd known the person who murdered your parents was still running around free," he said.

With that, he made a quick exit.

Chapter 32

Things were getting weirder—which twenty-four hours ago wouldn't have seemed possible.

But there was Harley, sitting in Arden's dad's chair. Franny in Arden's mother's. Eli was where her brother had always sat. And Arden . . . She was in her old seat, staring at the plate of spaghetti Harley had placed in front of her.

And she was drunk.

Very drunk.

Had anybody noticed?

At the bar in New Mexico, she'd learned how to hide her inebriation. But only to a certain point, that point being when she could no longer walk. When she kept losing her balance and falling over.

Was she there yet?

No, but she was close. Very close.

The secret was to keep your mouth shut. Unless you tumbled off your chair and fell on your ass, nobody would know how messed up you were.

"Aren't you going to eat?" Harley asked. "You haven't eaten anything since last night."

He was coming around. The fog was lifting from

his brain, almost like it had washed down the drain with the bathwater. And Harley was definitely a looker. She realized that now that he'd gotten rid of the hair on his face.

Even Franny's jaw had dropped when she'd seen him. She was still staring at him, her eyes big, following his every move.

This was like watching a movie. That's what it was. Remove yourself and observe.

Eli and Franny got to their feet and put their dishes in the sink. They left the room, and when they came back they were wearing winter jackets that had belonged to Arden's parents. They were holding backpacks.

"We found these in the closet," Franny said, indicating the heavy green down jacket and Eli's navy blue one. "I hope you don't mind."

They were leaving. Arden had forgotten about that. And Eli had somehow convinced Franny to come with him.

Even if Eli was mad at her, she didn't want them to go.

"There should be gloves and hats in the cedar chest."

Very adult. Very sober and responsible.

Eli pulled a stocking cap and gloves from his pocket. "Already found them."

Arden got up from the table and walked with them through the dining room and living room, to the front door.

"It's snowing!" Franny shouted, sounding both alarmed and excited. She hurried outside.

"It wasn't supposed to hit this soon," Eli said with dismay as he stepped out after her.

Arden followed.

The porch light was on, illuminating giant flakes as they came down. The snow was already several inches deep.

Arden wrapped her arms around herself. "Maybe you should wait until tomorrow."

"We're going now." Eli tapped his coat. "I've got a map. We'll be okay. What about you? I don't want to leave you stranded. Are you sure your brother will be back?"

"He'll be back," she said, even though she had her doubts.

They hugged. Harley appeared. They hugged him too.

The yard was equipped with automatic lights on top of three telephone poles. It was never completely dark unless the power went out.

Maybe more was said. Arden wasn't sure. All she knew was that suddenly they were leaving, turning to wave at the last minute, Franny wearing a pair of red-and-pink mittens knitted by Arden's mother.

Arden watched them run down the hill, then disappear around the corner, laughing like a couple of kids. They *were* a couple of kids.

For a second she wished she was going with them. It seemed they'd be leaving the bad things behind and heading off on an adventure.

"I'm going to go do dishes." Harley opened the door and paused, as if expecting Arden to come inside with him.

The cold air felt refreshing. It was sobering her up a little.

Was that a good thing?

Maybe not.

There was always more alcohol, she reassured herself. Not that her parents had been drinkers, which explained how they'd accumulated so much booze over the years from people who'd brought bottles as gifts on various celebratory occasions.

"I'll be in soon," she said.

The idea of being alone with Harley was strange. She wasn't sure she liked it.

He squeezed her arm, smiled, and headed into the house, the screen door closing behind him.

From down the hill came the sound of the barn door sliding open on the metal track, followed by the muffled slam of car doors, then an engine firing up.

As Arden watched, headlights appeared, illuminating the thickly falling snow. They drove up the hill, toward the gate and the mailbox with the backward letter.

She would miss them, she realized.

Suddenly she felt sad. Really, really sad.

Was she crying? She *was*. Her cheeks were wet. She wiped her face with the back of her hand.

They were almost to the gate when the car sputtered and died. Then came sounds of an attempted start. That was followed by a *click, click, click*. The driver's door opened. Eli came slipping and sliding through the snow. She stepped off the porch and began walking toward him.

He lifted his arms straight, then let them drop at his sides. "We're out of gas."

That was too bad. They used to always have diesel on the farm, but not regular gas. Never any regular gas.

Eli was still coming at her. Now she could see that he was pissed. Really pissed.

"You did it on purpose!" he yelled, even though he was only a few feet away. "You knew the gauge didn't work right. You let my car run out of gas!"

She laughed. Right in his face, because it was so ridiculous. Why would she do that? It had been dark. Nothing had been open.

He shoved her. Walked right up and shoved her. "You bitch!"

She shoved him back. "Dumb ass."

He shoved her again.

Arden made a fist and punched Eli hard enough to knock him down. *There, you damn hippie baby.* She grabbed her stinging hand, then shook it. *Ow, ow, ow.*

From somewhere in the background, in the dark, Franny was screaming, begging them to stop.

Eli staggered to his feet. Without pause, he charged, his head making contact with Arden's belly, driving her to the ground. She shifted her weight, rolling him over in a cloud of snow.

The quick movement made her dizzy.

This was crazy.

Crazy fun!

Suddenly the roar of an engine came out of nowhere. Headlights blinded her. A door squeaked, then slammed. At first, in her confusion, Arden thought Franny had somehow gotten the car started.

"Jesus Christ."

Not Franny.

Daniel.

His long legs scissored in front of the headlight beams. "Have you been fighting ever since I left?" He pulled Arden off Eli, but kept a grip on her sweatshirt hood. "You're like a bunch of retarded monkeys."

Arden wiped the back of her hand across her nose and tasted blood. Franny had her arm around Eli, making comforting sounds.

Was he crying? It sounded like he was crying.

Such a baby!

She pointed at the retreating couple as they headed for the house. Harley was silhouetted in the front door, most likely wondering, *What the hell?*

"He started it," Arden said. "And I barely touched him."

"Here." Daniel grabbed her hand and slapped a ball of snow into it. "Put that on your nose."

She held it to her face and tipped her head back. And kept going . . . Until she was flat on the ground.

It seemed a good time to make a snow angel. "Remember when we used to do this?" she asked, waving her arms and legs, snow filling her sneakers and numbing her bare ankles.

A shadow bent over her. "You're drunk as fucking hell," came Daniel's voice from the shadow. "What *are* you doing? What were you thinking, coming here? What *are* you thinking?"

She continued to flap her arms and legs. "Saving their lives," she chanted as she flapped. "Saving their lives."

"Oh, yeah. You're a regular goddamn superhero."

The sarcasm in his voice hurt. Hurt bad.

Suddenly, in one of those moments of absolute clarity that sometimes occurred with a high level of intoxication, she understood exactly what had happened, exactly what she'd been doing.

She'd convinced herself that she was saving them. Saving them all.

A delusion.

Total delusion.

Harley hadn't been in danger. Not immediately in danger, anyway. Neither had Eli or Franny. She'd convinced herself of the threat so she could rescue them. So she could absolve herself of her horrible, horrible sins.

She rolled to her knees, then staggered to her feet. With both hands, she shoved at Daniel's chest. The move took him by surprise, and he stumbled backward. "Go to hell," she told him.

Go to hell for making her see what she didn't want to see. What she couldn't stand to see.

That there had never been any immediate danger.

The only real danger was that they might take off in the middle of a blizzard, get lost, and die. The only danger was they might freeze to death. Or lose a nose and a couple of fingers to frostbite. The only danger was the danger she'd put them in.

They were just a bunch of idiots running around

in the snow, in the middle of the night, dressed in dead people's clothes.

Now it was her turn to be the crybaby. To dissolve into tears and drop back down in the snow, then sprawl on her belly.

She wanted to die. Right here, right now. To close her eyes and never open them again.

Even though she recognized the scene as melodramatic, she couldn't help but embrace it.

Snow was coming down heavily. She wanted it to cover her. She wanted it to smother her.

She had no idea how long she remained on the ground before she felt hands on her shoulders.

"Leave me alone." She tried to knock the person away, but he hung on all the harder.

He pulled her to her feet. "Let's go inside."

Not her brother, but Harley. It was Harley's voice. Harley's hands.

She glanced to her left, to where Daniel stood silent and watchful, a heavy layer of snow building on his stocking cap and the shoulders of his jacket.

Her little brother.

Shame washed over her.

Was there an afterlife? If so, were her parents also watching? Witnessing her decline into a white-trash, alcohol-guzzling, dysfunctional idiot?

Not a pleasant thought.

Chapter 33

The linoleum floor felt great. Cool against Arden's hot face, which was a foot from the base of the toilet.

A murmur of conversation crawled along the lead water pipes and slipped through the floorboards beneath her ear.

Daniel's voice. And Eli's. They were talking about gas. About trying to siphon some from Daniel's truck. Arden heard her brother say something about waiting until morning, until the snow let up.

She was glad it wasn't her problem. Glad it wasn't her concern. Let them handle it. Let them figure it out.

With that thought, she passed out.

Would there ever be a time when the weathermen got it right? The important stuff, anyway?

For as long as Fury could remember, people had been griping about the inaccuracies of weather reports. And with good reason.

The predicted storm had hit a day early, and roads were already impassable.

After catching a flight from Charleston, West Virginia, to Cleveland, Ohio, by way of Columbus, he'd pulled his rental car into the parking lot of an all-night truck stop.

The place was packed.

"Refill?"

The waitress on the other side of the worn counter was a middle-aged woman with a gold name tag that said BRENDA. The overhead lights were as blinding as those in a doctor's office.

The glass double doors behind him opened, then closed with a whoosh of cold air and a blast of snow. "They're closin' the roads," a truck driver announced. "Just heard it on the radio."

A groan moved through the room.

"I gotta load of hogs. They've already been on the trailer too long. Half of 'em will be dead by tomorrow."

Fury hadn't told anybody where he was going. Not the FBI or the local Madeline police. His secrecy wasn't standard FBI procedure, but he was dealing with Arden, and so far all he had were theories and suppositions. He needed to find out if they were valid before giving voice to his fears.

His immediate concern was how to complete the last leg of his journey. The rental car was front-wheel drive, but that didn't help when the snow was over a foot deep. He turned to address the crowd. "Anybody going to Lake County?"

That brought stares.

"You must be lost," some guy in a corner booth finally said, taking in Fury's black overcoat, black pants, black shoes. "New York City's that way." He pointed.

Everybody laughed.

Fury hated to do this. He reached inside his coat and pulled out the folded leather that held his badge. He flipped it open. "It's imperative that I get to Lake County—near the town of Grove."

Dead silence. More stares.

Why had he said *imperative?* Bad word. Stuffy word. Not the kind of word this bunch would embrace. Not the kind of word *he* embraced.

A man—or kid, really—stepped forward. He wore a quilted flannel shirt, heavy canvas overalls, and a green cap advertising some kind of herbicide pulled down over shoulder-length black hair. "I'm a township road commissioner. I'm heading that direction. Grove's not too much out of my way, but we need to take off before the roads get worse."

Fury put a five-dollar bill on the counter and slid off the stool. Outside, he grabbed a few things from his rental car; then they were off.

The mode of transportation was a road grader. A massive thing, with tires as tall as a man's shoulders and a front blade that took up a lane and a half. They wouldn't get stuck, but they wouldn't get there anytime soon.

Top speed was twenty-five miles an hour.

Hands touched her.

"Arden?"

Harley's voice. Harley's hands, pulling her away from the frigid floor.

"You're cold."

He wrapped his arms around her and lifted her to him, pulling her close, practically holding her like a baby. "What are you doing on the floor?" He stroked the hair from her eyes, back from her forehead. He ran a hand down her arm, her side, her leg. "Your feet are like ice."

"Cold feet, cold heart."

He stood and pulled her up after him. "I'm not as strong as I was. I used to be able to carry you. Remember?"

She didn't.

"But I'll get there again."

With his arm around her, they walked down the dark hall to her bedroom.

The illuminated lamp was still on the floor. The house was silent. Just the ticking of a clock somewhere, and the sound of a loose antenna wire clanging against a metal pole outside the window.

"What time is it?" she asked.

"After three."

He closed the door.

Everyone was asleep.

He reached for the button of her jeans.

"Your clothes are wet from the snow."

She put her hands on his. "I'll do that."

"I want to. You take care of me; I take care of you."

He unbuttoned and unzipped her pants. With a hand braced on his shoulder, she toed off her old sneakers, then, with his help, stepped from the soggy jeans. Leaving her sweatshirt on, she dropped into bed, tugging the heavy comforter over her.

He turned off the light, lifted the comforter, and joined her, wrapping his arms around her, his body like a blast furnace.

He ran a hand down her leg. "Your skin is so soft." He nuzzled her neck, then pressed his lips to the area just below her ear. He slid his hand inside her panties, pulling her against him.

She tugged his hand away. "Harley, don't."

"Why not?" he whispered.

"Not here. Not now." For a second, she felt a flutter of hysteria rising in her.

"Shh," he whispered against her neck. "Everything is going to be okay." He wrapped his arms around her and just held her. "Everything is going to be fine."

Chapter 34

Arden woke up with a hangover.

Not a little one that would go away with a couple of aspirin and several glasses of water. This was the kind that stuck around all day. The kind that made you wonder how many brain cells you'd killed.

Downstairs, someone was making coffee—and it didn't smell good.

She rolled to her back and opened her eyes a crack. It was daylight, but the room was dark. Not like night, but the kind of dark that went with a storm. That kind of quiet gray.

She was alone, which was good.

She tossed back the comforter and swung her feet to the floor.

Cold! The room temperature was unusually cold. She exhaled, half expecting to see her breath. The coolness felt good on her hot skin, her hot face, but that wouldn't last.

Barefoot, she walked painfully to the dresser, opening drawers and digging until she found a pair of white, waffle-weave long underwear. She stripped down to panties, put on the underwear top and bottoms, then the pair of jeans Harley had helped her out of last night. Or rather, this morning. He'd been thoughtful enough to drape them over the back of a chair.

They were cold and stiff, but dry.

From downstairs, she heard the clang of something solid, something metal.

The opening and closing of the woodstove.

For a moment, her mind slid backward and she was confused. For a moment, she thought maybe everything that had happened in the past months had really been a dream and her parents were alive. Her dad was downstairs, filling the stove with apple wood, the sweet scent wafting up to her room.

That was the hard thing about death. The trick about death. Those jarring flashes of time travel that ricocheted you into the past and back to the present in a fraction of a second.

In the closet, she found an old flannel shirt that had once belonged to her dad. She put it on, following it with the blue sweatshirt, which she zipped all the way up for a change. Heavy wool socks and the old jogging shoes.

Coming here had been a mistake.

And she was afraid she was losing her mind.

She'd once read about a period of time in the mid-1800s when an entire Wisconsin town had gone mad.

Settlers had dropped in their tracks, fever wiping out most of the town. But perversely, the fever had spared a member or two of each family. Those were the ones who went crazy, because there was only so much the human psyche could take before it broke. Only so much death a person could handle.

In the bathroom, she turned on the sink faucet. Air sputtered in the pipes, along with a few spits of water. The electricity was out. Which meant the well's water pump was off.

But somebody was downstairs making coffee.

She brushed her teeth with a dry toothbrush.

Eli.

God. She'd completely forgotten about the fight she'd had with him.

She leaned over the bathtub and pulled the curtain aside to look out the window.

Still snowing. She'd hoped it had stopped. Hoped Eli had found some gas and was now on his way home.

Daniel was right. She was always running. If the snow hadn't been so bad, she'd run right now too.

She should have stayed in New Mexico. So what if her life there had been in a holding pattern? Everybody's life was in a holding pattern to some extent. And compared to everything that had happened since she'd left, a holding pattern would be welcome. Not every loose end had to be tied up. Not everything *could* be tied up, no matter how much she wanted it.

She opened the medicine cabinet above the sink, found a bottle of generic aspirin, shook four tablets into her palm, and tossed them down, swallowing the dry pills with a shudder.

She couldn't stay upstairs forever. She needed water. She needed heat.

She returned to her room and eased herself down on the bed, careful of her head. Ten minutes passed before she gave up and left.

At the landing, she paused to listen.

Sounds of conversation. Franny. Talking softly. About college.

Arden took a deep breath, went down the stairs, and stepped into the living room.

Four people, huddled around the woodstove, coffee cups in their hands, staring at the fire that could be seen through the glass window. Daniel must have been stranded there last night.

Franny looked up from where she sat on the floor. "Hey, Arden." Her voice was cautious. She was probably wondering if Arden was going to attack Eli again.

All the guys nodded, then turned back around and stared awkwardly at the floor. All except Harley, who smiled at her.

What was going on?

Had they been talking about her?

In less than a second, she got it. They thought she and Harley had slept together last night. The walk of shame, it was called. When everybody in the room assumed sex had occurred, but nobody mentioned it.

"Want some coffee?" Harley asked. "Daniel made some on the woodstove."

"I'd rather have water. Where'd you get the water for coffee?"

"Daniel filled some jugs before the power went out."

If Arden hadn't been wasted, she would have thought of that herself.

In the kitchen, she found the jugs lined up on the counter. She was getting a glass from the cupboard when Harley came up behind her, wrapped his arms around her, and kissed the back of her neck.

"Harley." She bent her head and scooted away.

He followed.

"Don't."

"What? Why?"

She opened a jug, filled the glass, and turned to face him. "I can't do this."

"Do what?"

"Us. You and me."

"Somebody's here!" came a euphoric shout from the living room.

Nathan Fury now knew everything there was to know about Richard Sheppard. Where he'd gone to high school. His first job—at a gas station in Little Canada. His first car—a Chevy Impala with a 350, V-8 engine. His two kids—Sheila and Brian.

With briefcase in hand, Fury jumped from the cab of the road grader, landing in snow above his knees. Wind whipped around him, creeping down his neck. He flipped up his jacket collar and reached for the suitcase the driver was handing him.

"I'll wait to make sure somebody's here," Richard said.

Fury waded to a buried car and brushed snow from the front plate.

Eli Norton's car.

Fury returned to the road grader.

Richard peered intently through the windshield, his wipers going like crazy. "Isn't that the Davis place? Where those people were murdered? This isn't in my territory, but I remember hearing about it on the news. Stuff like that doesn't happen around here." He shivered, gave the grader some gas, and put his hand on the gearshift. "But they caught the guy right away. That's good. 'Cause I wouldn't want to know he was still prowling around."

Fury muttered some kind of affirmative response, thanked Richard, then turned and headed for the house. At the back door, he lifted his hand, paused, took a deep breath, and knocked.

Arden's brother, Daniel, answered.

Had Arden ever mentioned Fury's name to her brother? Would Daniel remember him from the one dark time they'd met?

Behind him, Richard honked, put the grader into gear, and pulled away, the heavy odor of diesel exhaust filling the air.

Fury pulled out the leather case containing his badge, flipped it open, introduced himself, then slid the badge back in his pocket. "Is Arden home?"

Daniel hesitated, then opened the door wider. "Come on in."

Fury stepped inside.

A familiar kitchen.

"You were here after my parents were killed," Daniel said, closing the door.

"That's right."

He'd come as soon as he'd heard. By the time he

got there, the killer was gone. It was theorized that he'd been gone by the time the first officer had arrived on the scene.

At first, Fury thought Arden had been killed too, since she was unaccounted for and her car was in the driveway.

The next hour had been a blur.

"When she was little, she used to hide in the crib," Daniel had told them.

That's where Fury had found her. In the top of the cupola, half-frozen and in shock. She'd clung to him so tightly that he'd had trouble prying her loose so the paramedics could get her down the ladder.

It was the last time she'd looked at him with any sign of recognition.

"Fury."

He turned.

Now here she was, standing in the kitchen doorway with a *what the hell are you doing here?* pose.

She wasn't thrilled to see him; that was obvious.

And she looked like hell. Worse than when he'd last seen her, if that was possible. The circles under her eyes were deeper, and she was thinner.

Was she eating?

Without a word, she swung around and left. He heard her striding across the living room, heard her footfalls on the stairs until the floorboards above his head creaked and a door closed.

Daniel stood with his feet braced apart. Fury gave him a twisted smile that was really an awkward acknowledgment of the situation. "She's not as glad to see me as I'd hoped," he said.

Daniel raised one eyebrow in response.

The road commissioner had been an anomaly. Most people from these parts didn't do a lot of unnecessary talking.

Eli came skidding around the corner wearing a puffy, unzipped jacket and clutching a stocking cap. "What's going on?" He was out of breath. "Did the guy with the plow leave? Is he coming back? I thought I heard him leave."

"The roads are closed," Fury told him. "The driver is on his way home to wait out the storm. Nobody's going anywhere for at least twenty-four hours."

Eli stared at Fury in disbelief, looking like he might cry. Then he tossed down his stocking cap, turned, and stomped from the room.

Daniel crossed his arms over his chest and let out a derisive snort. "Welcome to Hotel Hell."

Sarcasm seemed to run in the family.

Chapter 35

People joked about cabin fever, but apparently the joke was on Eli, because cabin fever was real. The physical isolation was overwhelming, and he felt his mind slip just trying to grasp the fact that there was no pizza joint around the corner. No coffee shop or theater. The only thing out there was a field. Beyond that, another field. Maybe a valley of timber, and then another field.

The storm wasn't showing any signs of letting up. The weather guy on a small, tinny-sounding portable radio concurred.

But the atmosphere inside the house was worse than outside. Arden refused to leave her room. Harley had spent a large part of the day whimpering at her bedroom door, trying to tempt her with food or coffee. He'd even found hot chocolate, but she hadn't budged.

Those two had had sex last night. Everybody in the house knew it, even though nothing had been said. Fury even seemed to get it, and he hadn't been there.

So far, Fury hadn't tried to talk to Arden, who Eli

still felt was in charge, no matter how messed up she was. But that's how FBI agents were. Waiting and watching was what they did. More like a cat than a human. Right now, Fury was lounging on the couch, his coat and tie discarded, acting as if he'd just dropped in for a visit.

While Harley sniffed at Arden's door and puttered around in the kitchen, the rest of them decided to play Monopoly. Eli hated Monopoly. It had to be the most boring tribute to consumerism ever imagined. He was surprised and horrified that Franny had agreed to play.

Oh, that's right. Daniel had suggested it.

They settled near the woodstove. Fury took one end of the couch, Eli the other. Franny and Daniel sat on the floor, the game board on the coffee table.

If nothing else, Monopoly was usually a good time for conversation. The FBI agent wasn't giving anything up, but Franny could get to yakking when the notion hit. And if the right person was around.

Ten minutes into the game, she proceeded to tell Daniel her life story. He seemed glad to hear it.

Eli had witnessed this scenario before. It was the Noah thing all over again. Franny's attraction. Her immediately falling for the new guy, when Eli was right there. Right in front of her.

When was he going to learn that he would never be anything to her? That she would always treat him like a buddy, nothing more?

He realized that Harley hadn't wandered past in a while. Everything upstairs was quiet.

Were they up there together? God, that was sick.

Not the thought that they might be having sex. No, it was the house. Doing it in the house where Arden's parents had been killed. It was so wrong. About as bad as bad karma could get. And Harley wasn't exactly a prize. But maybe Arden liked guys like that. Strong and dumb.

Eli looked at Daniel, his eyes narrowing. Strong, but not dumb. At least he didn't seem dumb. Hard to tell when somebody didn't talk much.

"Your turn."

Eli was jolted out of his mind-stroll to find Franny handing him a pair of dice. He took them and rolled, then moved his shoe game piece. "So, are you here to arrest us?" he asked Fury.

You could have heard a Monopoly shoe drop.

That was bad. Really bad.

Fury smiled. "You're wanted for questioning; that's all."

It didn't make sense. They wouldn't send a single FBI agent to bring them back. Eli knew better than that.

He'd never trusted Fury. Fury was a facade. What kind of facade Eli didn't know, but the guy had his own agenda.

After two hours, Fury leaned back in the couch. "That's enough for me."

He had a hotel and two houses. Most of Eli's stuff was mortgaged, and he was in jail. Franny and Daniel had fared better. If they pooled their resources, they'd own over half the board.

Better sign a prenup.

"I'm done too," Eli said. He had to get out of there.

He jumped to his feet, grabbed the heavy down jacket he'd found in the closet, and shrugged into it.

Franny looked up from where she sat cross-legged on the floor near the woodstove. She folded the game board, and slid the red and green plastic game pieces into the box. "Where are you going?"

"Outside." He added a brown stocking cap and gloves to his ensemble. "To get an idea of what it's doing and how deep the snow is."

She yawned. "I'm sleepy. I think I'll go lie down."

On the couch, the FBI agent was already nodding off. He'd probably been up all night spying and tracking them and shit.

Eli couldn't believe he'd actually thought about becoming an FBI agent at one time. Had he been out of his mind? *Yes.*

What a pathetic piece of work he was.

He left through the back door.

As soon as he stepped past the protection of the house, the wind whipped across his face, taking his breath away. The snow was above his knees in places, filling the boots he'd also found in the closet.

It was hard to believe they were in the United States, yet cut off from the rest of the world. Eli *didn't* believe it. A plow would come by soon, and when it did, he wanted to be ready.

He remembered reading a story about pioneers who'd gotten lost in a blizzard and had frozen to death a few yards from their home.

Kind of embarrassing, but it could happen.

The sky was a dark slate gray. Close enough to touch, as if it had fallen to the ground. Evening was coming, but the grayness had been there all day, unchanged.

He may have been a city kid, but his circadian rhythms were triggered by the rising and setting sun just like everybody else's. With no rising and setting sun, he felt off. Unbalanced. Uneasy and ready to jump out of his skin.

The snow still fell heavily, creating a feeling of claustrophobia, a wall you couldn't see beyond but could walk through, its very softness deceptive. His arms were already covered in a solid white layer that got fault lines in it when he moved.

On top of no visibility, sounds were muffled. Someone could be standing right next to you, and you wouldn't even know it.

How did people keep from going crazy?

They don't.

The snow changed. Or his perception of the snow changed. It went from being an obstruction to being a blanket.

He almost felt that it was comforting him. Telling him everything would be okay.

He was just one guy, one snowflake.

Here. Now. Fighting . . . for what? The world would go on without him. The world would be okay without him.

He heard a voice in his head. A voice that wasn't his, but at the same time seemed like his.

It was snowing quite a bit that day. A real Christmas

kind of snow that you knew would sparkle once the sun came out.

Eli immediately placed the voice.

Albert French.

That knowledge should have scared him, or at least made him uneasy. But the voice was like the snow: dangerous, yet comforting at the same time.

Suddenly Albert French was there with him. Watching him. Guiding him.

Eli felt special.

Kind of like he'd always imagined it would feel to go to Abbey Road. The studio and the street. See where the Beatles recorded.

How many people had reenacted the *Abbey Road* cover? How many had taken off their shoes to cross the street? Few people would have had the guts to do that. But why do something if you don't go all the way? Why do something half-assed?

If you're going to kill somebody, do it. Don't dream about it. Don't talk about it. Do it. And do it well.

Thank you, Mr. French.

Last night, the yard lights had been on. Now they just stared at him with blank expressions.

He struggled to walk, trying to follow what he thought was the road, unable to lift his legs very high because of the depth of the snow. Instead, he was forced to push through it.

He hit the downhill slope that led to the barn.

The ground fell out from under him, and he tumbled forward, gravity sending him rolling, snow finding its way down his collar and pants, finding the small strip of bare skin between his socks and the hem of his jeans.

This was nasty. This was like some pioneer lifestyle. Who would choose to live like this? Fucking idiots, that's what they were. No wonder somebody had killed her parents. People that stupid deserved to die.

It was darker at the bottom of the hill. Maybe because he was now in a valley, or maybe night was finally coming.

The barn door wasn't that hard to open. Rather handy the way it slid sideways without having to fight the resistance of snow.

The darkness increased.

He opened the huge door the rest of the way, letting in what little light he could.

There was Daniel's truck. There was the red plastic gas container in the back.

He quickly scanned the barn wall, passing over tools and chains to finally stop on a green garden hose.

He stomped over and pulled the hose down. With some kind of sharp pruning tool, he cut the hose so he had a length of about nine feet. He opened the plastic container and set it on the ground near his feet. Then he unscrewed the gas cap from Daniel's truck and fed one end of the hose into the tank. He put the other end in his mouth and sucked.

Nothing.

He took a few deep breaths, then sucked some more.

He could feel it coming, but it wasn't there yet. As

soon as he quit sucking, the fluid dropped back
down the hose and into the tank.

He took another deep breath, and sucked again,
harder this time. He was getting dizzy—a combination of hyperventilation and fumes.

Suddenly gasoline gushed into his mouth.

He gasped, breathing liquid into his lungs. He
dropped the hose, gas splashing on his coat and
pants and boots. He felt the toxic fluid hit the pit of
his stomach.

He heard a sound behind him and turned.
"Help!"

A gloved hand lifted Eli's chin.

Someone there.

Someone to help.

"Open your mouth."

He obeyed.

A Zippo lighter appeared out of nowhere. A quick
flick brought with it a large flame.

Eli inhaled.

And became a human torch.

Screaming, flames shooting from his mouth, Eli
ran for the door.

Chapter 36

Arden heard a commotion downstairs. Franny's voice, raised in alarm. She couldn't make out the words, but the tone was bordering on hysteria. Male voices responded.

Let somebody else take care of the problem, whatever it was.

Nothing is real.

This isn't real.

She was in the float tank, dreaming a dream she couldn't wake up from. Being fed someone else's reality.

But the noise downstairs didn't stop.

Franny's insistent voice. Chairs scraping the floor. Heavy, booted footfalls. Sounds of people preparing to leave. Sounds of departure.

Had a plow come through? Were Franny and Eli going?

Doors slammed. That was followed by silence, then muffled cries, voices shouting Eli's name.

Arden unzipped the sleeping bag she'd burrowed into earlier.

The room was as dark as dark could get. She had

to feel her way to the door before moving down the hall. She clung to the smooth wooden banister as she took the steps one at a time, her feet, in thick wool socks, finally making contact with the first floor.

In the living room, the woodstove gave off light. Nearby, two candles burned in clear glass votives.

Through the dining room and into the kitchen.

A burner had been left on under a skillet. She turned off the gas. The blue flame disappeared, leaving an oil lamp as the only source of light. Her dad had insisted upon a gas stove. If you had a gas stove, you could always cook when the power went off.

An array of flashlights and lanterns were scattered across the table, most likely left by Daniel. She tested a few, finally settling on a black LED she'd given her father for his birthday. It had been expensive, but was far brighter than what he'd normally used.

She retrieved a pair of insulated boots from the closet and put them on, tucking the hem of her pants inside before tying the laces. Those were followed by a black down jacket, black stocking cap, and a pair of heavy gloves.

At the last minute, she extinguished the oil lamp before stepping outside.

Wind and snow immediately blew down her collar, and she wished she'd thought to grab a scarf.

The cries for Eli had faded as the makeshift search party moved away from the house.

Arden headed straight for Eli's car, which was still marooned in the driveway. She brushed away snow and shone the light in the driver's window, then circled the vehicle. Seeing no sign of life, she opened the passenger door.

The dome light came on.

The floor mats held frozen snow footprints—but they could have been left from yesterday. She didn't see any hint that someone had been there recently.

"You can take the girl out of the FBI," came a voice from directly behind her, "but you can't take the FBI out of the girl."

Nathan Fury.

She was polite enough to refrain from blinding him with her flashlight as she straightened and slammed the car door.

"FBI issue?" he asked.

She lifted the light so he could get a better look. "Farm Supply."

"I saw you from across the yard. I used to complain that LEDs were good for seeing what you needed to see, but also good for drawing fire."

"Nice that I no longer have to worry about those things."

"You should have come downstairs to join us today," he said. "We've been having a lot of fun."

Like she was supposed to believe Fury ever had fun. "Oh, yeah?"

"We played Monopoly."

"Who won?"

He was acting as if everything were normal.

"Have you ever played a Monopoly game where somebody won?"

She made a sound that mimicked an agreement

without the verbal commitment. "Did you find Eli?" she asked.

"No."

"Are you certain he's not in the house?"

"He went outside about two hours ago. His coat and boots are still gone."

"Is he stupid enough to try to walk somewhere?"

"That's what I wondered. Earlier, Daniel mentioned that our cell phones might work at a high point about a mile or so from here."

"Roller Coaster Road," Arden said.

"Yeah, that was it."

Fury didn't have a flashlight. He was bundled in his black wool jacket, hands jammed deep into the pockets, shoulders hunched against the wind, head bare, a pair of green Northern knee boots, circa 1970, on his feet.

One thing about living on a farm—there was always plenty of winter clothing to go around.

"You should have a hat," she said. He couldn't have looked more out of his element. "Why do city people have such an aversion to warm hats?"

He made a gesture with his hands in his pockets. "Because warm hats are ugly?"

At least it was an honest answer. "I'm going to check out the barn." She walked away. He caught up and fell into step beside her.

The flashlight created a blinding glare against the thickly falling snow. If she kept it tipped down, like a car on low beam, the glare wasn't as bad.

They walked where the road should be, with Arden using familiar landmarks to gauge the location. *Walk* wasn't the right word. *Wade* was more like it, some of the drifts hitting her at thigh level.

She should have put on a pair of overalls.

"Maybe tonight we can play Charades," Fury said.

"Or how about Who Am I?" she suggested.

"I'm guessing Truth or Dare and possibly Spin the Bottle would be more up your alley."

She stopped. Fury stopped.

"Is this about Harley?" She kept the flashlight aimed at her boots.

He sighed. "You need to ask yourself why you're having sex with men who aren't your mental equals."

"Are you a shrink *and* an FBI agent?"

"I think it's because you don't want anyone to dig past the surface. You want to be held, you want sexual gratification, but you don't want emotional intimacy."

Her heart was hammering, and she didn't know why. "You aren't telling me anything I don't already know." She let out a harsh laugh. "Who would have thought you'd turn out to be such an idealist? Such a Hallmark card?"

"It's not fair to Harley," he said.

Her toes and fingers were frozen. Her nose was beginning to run. She sniffled. "Would you be fairer game? Is that what this is really about?"

"I don't have casual sex."

She heard Franny and Harley shouting Eli's name, their voices echoing from the direction of the barn.

The diversion couldn't have come at a better time. "It's none of your damn business," Arden said, "but Harley and I haven't slept together. Well, we *slept* together, but we didn't have sex."

She strode away, her heart still pounding.

She circled down to the barn, following a path where the snow had recently been disturbed. Arden rolled open the barn door, and was immediately hit with the heavy odor of gasoline fumes.

She shone the light on Daniel's blue truck.

The vehicle's gas cap was open, and a plastic gas container was on the ground with a length of garden hose nearby.

"We don't need a detective to figure out what he was up to," Fury said, coming up behind her.

Suddenly the entire search team was there, drawn by the noise and light.

"I told him I'd help him get gas," Daniel said.

"What's that smell?" Franny put a mittened hand to her nose. "Like burnt hair."

"Yeah." Harley aimed his flashlight at the walls of the barn, down toward the stalls, then back.

Arden directed her light at the ground.

"Drag marks," Fury said.

He was right. At the spot where the drag marks began was an area that looked scorched.

Her eyes made contact with Fury's. *Something bad going on here.*

"I remember catching my hair on fire once when I was little," Franny said. "I was lighting a pumpkin I'd just carved, and I smelled something awful, but couldn't figure out what it was. Then I saw my hair dissolving."

Daniel laughed.

Arden and Fury refocused their attention on the drag marks, following them to where they vanished through the barn door, into the snow. "How long has he been gone, did you say?" Arden asked.

"At least two hours."

"In two hours, we've probably had four inches of snow." She stood in the open door and panned the light to the left, then right, looking for an indentation.

Drifts formed as she watched.

"We need to make a search line and fan out," she said.

Daniel came up beside her. "Do you think he caught himself on fire," he said, his voice low, "then ran from the barn? Or dragged himself from the barn?"

"Maybe." That seemed the best possible scenario right now. The least sinister scenario.

Arden was tempted to let her mind go off in a direction she didn't want it to go, but she froze her thoughts, concentrating on the problem at hand.

They worked the space in a line, sweeping their feet through the snow, the path of Arden's left boot meeting up with the path of Fury's right so that no space was left uncovered.

Franny screamed.

Everyone ran, three flashlights pointing down at the ground.

Half-buried in the snow was Eli.

Arden and Fury dug, uncovering him.

His face was burned almost beyond recognition.

His throat had been sliced from ear to ear.

Just like Vera Thompson. Just like Arden's mother and father.

Arden pulled off her gloves and felt for a pulse even though she knew she wouldn't find one.

"I-is he dead?" Franny asked from a safe distance.

"Yes." That came from Fury.

"I don't understand," Franny said. "He would have known better than to have anything flammable around gasoline."

She still didn't get it. She was too far away, and it was too dark for her to see Eli's throat.

Arden straightened.

No crime-scene team could reach them. Not for at least another day. Maybe two or three days. They would have to find a place to put the body. A place where it wouldn't get eaten by coyotes and wolves.

"Eli didn't accidentally set himself on fire," she said quietly. "His throat has been cut. This is a homicide."

Franny let out a gasp and took a stumbling step backward. "Oh, my God!"

Next to her, Harley added his own choked sob of disbelief.

Franny spun around and started to run. She was too upset, and the snow was too deep. She floundered.

Harley caught up with her, grabbing her by the arm as she dropped to her knees, sobbing.

"Who did this?" Daniel asked.

Arden's mind raced, coming upon one possibility after the other. She cast a swift glance around. Was the killer still out there? Watching them?

"Are you armed?" she asked Fury.

He nodded and patted his coat where a shoulder holster would be.

"Someone could have gotten here on foot," he said slowly, as if not really thinking about his words but concentrating on something in his head.

"Or snowmobile," Arden added. "But we probably would have heard a snowmobile unless it remained out of hearing range."

"What about motive?" Fury asked.

There had been no motive when her parents were killed. Just bloodlust. Just a drive to kill.

"Could it be the same person?" she whispered to Fury, not wanting the others to hear. They were already on the verge of hysteria.

There was no need to explain what she was talking about.

"I don't know." He sounded troubled and confused.

"Why did we come here?" Franny's voice rose with each word. "What was the point? This is a bad place. An evil place. That's what Eli said the first night. He'd still be alive if we'd stayed in Madeline. If we hadn't run off."

She was right.

It was Arden's fault.

Once again, she'd dragged innocent people into her own nightmare.

Chapter 37

Daniel Davis did what any other red-blooded American boy would do in his situation—he went for his gun. In the barn, he jerked open the truck door. The dome light came on, and his gaze immediately dropped to the floor. No gun. He pulled down the bench seat, accessing the storage area where he sometimes kept the weapon.

Not there.

His heart began to hammer even harder.

Christ.

He quickly rewound a mental tape of events, starting with the fight with Arden's bodyguard.

He'd put the gun back in the truck. He was sure of it. That's where he kept it. Where he always kept it.

He forced the seat into the locked position, then reached and opened the glove compartment. The box of bullets he kept there was also gone. Head bent, he backed out of the truck, slammed the door, and ran from the barn, flashlight beam bouncing.

Arden and Nathan Fury were buried waist deep

in snow tinged pink and red, the body of the dead kid between them.

Daniel had been on some deer hunts. He'd seen that kind of snow. "The .22's gone," he announced, his voice tight and breathless and sounding foreign to his own ears.

His sister looked up. Snow fell on her face. It caught in her eyelashes. In the dim light, he couldn't see the circles under her eyes and the gauntness in her cheeks. For a second he could almost imagine that they were kids again, helping their dad feed the livestock before going into the warm house for supper.

Almost.

"The rifle," he repeated. "It was in my truck. It's gone."

Somewhere in the shadows, beyond the snow-muted glow of light, the girl, Franny, let out a gasp, and Harley, the bodyguard, made some murmur of comfort that set off a spark of annoyance in Daniel. For a fraction of a second, he'd felt the urge to comfort her himself. But who was he to say everything would be okay, especially when it wouldn't?

"Douse the lights." Arden clicked off her flashlight.

Daniel did the same.

He thought he was being paranoid. He'd hoped he was being paranoid, but Arden was thinking what he'd been thinking—that somebody was out there watching them.

He was always surprised by how dark dark was

when there were no stars, no moon, and no man-made light.

Humans were so fucking helpless, so vulnerable and unable to cope.

His mind raced. Somebody was out there. Somebody with a gun. *His* gun.

Franny was right. It was Arden's fault. She'd brought evil and death before. Now she'd brought them again.

"Everybody get back to the house," Fury said.

"W-what about Eli?"

The question came from Franny. Her voice was all scared and trembly.

Daniel had grown up in a world where most women stayed home to raise their kids. Where many didn't go to college, and the men took care of them. Franny, with her piercings and short black hair, represented a world he didn't know much about. A world that was exotic and strange. But in the dark, she sounded like any other scared girl. And where he lived, men protected women.

He approached the sound of sobbing. He reached for her, touching her coat sleeve. "Take my hand."

She clasped his gloved hand.

He and Arden were the only ones who knew the immediate layout of the farm. And Arden might not remember, might not know the exact location of the rock wall and the covered well.

He had a good sense of direction, even in the dark.

"Eli?" Franny asked again.

"He'll be okay."

It was a lie. It wouldn't be good to leave the body there. Animals would come as soon as the storm let up.

Coyotes were everywhere. You could hear them at night, sounding like people in pain. Packs of them, climbing on top of round hay bales lined up in the fields, howling at the moon. Whenever Daniel heard them, he was always reminded of those drawings they used in Sunday school to put the fear of hell in kids. Pictures of people screaming and reaching imploringly to the sky while flames cooked them to a crisp.

Arden's voice came out of the darkness, very near now. "We have to get inside," she said. "We can't do anything for Eli. We have to protect ourselves."

Animals would come and eat him. By tomorrow or the next day, Eli would be gone. Daniel had seen a dead cow cleaned to the bone in a matter of hours. Meat was meat. Food was food.

They made a human chain, with Daniel leading the way.

They slipped and stumbled. When one of them went down, they all went. The falls confused him, made him briefly lose the direction of the farmhouse.

All of them were breathing hard, as much in fear as from the struggle with nature. The only comfort Daniel took in the situation was that whoever was out there, whoever had killed Eli, would also be hampered by the snow and the darkness.

They stumbled, falling against one another, their terrified, blind flight reminding Daniel of the time they'd lost a dozen sheep in a blizzard. The animals were finally found the next day, some exhausted and running in the small confined area they'd trampled in the snow just a few yards from a storm shelter. Others were bleating, legs flailing at the air, their wool frozen to the ground.

Familiar landmarks stabilized him. The stone wall that wrapped around the barn. The leg of the old windmill. The corner of the garage.

Up the sidewalk to the back door, all the while Daniel intensely aware of the mittened hand clinging tightly to his. He felt proudly protective and tender at the same time. He felt like a man instead of a boy.

Franny crowded up next to him. "What if the killer's in the house?" she whispered.

This could be true.

"We can't stay outside," Daniel said.

Nathan Fury stepped forward. "I'll go in first."

Chapter 38

Fury unbuttoned his coat. With stiff, frozen fingers, he managed to slip his Glock 23 from his shoulder holster. Pointing the barrel skyward, he edged past Daniel. "Let me have your flashlight."

He held out his hand, and Daniel slapped the light into Fury's palm. Once inside the kitchen, Fury clicked on the flashlight and rested it against the handgun so barrel and beam pointed in the same direction.

He had the feeling his display of making sure the building was secure was just that—a display. He doubted anybody else was in the house.

For a long time, he'd had his suspicions. As long ago as the winter day he'd found Arden in the top of the corncrib, staring at him with half-mad eyes. Even before that, when Fury was still in Project TAKE.

During that time, he'd had thoughts and urges that hadn't been his. More than once, he'd found himself toying with the idea of cold-blooded murder. No need to wonder how it would feel. He'd known. Known it would be thrilling and erotic. Known it would be the biggest rush of his life.

He'd never told anybody about his thoughts. He'd been ashamed, and at that time he'd believed his response to the indoctrination was an anomaly.

Arden was suddenly behind him, just beyond his right shoulder. "I wish I had a weapon," she whispered.

She used to carry a Glock 23 on her waist, and a single-shot Smith & Wesson strapped to her ankle.

This was almost like old times. For a moment, he could almost forget everything that had happened.

He bounced the beam around the kitchen, checking the floor for fresh snow or wet footprints. "Doesn't look like anybody's been here."

Death was in the air. It was all around them. The farm, the ground, was imprinted by death. The house was a crypt. A crypt of evil and sorrow and unspeakable deeds.

French's voice came back to him. Fury could almost see his eyes, staring at him from behind the death chamber glass.

I'm not sorry for anything. I'd do it all again if I had the chance.

Blood.

Fury looked down and saw dark smears on his hands. It was rich and bitter, smelling like both life and death.

Eli's blood.

Definitely not killed by French.

But the same house. Same MO.

Can a place make people crazy? Can a house make people do things they wouldn't normally do?

He and Arden moved through the kitchen, the

dining room, the living room. Behind him, he heard the others step into the kitchen and stop in a cluster just inside the door.

Fury ran the flashlight beam along the floor, in front of the door that led to the porch.

He wanted to find a stranger.

Nothing wet there. No sign of recent entry.

Down the hall, then a quick check of the bedroom.

An unmade bed of rumpled sheets and hand-made quilts. A backpack. An MP3 player and head-phones on a dresser.

Eli's room.

It smelled like kids in their early twenties. That exotic mixture of spices and incense. The not-unpleasant odor of young, healthy bodies.

Arden tugged at his coat. "Upstairs," she whispered.

Being in Eli's room bothered her.

Together they moved up the staircase. When they reached the second floor, Fury raised his voice for the first time since entering the house. "There's nobody here."

"I want to see it all."

She'd always been that way. Had to see everything for herself, even though logic gave her the facts.

Down the narrow hall with its wooden, creaking floor.

Open the door to the bathroom.

Claw-foot tub, shower curtain pulled aside. No place to hide.

Next to the pedestal sink was a small wooden step

stool Arden had probably stood on as a kid when she'd brushed her teeth. "Bathroom okay," he said.

They moved back down the hall, past a small bedroom.

"Clean."

Then another—Arden's room, also clean.

They finally stopped in the doorway of the master bedroom.

Perfume.

The smell was intense.

"It's called Violet," Arden said from behind him.

"Wait here," he said.

He felt her hand on his back as she urged him forward, then followed him into the room.

She'd never liked to follow. Never liked to be told what to do. If she'd had a gun, she would have been the first inside.

He stopped a few feet from the bed, in the room where Arden's mother had been murdered. The overpowering scent of perfume hung in the air.

He would have to remember never to buy that particular scent for anyone for Christmas.

He pivoted to face Arden.

He was so damn cold. He couldn't even feel his feet. He hadn't been able to feel them for a long time. Arden was right. He was a city guy. He hadn't come prepared for the weather. Stupid of him.

"I have to talk to you," he said.

She looked at him, chin down. The circles under her eyes were more pronounced in the glow of the flashlight.

"What?" she asked.

He could tell by her voice that she was distracted by the room, that she wasn't giving him her full attention.

"I have a theory."

Arden glanced uncomfortably at the bed. "Let's get out of here," she said.

"Wait."

He grabbed her by the arm before she could get away. He walked backward, pulling her deeper into the room, his flashlight and gun pointed at the ceiling, the bounced light casting long, weird shadows.

She struggled to free herself. He released her.

"Don't go."

"Not here," she said. "Not in this room."

"I don't want the others to hear."

"Say it. Hurry and say it then." She shivered, and rubbed her arms over the bulk of her heavy jacket.

"I don't think there's anybody else in the house." He watched her for a reaction. "And I don't think there's anybody outside."

"What are you talking about? Eli is dead. Somebody killed him."

He knew she wouldn't want to face what he had to say. She'd been an FBI agent. A good one. Her mind was still quick. She had to have put it together. She had to have at least formed an assumption. "Noah didn't kill Vera Thompson."

"What do you mean? What about the bloody shirt? The footprint of his shoes?"

"He may or may not have been there, but he didn't do it. Someone taller than Noah killed the old woman." He paused for effect. "And now here we are. Back in Ohio with another dead body."

Full circle. Except that this time everything would finally be tied up. This time, they would finally get the right answers.

She was watching him, her eyes wide. He could tell she wanted to leave. That she didn't want to hear what else he was going to say.

"Who was here when your parents were murdered?" he asked softly. "Who, out of everyone currently in the house, was present when your parents were killed?"

Daniel had been in town with a girlfriend. His alibi had been tight. Harley hadn't been there. Franny hadn't been there. Fury hadn't been there.

Arden stared up at him and slowly shook her head. "No." Her bottom lip trembled. "You're wrong."

He slipped his Glock into the shoulder holster, and dropped the flashlight on the bed. He grabbed her hands.

Her gloves were bloodstained. He removed the gloves and dropped them on the box spring, near the flashlight.

Her hands were caked with dried, black blood. Eli's blood, transferred when she'd checked for a pulse.

He held her hands in both of his. Their bloody hands. As he stared at her face, he watched in fascination as a huge tear gathered in each eye, then slowly broke loose to run down her cheeks.

This was so painful for him. "You," he said softly. "You are the common denominator."

She stared at him for so long that he began to wonder if she'd heard him, or if he'd even spoken. Finally she said, "Your hands . . . they're like ice."

Hers were warm.

"You should have worn gloves. I'll find you a pair. There are tons of gloves in this house. Or mittens." She was talking rapidly. "Mittens are awkward, but a lot warmer. But then you can't shoot a gun very well with mittens, can you?"

He heard voices downstairs.

Franny and Harley and Daniel were getting nervous. It was too quiet. He and Arden had been gone a long time.

The temperature in the room was frigid. He could see their breath. He could hear wind howling around the window seams and joints the way it did in old houses.

"It's not your fault," he said. "It was the program. Harris went too far. Instead of taking you into the mind of a killer, he gave you the mind of a killer. He made a copycat killer out of you."

French's webcast execution had been the trigger for the renewed bouts of killings. And New Mexico bordered Oklahoma—where the more recent copycat murders had taken place.

Arden tugged her hands from his and shoved him away. Then she shoved him again. "Who do you think you are? Who the hell do you think you are?"

"That's why Harris pushed the bleaching. He suspected what had happened, but wouldn't admit it even to himself."

"I did not kill my parents."

But he could see her doubt. See that it was something she'd thought about before and pushed away.

"Everything okay?" came Daniel's voice from the bottom of the stairs.

Her eyes locked with Fury's. She was pissed. Anger had always been Arden's defense.

It was a good one.

He waited, arms at his sides.

She moved fast, pulled his weapon from the holster, and turned it on him.

He smiled.

He loved her.

Even though she didn't remember him, even though she didn't know his middle name or his favorite food, he loved her. He would love her until the day he died.

Arden watched him, her eyes narrowing. "You brought this all on me," she accused. "On us. You were the one who instigated this whole thing. You wanted me to go back to the Hill. Why, if TAKE wasn't working?"

Why was she so mad? she asked herself. Fury had only voiced the very thing she herself had subconsciously feared. Wondered and accused were two completely different things. But her instincts had told her he was hiding something. Something big. From the very beginning, her instincts had told her there was something secretive about him. Something bad, or at the very least, disturbing.

And the way he stood there, so calm, so collected . . .

"Who are you?" she demanded. "I don't mean your name. I mean what are you doing in my life? Really?"

"You erased me. You bleached me from your memory. I'm not sure it's up to me to tell you who I am. Or more to the point, who I was to you."

From the beginning, there had always been the implied relationship. She'd felt she knew him from somewhere. The scent of him was familiar. Even the feel of his hands on her arms. His voice. His irritatingly calm demeanor.

"We were FBI partners, Arden."

That didn't surprise her.

"You forgot me," Fury said. "And you forgot that you murdered your parents."

Things were finally making sense, if you could call it that. "I want to ask you one thing," she said.

He waited.

He was a patient man.

She remembered the gun she was holding, and realized her hand was both sweating and trembling. "You were in Project TAKE, weren't you? You've been in the tank." She'd seen the fear in his eyes the day she'd fallen and hit her head.

"Yes."

Her heart thudded in her chest. *Jesus, Jesus, Jesus.* "That's what I thought."

The smell of her mother's perfume was getting stronger by the second. It filled her head. She wet her lips with her tongue and could taste the flowery scent.

The man in front of her was full of lies and deceptions. Lies and deceptions he may have thought were truth. How did a person deal with that? How did you handle that kind of thinking? It was like trying to wake up from an intensely real dream.

Sometimes it couldn't be done.

Was she in the float tank now?

She closed her eyes.

A lot of times, before she fell asleep and when she awoke with a jolt in the middle of the night, she would think she was there, in the tank. She couldn't escape it, not even in New Mexico. She always went back to the tank. To the water.

Those moments filled her with heart-pounding terror. Now, for the second time in a matter of hours, she actually hoped she was in the tank. Now, with her eyes closed, she tried to re-create that feeling, to make it happen.

All things bad become good.

She felt the Glock slide from her fingers and opened her eyes to see Fury taking it away. He checked the safety, then slipped it back in his shoulder holster.

Was he right? Had she killed her family?

"Is there any other possibility?" She looked at Fury and sensed that he disliked the idea of her being the killer as much as she did. "There has to be another possibility." Had she murdered Eli? "I would remember killing Eli."

But what if she'd been brainwashed not to remember the innocent people she'd killed? She put a hand to her forehead and rubbed hard.

In her mind, she pictured herself going down the hillside to the barn. The door was open and Eli was bent over the red plastic jug.

How had she gotten out of the house without being noticed? Oh, it could be done. She'd done it often growing up.

"Fire doesn't fit French's MO," she said in a monotone voice, still staring at the vision in her head. "If I were a copycat, why the fire?"

"That part was pure opportunity. You know how opportunity works when it comes to killers."

Yes, often there was an element in these scenarios that didn't fit.

She set him on fire. She cut his throat.

Not me. Somebody else. Somebody in my head. "You are wrong," she insisted. "You are so wrong."

He watched her in somber silence. "I want you to think about it. I want you to consider what I've said."

Heavy footsteps sounded downstairs. "Everything okay?" Harley shouted up at them.

Like a dreamer falling into bed as she awakened, Arden jumped.

How long had they been standing there? Hours? Days? Years?

"All clear," Fury shouted back while continuing to focus on Arden in a way that reminded her of someone caught up in a movie.

"I can't accept your theory," she told him. "I won't accept it."

Every one of them was screwed up. Everybody except for Daniel, and he was screwed up in a different way. Traumatized by murder and abandonment.

All along, she'd held Fury in a position of superiority and logic. Somebody who could stand on the periphery in order to sort out the chaos and make sense of it. But now the bullshit he'd just spouted told her he didn't know anything. He didn't know any more than she did. Now he was telling her he was just as fucked up as she was. Because it was bullshit. What he'd just told her was total, total bullshit.

She had to believe that.

Chapter 39

Arden watched as Daniel put more wood in the stove, trying to recharge the fire that had burned down to a few red embers.

He'd always been good at building fires. Hadn't he earned a merit badge in it? she wondered. Yes. With her help, he'd practiced for weeks, until he was finally able to start a fire without matches.

If only the world operated according to *The Boy Scout Handbook*.

Candles of various shapes and sizes had been arranged on a tray in the middle of the coffee table, the flames flickering wildly in response to any movement or gust of wind that found its way around the storm windows.

Everyone watched Daniel in silence.

Once he had a good flame going and the stove door was shut, they hunched closer. Bundled in their coats, they sat staring at the fire.

The harder Arden thought about the situation, the more she tried to make sense of it, the more confused she became. Her mind was spiraling into a black hole.

Had she ever really kissed Harley in the cemetery? And if that hadn't happened, had he really called her on the phone in New Mexico? Did the Hill and the project even exist, or was she tangled up in a straitjacket in some institution, staring at gray walls and imagining a movie screen that signified her life?

If she followed that line of thinking, then maybe her parents were still alive. Maybe the whole thing was a false reality fabricated by Harris. A cruel mind tease.

In a situation like this, maybe it was better not to think. Or at least not to think too deeply. But she'd been taught to solve problems, to find solutions to puzzles, and she couldn't stop herself from trying.

In the end, the only answer was to follow the reality she knew. That was all she could do. All anybody could do.

Fury pulled his cell phone from his coat pocket.

"Won't work here," Daniel said.

Fury punched in three numbers: 911. He waited. He looked at the phone. He gave up and jammed it back in his coat pocket.

They should tear down the house, Arden thought. If any of them survived, the place should be demolished. It hurt to think about destroying their childhood home, but it shouldn't be here. No one should ever live in it again.

"A little over a mile from here," Daniel said, "on Roller Coaster Road, you can get a fairly decent signal."

"On a clear day," Arden pointed out.

A mile didn't seem like much under normal conditions. A mile in a blizzard would seem like ten.

Franny spoke for the first time since they'd returned to the house. Her voice was monotone, robotic. "Someone would have to go outside." Avoiding eye contact, she shook her head. "Nobody should go outside."

Arden didn't want to look at Fury. Even a glance would give credence to his supposition, but she couldn't help herself. She looked.

He was watching her; he still suspected her.

"I'll go," Daniel said. "It's a straight road. Hilly as hell, but straight. I won't get lost."

Franny came to life. "You can't go out there. Nobody can go out there!"

"Franny's right," Fury said. "We should all stay here."

"Eli is dead," Daniel stated firmly. "I'm going."

Arden's stomach dropped. She wanted Daniel to stay here where it was safe. Safer. Not as dangerous. "I'll do it," she said.

Harley stiffened and shot her a look of concern. For a moment, she thought he was going to protest, but Daniel spoke up instead.

"Sorry, Sis. I'm in a little better physical shape than you."

It was true. A few days ago, when food was still a part of her existence, she would have been more qualified for the challenge, but she hadn't exactly treated her body as a temple lately. She hadn't exactly treated it as a temple for several months.

"You shouldn't go alone," she said. He'd been a

Scout. He'd have to understand the importance of the buddy system.

Harley stepped forward. "I'll go with him."

Everyone stared, but nobody wanted to say what they were thinking—that having Harley tag along could actually be a hindrance.

"I'll do it," Fury said. It was obvious he wasn't thrilled with the direction the plans had taken, but he was really their only choice.

And when they were out there, when they were alone, he would tell Daniel about her. He would tell Daniel his suspicions, and Daniel would hate her all over again.

They found warm clothes for Fury.

Long underwear, wool socks. A pair of insulated boots that had once belonged to Daniel, topped off with more layers. A wool sweater. A sweatshirt. An ancient down jacket with a three-corner tear Daniel repaired with silver tape.

"Duct tape," he said, smoothing down the last piece. "Wonder of the modern world."

When the outfit was complete, Arden almost laughed.

Lack of sleep, lack of food, that's what it was. But Fury, who normally reflected quiet dignity, looked hilarious in the torn jacket and pilled stocking cap, leaving a waft of feathers behind as he walked to the door.

Daniel, dressed in insulated Carhartt overalls, followed with the LED flashlight.

Arden experienced a renewed attack of anxiety.

She wanted to join Franny in her earlier plea. *Don't go out there. Stay here, where it's safe.*

But it wasn't safe here.

Somebody had to go.

People, especially farmers, spent their lives fighting nature. Nature controlled their future, their livelihood. Nature was always there, waiting in the wings to creep in for the big finale, the twist ending. It liked to kill lambs and calves. It liked to carry off grandmothers and babies and homes.

Nature had always been the enemy.

Things were different now. There was a bigger enemy.

She grabbed Daniel by the jacket sleeve. "I'll do it. I can do it."

She thought about how hard it had been to reach the barn, what a physical struggle to get through the snow.

Daniel looked up from the hand on his arm. "It's okay. It'll be okay."

She stared at him, unable to hide her fear. She wasn't afraid to die. In fact, dying sometimes seemed the only way out. But Daniel . . . She didn't want Daniel to die. Not her little brother. Someone she'd looked out for, someone she'd read to and taught to ride a bike. Someone she loved.

"It'll be okay," he repeated with a soft smile.

He was waiting for her to release her grip on his coat. She let go and stepped back.

Franny ran from the room, then reappeared with her cell phone. "Take this as a backup." She handed it to Daniel.

Fury opened the front door. Wind gusted in, sending snow swirling around the living room. Candles flickered and went out.

"Try not to use the flashlight until you're down the road," Arden said.

It seemed hard to believe that someone could be out there watching them in this violent weather, but madmen didn't think like everybody else.

And what if nobody was out there? What if Fury was right?

They left.

Swallowed by the night. The storm.

Leaving Arden shaking, feeling sick to her stomach.

Franny relit the candles with a metal lighter, then disappeared into the spare bedroom, closing the door behind her.

Harley put one arm around Arden, giving her a hug. "They'll be okay."

He didn't know that. And if Fury really believed she was the killer, would he have left her alone with Harley and Franny? Arden wondered.

Harley went into the kitchen and began puttering around. Thank God somebody was interested in meal preparation. If Harley hadn't been doing the cooking, nobody would have eaten.

Arden's gaze dropped to Fury's briefcase, which he'd deposited on the floor in the dining room near the kitchen door. Without hesitation, she crossed the room and snatched the case, grabbed the flashlight Daniel had left on the dining room table, then headed for the stairs.

Chapter 40

Upstairs in her bedroom, Arden shut the door and sat down on the bed. Bundled in her heavy winter coat, she snapped open the briefcase and pulled out a small, black computer.

Government issue.

Her plan was to open Fury's computer and snoop through his files. She didn't make it that far. Under the computer was an eight-by-ten brown box, approximately an inch deep.

She brought the flashlight closer. On top was her name, followed by her date of birth.

She lifted out the box and pulled off the lid.

Her life.

In a box.

The condensed version, because whose life could fit in a box? But it was still her life.

Photos. Dozens of them. She looked through a few, then put the rest aside to continue her search.

There were several CDs and DVDs, all with her name on them.

One appeared to be her life history from birth through college. Another was a copy of her interview, videotaped after her parents' bodies were found. Another was labeled DAVIS CRIME SCENE FOOTAGE.

It wasn't strange that he had information about her. An FBI agent working on a case would have such material.

Under the photos were hard-copy files stamped CONFIDENTIAL.

Her college rape. Nobody knew about that. Not even her parents. Not her brother. Why hadn't Fury brought that up when he was trying to psychoanalyze her?

She dug deeper. Something stapled together. A sort of manuscript. She turned the pages, scanning the print, the words seeming vaguely familiar.

Her journal. Written in college. Not the actual journal. This was a photocopy.

The entire briefcase was about her.

This wasn't the collection of an FBI agent. It was the collection of someone obsessed. Someone unstable. Someone focused on one thing and only one thing.

The singular thoroughness gave her chills. It was like something a serial killer would covet. A treasure trove. A box of souvenirs.

She and Daniel were the two who'd gotten away. Who'd escaped what had been intended as a total massacre.

Was Fury the copycat killer? Didn't she have a memory of his being on the farm that day? Hadn't she seen him in the corncrib?

It wouldn't have been enough for him to hunt her down and kill her in New Mexico. He had to bring

her back to the place where it had all gone wrong.
He had to bring her back to the place of execution.

Jesus. He was the one alone now with Daniel.

Daniel, whose death, along with Arden's, would
complete the massacre.

Think.

Think, think, think.

It was times like these when she wished for a *Jet-
sons* existence. Where were those fucking pills that
were supposed to supply everything a body needed
to survive? She wanted to pop a pill. Just pop a pill
that would give her brain and body the fuel it
needed to continue.

Think.

Fury started this whole thing. He talked Harris
into letting her return. Fury came to get her in New
Mexico. Fury had been at the Hill when Vera was
killed. It wasn't until Fury appeared that Eli's throat
was cut.

Then there was the way he'd immediately gotten
her alone to dole out his theory, to completely mess
with her head, to get her mind so screwed up that
she wouldn't be able to figure it out. He'd wanted
her to be so horrified by the idea that she may have
murdered her own family that she wouldn't see
what was really going on. She wouldn't see that
Fury himself was the killer.

Oh, Jesus, Jesus, Jesus.

Her mind ran over everything again.

It was Fury. Why hadn't she seen it before?

And now he was out there with her brother.

*   *   *

Daniel knew snow. He knew how to walk through it. You could step high, which wore you out quickly. Or you could wade. Wading took longer, but it was the best way to conserve strength.

Fury was doing a little of both.

"This is it." Daniel stopped. "The highest point in the county."

Fury pulled out his cell phone and stared at it. "No signal." With his head bent he moved around, watching the tiny screen for any sign of power. "Nothing," he said, breathing hard from exertion. "Not even one bar."

Daniel tried the phone Franny had given him.

Same results.

He stuck it back in his pocket and replaced his gloves. "Tower must be out." Daniel wasn't cold, but it would be a bad idea to linger. Soon their bodies would begin to cool down. "That happens sometimes around here."

Fury made an annoyed sound and kept staring at the phone as if it would suddenly work. He punched in the 911 emergency number. No surprise when nothing happened.

The wind was whistling through something. Maybe a crack in a telephone pole, or a transistor. Maybe something they didn't even know was out there. Maybe an old combine somebody had left in a field. Or a broken washing machine that had been tossed in a ditch.

Above their head, strung on poles that ran parallel to the road, power lines swung back and forth, cracking like whips. Fury's back was to the wind, but Daniel was getting struck full in the face.

"Better head back to the house," Daniel shouted.

"Not yet."

"We can't piddle around here. We've got to start moving again or our body temperature will drop."

"Stay here," Fury told him. "I need to talk to you."

Chapter 41

Arden ran from her room and down the hall to the master bedroom. There, she dug in her parents' closet.

Her dad had owned a shotgun, along with the .22 rifle taken from Daniel's truck.

Where was the shotgun?

Not in the closet. Not this closet, anyway.

No time.

She had to leave. Had to go after Daniel and Fury.

She checked the other two bedrooms, then hurried downstairs.

"Pancakes again," Harley said, spatula in his hand. "And I found more canned apples to go with them."

He was wearing an apron. KISS THE COOK. Someone had given the apron to her father for his birthday. It should have bothered her that Harley was wearing it, but that wasn't important.

"Can't right now." She slipped past him, opened the basement door, and hurried down the steps.

The foundation was stone. The basement was the only part of the house that really showed its age, that gave you a sense of history. Uneven stones gathered from creek beds and stacked to make the walls, smelling of mold and earth and cobwebs.

Not a place to keep a gun, but she checked the ancient and worn wooden shelves anyway. She checked a small wooden cupboard.

Had Daniel taken the shotgun, too?

No time.

A pair of brown duck overalls hung on a nail above the stairs. She pulled them down and put them on.

Back upstairs, she slipped into insulated boots, black stocking cap, and heavy wool mittens.

"What are you doing?" Harley asked, holding a plate of pancakes.

"I have to check on something."

She didn't want to tell him her worst fears. He would go off. Think it was up to him to hunt Fury down.

That honor was reserved for her.

"I have to get something from the car. And I have to look at the LP tank. Make sure we aren't running out of fuel for the stove."

He set the plate down on the table. "I'll go with you."

She braced the flashlight between her knees and wound a scarf around her neck. "Stay with Franny." She zipped her coat to her chin. It smelled like cotton and damp feathers.

"You shouldn't go by yourself."

"I'll be okay."

She was heading out the door when he grabbed

her. "Arden." His voice broke on her name. She looked up. He was a silhouette, his face hidden by darkness. "I think I'm in love with you."

She swallowed.

This had gone too far. It had gotten out of hand. She hadn't understood how serious he was.

He pulled her to him and kissed her. A quick kiss on the mouth. Then he let her go. "Be safe."

Two seconds later, she was out the door, her heart pounding.

Be alive, she silently prayed, fighting her way through the snow.

Nothing can happen to Daniel.

The blizzard hadn't let up. It took her breath away, and the drifts had increased in depth. Daniel had taken the good flashlight. The one in her hand was a plastic discount-store model that did a poor job penetrating the falling snow.

She knew where to go. She knew the direction they should have taken. But what if they hadn't even left the yard? What if Fury had sliced Daniel's throat the minute they'd stepped outside?

Live the reality you know, not the one you're afraid of.

Her path took her past Eli's car, and the mailbox. She turned left, her head bent against the driving snow.

She mentally monitored her progress. *Down to the lowest point in the gravel road, then up the short, steep incline.*

At the hard road, she stopped to get her bearings and catch her breath, her chest rising and falling, lungs already raw, heart hammering.

She wasn't going to make it. Daniel had been right. She wasn't in shape for this. She'd thought her will would be strong enough. She used to run marathons; she knew how that worked. You removed yourself from your body until you were just along for the ride. But sometimes that wasn't enough.

Another left and she was on Roller Coaster Road.

Forward, forward, forward.

Don't think. Just move.

Keep moving.

She fell down. She got up. She fell again.

And stayed down.

For a while.

Just for a little while.

Her breathing was ragged. Her lungs burned. Sweat poured from her, soaking into the layers of clothing. She lay there, her hot face against the snow.

Freezing to death was supposed to be pleasant. At the moment, it seemed very appealing.

But she had places to go. Things to do.

Get up! Come on. Get up! Up!

She shoved herself to her feet and swayed, her hot, gloveless hands dangling at her sides.

Where was the flashlight? She'd had it a minute ago. . . .

She dug through the snow, finally seeing a faint glow. She scooped it up and pointed it south, in the direction Daniel and Fury would have gone.

A wall of white.

"Daniel!"

She waited, listening, arms hanging weakly at her

sides. She shouted, "Daniel!" She tried another name. "Fury!"

She dropped to her knees.

Things were hard enough, impossible enough, without this white stuff being thrown into the equation.

If life gives you snow, make snow cones.

Ha, ha. She was funny. A damn comedian, that's what she was.

She used to be funny.

Nobody would believe that, would they? That she'd actually made people laugh at one point in her life. Granted, it had been a very brief point, but a point nonetheless.

She thought she heard something.

Her ears perked up. Her body stiffened. "Daniel!"

She staggered to her feet, fighting fifty pounds of snow. It was packed in her boots, down her neck, up her sleeves.

A light. A flashlight beam.

A voice—a shout—came out of the darkness. "Arden?"

"Daniel?"

She started moving toward it. Running, or as close to running as she could get. The feeling was more like trying to move through thigh-deep mud. "Daniel!" she gasped, catching up with him.

He shone the light in her face, then lowered it. "What are you doing out here?"

"I came to find you. I was worried—" She stopped herself.

Had she simply been paranoid? Crazy Arden.

Thinking weird things again. Doing weird things. Was her theory about Fury total nonsense?

Fury.

Daniel was alone. "Where's Fury?"

"We couldn't get a signal." Daniel was breathing hard. "We kept trying, but nothing. I said the tower must be out, but Fury wanted to keep trying."

That didn't make sense. They should have stuck together. But then Fury could be persuasive. . . .

"Where are your gloves?" he asked.

She looked blankly at her bare hands. "I don't know."

He made an annoyed sound and checked the area with his flashlight, finally digging up a pair of snow-covered mittens. He tossed them back down. "Those will only make you colder now."

She didn't like the idea that Fury was back there somewhere.

"Maybe we should wait. Maybe we should go after him."

"He'll be okay. Let's go."

Daniel was acting strange. She had the feeling he was hiding something. Had Fury told Daniel his theory about Arden and their parents? Was Daniel afraid of her? Did he think he might be the next to die?

"I'm sweaty," he stated. "So are you. We can't wait or hypothermia will kick in. We have to get home."

Home.

If you want to call it that.

They turned around and began walking.

Arden didn't realize how far she'd come. Probably at least half a mile. And now she was slowing Daniel down. He had to keep stopping. Had to keep waiting for her.

Daniel grabbed her by the arm, but that was worse. If they walked side by side, the snow created too much of a barrier.

She fell into step behind him, following in the path he broke.

Chapter 42

Harley knew Arden was lying when she left the house. She wasn't going to check on the propane tank, or get something from Eli's car.

He was hurt. Terribly hurt.

She could be honest with him. Straightforward. She didn't have to lie.

Feeling lonesome, he grabbed a light that looked like a lantern and began to search the house. He found Franny in the guest room curled in a ball, burrowed under a comforter, headphones on, staring at a flickering candle flame in a votive on the dresser.

He left her alone and went upstairs.

To Arden's room.

There was a computer on her bed, an open briefcase beside it.

The FBI agent's briefcase. His computer. What was she doing with Fury's computer?

He sat down on the bed and opened the laptop.

It had been left in sleep mode. Now it came to life, everything already booted.

CDs and DVDs were scattered across the bed. He

picked up a DVD, opened the plastic case, and slipped the disk into the drive.

It made a spinning, whirring sound. A minute later, he was watching something very familiar.

Chapter 43

Franny came awake with a start.

The candle had gone out. The room was freezing.

"Franny!" a voice called from deep upstairs.

Harley?

Disoriented by sleep and the darkness, she lay there, her heart hammering.

"Franny!" he called again in a loud, urgent whisper.

For a moment, she'd forgotten everything. Forgotten that Noah was dead. Forgotten that Eli had been murdered. But now it all came rushing back.

She was alone in the dark, and Harley was calling her name.

Was someone else in the house?

Was Harley trying to warn her?

Her heart pounded louder, faster, until it thundered in her head.

She forced herself to move, to toss back the comforter and get to her feet. With her face turned toward the door, she reached blindly for the dresser, her fingers feeling across the cold wooden surface until she came in contact with the Zippo lighter she'd found in the kitchen.

She slowly and silently opened the metal lid. She rested her thumb against the wheel, flinching at the sound as it rotated. The flint sparked, igniting the wick.

Franny held the flame in front of her. The room was bitterly cold. She could see her breath coming in rapid, frightened puffs.

The bedroom door wasn't latched. She pushed, and it swung open with a creak.

The living room was warm. Hot, almost.

She heard a sound—a low, steady roar. It took her a moment to realize it was coming from the wood-stove.

She stood there a moment, staring at the red glow behind the thick glass.

She wanted to go there. Stand it front of it. She wanted to think about how they'd played Monopoly just a few hours ago.

She'd had fun. But how could she have had fun when Noah was dead? What was wrong with her?

I'm damaged.

Eli hadn't wanted to play. She'd known he was disgusted with the whole idea of a game built around consumerism, but she'd thought it was harmless. Nostalgic. He got too upset about things like that. The game had been something to do.

But his anger wasn't just about the game. She knew that too.

He'd been jealous of Daniel.

She and Eli were friends. Good friends. But it

could never have been more than that. She'd planned on telling him, but didn't want to lose him completely. She'd loved Eli. . . .

"Franny," came Harley's loud, harsh whisper. "Hurry."

Everything was blurry, and she realized she was crying.

She didn't have anyone. Noah had been her family. Eli had been her family. She was alone.

She turned and went up the stairs. The lighter in her hand was getting hot, the flame dancing crazily the faster she moved, the smell of burning lighter fluid going up her nose.

At the top of the stairs, she stopped and the flame settled down.

"Where are you?" she whispered.

The hairs on her arms floated as if exposed to static electricity. Her scalp tingled as if someone were dragging a finger up the nape of her neck.

"In here."

His voice came from the big bedroom. The bedroom where Arden's mother had died.

Franny didn't want to go in there.

She slid her feet across the floor, stopping at the open doorway. "Harley?"

"Come on." He sounded impatient. "Come in here."

She lifted the lighter higher, but it wasn't enough to penetrate the darkness. "What are you doing?"

"Hurry."

"I don't want to."

He laughed. "Come on, sweetie pie. I'm tired of waiting."

He sounded so normal. More normal than he had the whole time they'd been there. She took a few more steps across the threshold to stop just inside the room.

The hairs on her arms were still moving.

Run.

Turn around and run.

Trust your instincts. That was what they taught in self-defense class. *Always trust your instincts.*

She pivoted in her stocking feet. The muscles in her legs tightened as she prepared for flight.

A burst of air hit her in the face, dousing the lighter flame as the bedroom door slammed shut.

Beyond the shuddering terror-roar in her head, she heard a click.

A muted light replaced the extinguished flame.

Now she could see him.

Now she could finally see him.

Harley. Standing in front of the door, a lantern in one hand, a knife in the other.

She did something that completely surprised her. She raised her hands like claws and charged him, screaming as she went.

But she was no match for Harley.

He was big. And strong. And crazy.

He dug his fingers into her hair and pushed her to her knees.

A lot of things went through her mind, one being that Arden had slept with this guy, this monster. Another, that Franny herself had offered to share her granola bars with him.

And then the knife glistened.

The blade came down.

He slit her throat as she clung to him with hands like claws, begging and pushing him away at the same time.

"Sweetie pie," Harley crooned, cradling her.

Hot blood ran down her chest, soaking into her top.

Harley dragged her to the bed, turning her around so her head was toward the door and hanging over the side.

Of course, she thought. She must lie in the same position as Arden's mother. How had that been? Kind of upside down?

Yes. Yes, that was it.

It suddenly seemed right. Comforting and right. It made her feel less alone.

Chapter 44

They could see the house.

The strong beam of Daniel's flashlight glanced off the black pair of upstairs windows.

With shelter in sight, Arden pulled off her hat and unsnapped her coat, letting the heat from her sweat-soaked body escape. Wet hair clung to her neck and face.

They cut around to the kitchen door, so their entry wouldn't chill the whole first floor. It was something they'd learned to do as kids.

At first they were too involved in stomping off snow to notice the silence. Arden became aware of it first. Maybe because she'd felt it before, in such a similar way.

Without saying anything, she put a hand to Daniel's arm. He stopped unlacing his boot and looked up from his bent position. His hair was wet too, appearing almost black, stuck to his forehead in sharp clumps.

She stared at him, her brows drawn together. *Something is wrong*, she told him. *Something doesn't feel right.*

He paused and listened.

Nothing to hear except the wall clocks. At least three of them ticked away, none in unison.

Daniel slowly and silently straightened. His gaze swept the shrouded kitchen, taking in the uneaten food. The pan on the stove. The remaining batter.

He looked back at her.

She could see the wheels turning. See his doubt. His suspicion.

Of *her*.

She didn't blame him. She was suspicious of herself.

She'd abandoned the house. Run away in a panic. Daniel had come upon her breathless, gloveless, agitated.

While he continued to stare, she squeezed around him, grabbing the metal handle of the lantern light on her way past the table.

There was no way to move silently in the heavy winter boots. She finally gave up trying and let her footfalls sound heavily upon the wooden floor.

The dining room and living room were empty. Candles burned on the coffee table. The woodstove emitted a low roar that meant it was hot as hell and probably needed the flue opened.

"Franny!" Arden shouted.

No answer.

She continued her search.

The guest bedroom was empty, the comforter bunched, Noah's MP3 player and headphones on the pillow as if Franny had just left.

Arden felt stuck in a loop, destined to replay the same scenario again and again.

Heart pounding, she turned to head for the stairs, her hand on the banister.

Daniel stood in the middle of the living room, arms at his sides.

Watching her, watching her, watching her.

"Get out of here," she told him.

He continued to stare.

"Go! Get out of this house!"

He was her little brother. From years of habit, he obeyed. He shifted his weight and began moving toward the kitchen.

Arden walked up the stairs. She should run, but she couldn't make herself. She didn't want to see what was coming next.

Music should be playing. Maybe a track by Godspeed You Black Emperor!

The door to her room was ajar. Something glowed from inside. She approached, the sound of her boots like thunder on the floor. Without hesitating, she shoved open the door. It slammed against the wall. With the lantern held high, she did a quick assessment of the room.

Nobody there.

Fury's computer was on her bed, where she'd left it. Except now it was running. She could hear the fan, and the occasional sound of a spinning disk. She moved close enough to look at the screen. It had defaulted to the saver mode—a succession of pleasant and soothing nature scenes.

A meadow. A waterfall. A woodland.

She ran a finger across the computer touchpad. A new image appeared.

The motion-sick bobbing of a handheld camera making its way through a house and up the stairs. A hand appeared from off-camera, pushing open a door.

Suddenly, there was Arden's mother lying on her back on the bed, her throat cut.

Arden wanted to close her eyes, but couldn't.

This was the image she'd forgotten, the image that had been erased.

Confusion came like a black cloud, and for a moment she thought this was what had been physically removed from her brain. The disk that was playing in the computer.

It wasn't the kind of thing you wanted to take with you. It wasn't the last memory you wanted to have of someone you loved.

The jagged cut looked like a giant smile. A pumpkin smile. Because the human brain is always looking for a face. Babies, even newborns, were always looking for a face. Humans saw faces in everything. In the pattern of bark on a tree. In the swirls on a door. In a cluster of leaves.

Faces. Always looking for faces.

The emotionless camera moved on. Back down the stairs.

She knew where it would go next. To the barn, where her father had been killed.

She heard a sound coming through the wall. Like something falling.

With the lantern in her hand, she ran from her

room and down the short length of hall to the door
of her parents' room.

A body.

Sprawled across the bed.

Franny.

Arden lifted the lantern higher and approached.

Franny, her throat sliced.

No!

Franny, her dead eyes wide.

Staring at nothing.

Staring at Arden.

Those dead eyes.

A hiss came from Franny's throat. From her giant
smile.

Jesus.

She was still alive.

Arden spun around, running down the hall to the
bathroom closet.

She pulled two blankets from a top shelf, tucking
them under her arm. A handful of towels. An open
box of sanitary napkins.

Back down the hall, her heart pounding, her
breathing heavy.

In the bedroom, she put the lantern on the floor
and dropped everything else on the foot of the bed.

How long had she been gone? One minute? Two?

*Unfold a blanket. Spread it over Franny. Tuck it in.
Follow with another.* She sat down on the bed, digging
into the box of napkins.

Franny's hand was on her throat, blood oozing
between her fingers.

"You're going to be okay," Arden said. "We're

going to get a snowplow here. Then the police will come. An ambulance will get through."

She didn't want Franny to give up. She didn't want her to know the hopelessness of the situation.

A sound of movement below her. Footfalls on the stairs.

Daniel was coming.

Franny's mouth moved, but no sound came out.

"Don't try to talk."

Franny's mouth kept moving.

What was she looking at?

Arden swung around in time to see Harley appear out of the shadows.

Something in his hand.

A large knife caught the lantern light and sent an orb bobbing around the room.

Franny's eyes grew wide, and she let out a silent scream.

Chapter 45

Arden swung her leg, deliberately kicking over the lantern, the glass and bulb shattering, plunging the room into darkness. She sprang from the bed and veered sharply to the right.

Her boots! Her noisy boots!

With eyes wide, she stared into nothing and strained to hear him. From her left came a hiss.

Franny.

Arden crouched on the floor, her fingers feeling for the shattered lantern. Coming in contact with broken glass, she picked up a jagged piece.

Harley let out a roar and charged.

She stayed down.

He shot over her, one foot kicking her in the chest, the other striking her chin, throwing her backward. She scrambled to her feet and turned to face him.

Her eyes weren't adjusting. The darkness was solid. No shadows. Just sound. Smell. Taste.

She tasted blood.

He moved silently, unhampered by heavy boots or a heavy coat. Suddenly he was on top of her, digging his fingers into her hair. She felt cold steel against her throat. With the broken glass, she jabbed up and behind.

He let out a yelp and released her.

She scrambled for the door.

He grabbed her by the coat, pulled her back.

She slipped away, leaving him holding an empty jacket.

Run.

Down the hall, to the bathroom.

Slam the door.

Hand scrambling for the lock.

The door burst open, throwing her backward, her head smacking the tub.

In the darkness, she squeezed between the tub and the wall.

A hallway ago, she'd been thinking of Franny and Daniel. Of how to get them out of this alive. Now self-preservation kicked in and she was thinking only of herself. Only thinking of life in small increments. Only trying to stay alive for five more minutes.

Daniel heard the sound of a struggle and ran for the stairs, taking them three at a time, flashlight in hand. He paused at his parents' room, shining the light inside.

And stopped breathing.

Franny.

No.

On the bed.

Blood everywhere.

Her throat sliced.

Oh, my God.

He couldn't handle this. He couldn't take this.

He let out a choked sob.

She blinked.

Blinked.

Oh, fuck. Oh, Jesus.

She raised a hand to him. An imploring, bloody hand.

From down the hall came a shout, followed by a crash.

Something roared between Arden's ears.

She shook her head, but the sound didn't stop. A sound like the woodstove, only louder.

Fire.

A chimney fire.

How many times had her dad warned them not to let the woodstove get too hot?

You gotta open the flue and let the heat escape; otherwise you'll catch the chimney on fire, he'd always told them. And the chimney ran up the wall through the bathroom.

In the dark, she could hear Harley blindly searching for her, knocking things down, coming closer.

In one fluid movement, Arden stood and opened the window above the tub. A brief pause; then she dove out to land in deep snow on the kitchen roof four feet below.

Chapter 46

Harley leaned out the bathroom window in time to see Arden land in a deep snowbank. A fraction of a second later, she was bounding away like a deer.

"Arden!" he shouted after her.

She paused and looked up.

Flames from the house illuminated her face.

She was frightened.

Frightened and beautiful.

He loved that combination.

He was on a blood high. This was what he lived for.

The chase.

The smell of blood and terror.

And now, with the fire—it was epic.

A visual of the excitement he felt inside.

This—*this*—was his calling. It was who he was. Not some wimp. Not some sweet guy everybody liked but nobody respected or loved.

Albert French had been knocking. He'd even gotten in a couple of times, like that little episode with the annoying Eli kid, but Harley always made him leave.

Why?

He'd once had a dog that was part wolf. It was the nicest dog, the sweetest dog, except that it loved to kill things. Cats. Dogs. It almost killed a baby once.

It couldn't help itself. And the more it killed, the more it wanted to kill.

That was Harley.

Harris had put the desire in him, then tried to wash it out. But the instinct was too strong. By then it had taken hold.

For a while, Harley thought he could stop killing. He thought he could block out Albert French's voice. For Arden. But he'd been fooling himself. He didn't want to quit.

Love did that to a person. Made you see things in a false way, a pretty, soft way. Made you become the person somebody else wanted you to be, rather than the person you really were. But the real you always came back. Eventually.

Even now, when he knew he was going to kill her, he wanted to please her. He wanted her to know that he'd fought French. That he'd been fighting him for a long time.

You always kill the ones you love.

The old lady had just happened. He'd sneaked out of Cottage 25 and was looking for Arden. He'd come upon the woman instead. But the farmhouse . . .

Being in the farmhouse had messed with his head. But the biggest turning point had come when he'd opened the computer and witnessed the aftermath of his own previous killings, the ones that had occurred at this very location. Harris had tried to bleach the event from his mind, but the images on the screen had brought everything back as if it had happened yesterday.

And then there had been French's execution.

Those eyes.

French had looked directly at him, reminding Harley of his calling. Of his duty and obligation to carry on.

Long live Albert French.

Up until that point, everything had been confusing. Everything had seemed skewed and wrong.

But *this*—this was right. This was real. As real as it got.

He had things to finish. A legacy to carry on.

Life was good.

Death was better.

The bathroom window wasn't very big. Harley put his legs out first, then followed with the rest of his body. He slid down the roof and landed in a pile of snow. He hit the ground and ran toward the building where he'd hidden Daniel's rifle and the bloody coat and gloves he'd worn when he'd killed Eli.

Daniel reached the bathroom just in time to see Harley disappear through the open window. The sky beyond the bathroom was light. Was morning coming? And that sound—what was that sound?

He smelled smoke. A second later, he realized the house was on fire.

"Arden!" He cast the beam around the room, then moved to the tiny bedroom that had once been his.

Empty.

Past that to Arden's room.

Had she jumped? Was she gone?

His lungs burned. In the beam of the flashlight, things were getting murky and smoke curled.

He backtracked to the master bedroom. Was Franny still alive?

He wrapped the blankets around her and picked her up. He wanted to be more careful, but there was no time. He could hear crackling and popping. It was getting hard to breathe.

He carried her down the stairs. The air wasn't as bad on the first floor, away from the chimney.

Franny didn't move or make a sound.

Dead, probably.

He opened the front door, staggered from the house and across the yard with Franny in his arms. He stepped in a dip and sank to his waist in snow. Never losing his grip on Franny, he burrowed out, fell to his knees, then struggled to straighten, the light from the burning house casting long shadows.

At the bottom of the hill, he turned toward a corrugated-metal culvert that ran under the road.

Once inside the protection of the culvert, he put Franny down. He took off his jacket and covered her with it as best he could, tucking the blankets around and under her feet.

She was probably dead. He was probably tucking in a dead girl. And if she wasn't dead yet, she would be.

He retrieved a flashlight from his jacket. With his

back to the culvert opening, he sheltered the flashlight from the outside and clicked it on.

Her lips were blue.

She was staring at him with terror-filled eyes.

His heart thumped. He swallowed.

The bleeding seemed to have slowed. Or was she
just running out of blood?

No, she wouldn't be conscious if she were
drained.

She lifted a hand toward him in an imploring gesture.

Don't leave me here.

That's what she was saying, what she was trying
to tell him. He grabbed her hand—it was like ice. He
tucked it under the jacket.

"I'll be back," he whispered. "I'll be back."

She blinked. But it wasn't an *okay* blink. It was a
blink that said, *I'm going to die. And you're going to die.
And if you leave, we'll both die alone.*

He shut off the light and straightened.

He had to agree with Franny's unspoken words.

They were all going to die.

They were all already dead.

Nathan Fury plodded along. One foot in front of
the other. That was the only way to go about this
business. Just keep moving. He glanced up and saw
that the sky was beginning to lighten.

The sun was coming up.

He'd started to think the night would never end.

He went fifty more yards, then stopped. Flames
were shooting from the farmhouse.

His legs started moving before his brain gave them the command. At the house, he held a glove to his mouth and nose and kicked open the front door.

Smoke and flames poured out. He staggered back, the heat singeing his face and eyebrows.

He spun around, jumped from the porch, and hurried to the back of the house, where he shoved open the kitchen door and ran inside.

"Arden!"

The heat was intense, the smoke suffocating.

Within seconds, he was back out the door, collapsing in the snow, choking and gasping, trying to pull air into his smoke-filled, oxygen-deprived lungs.

A movement out of the corner of his eye caught his attention. He looked up to see Harley standing several yards away, silently watching him.

"Where's Arden?" Fury gasped.

"I don't know."

"Did she make it out?"

"Yeah."

"And Daniel. Where's Daniel? And Franny? Did they get out?"

"I don't know."

The fire illuminated half of Harley's body; the other half was in shadow. The half in shadow began to shift and change. A hand was raised . . . and suddenly a rifle was pointing directly at Fury.

Fury's brain did a reset.

Harley?

How?

Had Harley killed Eli?

Had Harley killed Arden's parents?

Fury struggled with the new information, his logical mind wanting to immediately discard it. How was it possible? Harley hadn't even been there that day.

Or had he?

Christ.

Harley *could* have been there.

It was possible. Of course, it was possible.

Fury went for his Glock, diving and rolling at the same time.

Harley opened fire.

Fury kept rolling.

The deep snow hindered him, trapped him.

A rapid succession of sounds rang in his ears. The deep blast of the rifle. Its echo off nearby buildings. The *pffttt* of bullets lodging in the ground, lodging in Fury's body, some ripping through him to come out the other side.

Daniel heard gunshots.

He ran and crested the hill. The glow from the burning house lit up the sky, reflecting off the snow that still fell like a thick blanket.

He felt a thump. Similar to getting shocked by an electric fence. The kind of weird sensation that came when the brain and body weren't working together. When you couldn't make sense out of what had just happened.

He felt a warmth.

For a minute he thought he'd wet his pants. He reached down and touched his leg, his thigh. . . .

Sticky.

Blood.

He pulled his hand away and stared at it in the flickering light.

A lot of blood.

He hadn't been hit in the heat of battle. He hadn't even been a target. How fucking lame was that?

He knew a guy who'd shot himself in the leg. He'd been hunting, driving through a pasture, the truck bouncing, and his gun had discharged. The guy had felt pretty stupid about it.

No shit.

Daniel collapsed. Just kind of folded up.

Struck down by a stray bullet. Probably a bullet from his own damn gun.

It pissed him off.

Did anything ever happen the way it was supposed to?

Not much time, he told himself.

He was bleeding like a son of a bitch. Lying on his back, snow falling in his face, he undid his belt buckle. Somehow he managed to tug it from his pants in one long motion.

Just like he was fixin' to give somebody an ass whuppin'.

He let out a little laugh as he slid the belt under his leg, above the shattered artery. Without looking, eyes squinted against the falling snow, he slipped the leather end of the belt through the buckle and pulled tight.

No more hunting, he told himself. No more fucking hunting.

*　　*　　*

"Harley! No!"

The words were out of Arden's mouth before she realized she'd spoken. All she'd thought about was stopping Harley from putting another bullet in Fury, who had crumpled to the ground.

Harley slowly swung around to face her. The rifle barrel followed. Daniel's .22. She remembered it well. It was the semiautomatic that held a magazine of ten rounds.

She turned, ducked, and ran.

Never run in a straight line. Always zigzag.

The weapon discharged, the reverberation echoing off the outbuildings to finally move into the far distance. That was followed by the *click, click, click* of the gun's empty chamber.

She didn't slow.

Flames shot from the roof of the house, illuminating her way. She aimed for an old wooden outbuilding, once painted white but now peeling to reveal an old coat of red beneath.

The slaughterhouse.

The shed was small. Maybe ten feet by twenty.

She threw her shoulder against the door. It shuddered open. She stumbled inside, slamming the door behind her.

No lock.

She pressed her back to the door, breathing hard and loud, her mind racing, trying to piece things together.

Harley had been mad at Eli. Like someone with multiple-personality disorder, he'd pulled French

out when he'd needed someone ruthless and blood-
thirsty.

Maybe Harley didn't even remember killing Eli.
Maybe he'd truly been horrified by what had hap-
pened, but now French had taken over completely.
There was nothing of Harley left.

The door burst open, sending her flying forward.
She crashed into the metal butcher table screwed to
the floor, the wind knocked out of her.

Then Harley was there. He grabbed her by the
shoulders, making loud roaring noises while he
shook the hell out of her.

She kneed him in the crotch, dropped, and
twisted away, scrambling through the darkness. She
felt her way back to the table. On her knees, she
opened the drawer, blindly running her fingers
across the contents of cold metal objects.

Harley grabbed her from behind. At the same
time, her fingers curled around what she'd been
looking for.

A gun.

The captive bolt gun.

Harley was choking her.

Her arms flailed as she tried to hit him, the un-
cocked gun smacking him in the head.

He made a sound like an injured bull and let go.

Arden crashed to the floor, gasping for air.

Hurry. No time to recover. You have to hurry.

In the dark, she dragged the weapon to her lap
and tugged the mechanism back, cocking it.

Harley came out of nowhere, knocking her over.
He pushed her down, her shoulder blades crushed

against the cement floor. He choked her again, his thumbs pressed into her trachea, shutting off her air.

She lifted the gun.

It was heavy.

Much heavier than a revolver or rifle.

From outside came the sound of an explosion.

The propane tank.

The ground shook. A concussion rattled the windows. Flames illuminated the interior of the small building.

Arden could see Harley above her, his face contorted with rage. It wasn't Harley; it was Albert French.

Albert French. The man inside Harley who had killed her mother and father. The man who had killed Eli and probably Vera Thompson and the family in Oklahoma.

She pressed the gun to his temple.

It wasn't Harley's fault. None of it was his fault. They were all victims. Harris had created a monster. A Frankenstein. A killing machine that had to be stopped.

It would be so much easier if she could hate him. . . .

She pulled the trigger.

She heard the bolt go in. One loud, sickening crunch of the skull followed by a pop.

Time got weird.

In that encapsulated moment of disbelief and horror and pain, her synapses sparked and memory paths reactivated.

She saw his expression fade from rage to surprise.

A kind of *what the . . . ?* Then, in a baffled little boy voice, he said, "Arden . . . ?"

He was Harley again.

I'm sorry. I'm so, so sorry.

Not much blood. Just a hole. Maybe he would be okay. Maybe he would live.

"Did I hurt anybody?" he asked in a distant, groggy voice that told her death was already in the room, tapping on his shoulder. "I didn't hurt anybody, did I?"

She shook her head, unable to speak. "No," she finally managed, her eyes swimming with tears.

"It's the h-house," he said with whispered intensity. "It's bad."

"I know," she crooned. "I know."

He slumped forward.

Albert French was gone.

Harley was gone.

Chapter 47

Arden stepped from the slaughterhouse, spotted Fury lying near the burning building, and ran.

Noxious fumes stung her eyes and lungs as she braced herself behind him, hands under his armpits. Walking backward, she dragged him away from the farmhouse, across the exposed grass to an area of snow that hadn't melted from the heat.

She dropped, crossed her legs, and rested Fury's head in her lap.

Fear, pain, loss, and grief.

Life, death, murder.

Blood, snow, and Nathan Fury.

A spark of memory had started in the slaughterhouse when Arden had pulled the trigger and watched the life fade from Harley's eyes. Now, looking at Fury in the bloody snow, time telescoped and the past returned full-blown.

She remembered who Fury had been to her, and how much she'd loved him. How much it had hurt when he left the program and when they'd gone their separate ways.

France was real. France had happened.

With Fury.

She'd confided in Harley. She'd cried on his shoulder, telling him stories about herself and Fury. Harley was a sponge, absorbing personalities, absorbing lives. Somehow he'd gotten the events mixed up in his head. Maybe he'd really believed he'd been to France with Arden.

At the last minute, Arden had invited Harley home for Christmas after finding out he would be alone. He'd smiled, thanked her, and said he might drop by.

Might.

She'd driven home from the Hill, her car full of presents. It had been snowing, but her mind hadn't been on the weather. She'd been thinking about Fury. Confused. Missing him. Wishing things hadn't happened the way they'd happened.

She'd arrived at her parents' house in the early afternoon, entering through the back door, her arms loaded with presents. "Mom? Dad?"

The house was silent except for the ticking clocks.

She kicked off her boots and put the gifts down on the kitchen table. She walked through the dining room and living room.

Up the stairs.

"Mom?"

Turned the corner to the master bedroom—to find her mother lying across the bed, her throat sliced, the smell of blood and perfume in the air.

A familiar MO. Albert French's MO. Arden had seen the exact scene before, down to the placement of the body positioned diagonally across the bed, face toward the door, upside down.

Her mother was blue. She'd bled out.

Even though it was too late, Arden attempted CPR. Then she called 911, and ran from the house.

She found her father in the barn. Hanging from a rope attached to a pulley, his body slowly twisting as if it still had life in it.

She released the pulley, and he tumbled to the straw-littered floor.

Dead.

Albert French had done this. To teach her a lesson. That was what she had thought that day. What everybody thought. But it had really been Harley, an unwitting disciple of French's. The trigger had been the farmhouse, a setting eerily similar to those of the actual French massacres. For a little while, Harley had become French.

It was very possible Harley had still been on the farm at that time, hiding, waiting for her. Instead of trying to find him, catch him, Arden had run.

To the corncrib. To the very top, where she remained until the police came. Until the FBI was called.

Until Fury showed up.

She'd clung to him with frozen fingers, unable to speak. Unable to make a sound. He'd hugged her to his chest and cried with her.

Now Fury let out a low moan and opened his eyes.

"I remember everything," she told him. "I remember France."

He let out a gasp, struggling to form words.

"There was a vineyard," Arden said, speaking for him. "And rain."

"B-bikes," he added.

"And bikes." She could tell him the rest of the story. "We went for a ride, but it started to rain so we hurried back to the château."

"Y-yes."

"I loved you."

He blinked. There were tears in his eyes. In his blue, blue eyes. He lifted a hand to reach for her. "This . . . isn't . . . over."

It was painful to watch him try to talk. "I know," she said.

"Harris."

She picked up his hand, holding it in both of hers. "I'll take care of it."

She tugged at his zipper, opening his blood-saturated coat. He'd been hit in the shoulder, the chest, the abdomen. She didn't even know where to start.

"Don't." He struggled to take a shallow breath.

"Daniel?" His name was all Arden could manage to get out, but Fury understood.

"S-sorry."

No.

No, no, no. A sob of grief escaped her.

She wanted everything to stop. To shut off. But she'd wanted that before, and look where it had gotten her.

She and Fury used to talk about getting killed in the field, because it was always in the back of an agent's mind. Fury said he'd rather go out that way than get old, infirm, and senile.

His eyes glazed over, became unfocused, as if he were looking at something beyond her, in the air just past her shoulder. "The shadow people are here," he whispered with a half laugh.

"No." Her bottom lip trembled. "No, they aren't."

But they were. How he was still alive was a mystery. But she didn't want him to say he was dying. Saying it was an invitation to death. An open door. Saying it made it too real, and didn't give her a chance to adapt.

She'd just gotten him back. Just remembered him.

It wasn't enough time. She needed more time.

His eyes closed.

She pulled his coat together with fingers stiff and crusted with dried blood. *Don't leave me here.*

Something splashed on his face. For a minute, she thought it was raining. Then she realized she was crying. She blinked and wiped the tears away with a bloody hand.

Maybe she would die. Then this would end. A complete and total bleaching. That was the only way to stop the madness. And anyway, she'd come full circle. Not a good circle, but a solid one. A circle that had a beginning, a middle, and an end.

But things never happened the way you expected.

Sounds intruded.

The deep, heavy rumble of snowplows. Beyond that, sirens. Far away, but moving closer.

The first officer on the scene found her sitting in the snow, wearing nothing but brown coveralls and a sweatshirt, the hair on her head frozen and covered with frost, hugging a man while she stared into space.

She had blood on her face. Blood on her hands.

So much blood.

Officer Bennett stared at the man. Was he dead?

Bennett was young. He'd seen only a couple of dead people in his life, and he'd never seen an actual murder victim except in the films they showed at the police academy.

"Here's another one!" someone shouted. "Gunshot victim!"

Somebody had spotted the smoke and called it in. A house fire.

Officer Bennett bent down, hands on his thighs. "What's your name?" he asked softly.

The woman raised her head and looked at him with unfocused eyes.

"Or the victim?" he asked. "Who's the victim?"

"My partner." The words were delivered in a robotic manner.

"Who did this?" He reached for his gun, suddenly realizing that the perpetrator could still be in the area.

With a blood-encrusted hand, the woman pointed toward a shed. "In there. Dead."

The storm had ended abruptly. The sun was out, shining harsh and brittle. From the bare limbs of nearby trees, birds sang.

Officer Bennett didn't like this. Not one bit. But then he thought about going to the coffee shop later that day. Damn, but he was going to have a story to tell the guys. They were gonna be hanging on his every word. And it wouldn't just be this afternoon. This was a story that would last days, weeks. Hell, he'd probably be telling it to his grandkids. And what about his sister? She'd moved to Seattle and always liked to bug him, tell him nothing exciting ever happened in Lake County.

Like hell.

Paramedics arrived. They eased the woman away from the man and began working on him, faces grim.

"No pulse," said a paramedic. "No heartbeat."

"Another body over here!" somebody shouted from a distance. "This one's alive!"

It took a little while, but the words finally registered with the woman. She pulled her gaze from the man on the ground. She turned and began walking stiffly through the snow.

Bennett followed.

Her walk became a run. Faster and faster, until he could hardly keep up. Hurrying in the direction of the shout, where workers were beginning to cluster. Two men cut across the hillside, carrying a gurney. Two more followed with emergency kits.

"Daniel!" the woman shouted.

Daniel heard someone call his name, but he couldn't seem to open his eyes.

And then Arden was there.

". . . culvert," he managed to croak. "Franny."

Somehow he had an IV needle in the back of his hand.

How had that gotten there?

Somehow he was being carried on a gurney.

He rolled his head. Was that the house? That charred, smoldering, stinking mess?

He was glad it was gone. It needed to be gone.

Arden fell into step beside him, her face bobbing in and out of his field of vision. "Franny's alive," she told him.

He suddenly felt like crying. Give him some good news, and he wanted to cry like a baby.

Chapter 48

Arden sat on the porch of the Appalachian mountain cabin located in Virginia, only a few hours' drive from Quantico, where she was once again living. The cabin was a place she and Fury used to stay. A place of comfort. A refuge.

It was one of those warm spring days when the sun made you sleepy and the shade made you cold. Arden felt herself drifting off when the sound of muffled voices brought her back around. She looked up to see Daniel and Franny strolling toward her.

Daniel had physically recovered from his ordeal. Thankfully, they'd been able to save his leg.

Franny was tucked under his arm, a bouquet of wildflowers in her hand.

Her jet-black hair had been gelled into a funky style. She wore a long floral skirt with black army boots. The scar across her throat was smooth, red and raised, and you could see the dots where the stitches had been.

They'd auctioned off the farm.

That hurt.

It always hurt to leave the past behind. It was supposed to hurt.

The ground had been sold to a young couple and their parents for less than it should have.

People were weird about things like that. Especially farmers whose livelihood was fifty percent skill and fifty percent luck. You didn't want to thumb your nose at things you didn't understand. You didn't hang horseshoes upside down, and you didn't purchase ground that might be cursed.

It was hard enough making a living on normal ground, in good weather. But farmers farmed because they had to, because they didn't know another way of life and didn't want to know one.

With the money from the sale, Daniel would be able to go to college. He'd been accepted to George Mason University. Franny was also going back to school. They would be a young, normal college couple. Nobody would know where Daniel had gotten his slight limp, and Franny her scar.

The shadow people were still there.

They would always be there, because death was always waiting in the wings. Reality was just perception, changing from person to person. Not a new concept, but a disturbing one nonetheless.

There were times when Arden's mind slipped and she imagined that none of this was real, that she was in the float tank, being fed information by Harris. But then she would give herself a mental shake.

They would probably never know why she'd forgotten Fury. Maybe because he'd been there the day of her parents' murder and had found her in the cupola. Or maybe because she'd been trying to forget all things painful.

Had Harris merely handed her a placebo, telling her the bleaching would make her forget what she wanted to forget? Had her own desire, her own need to shut out what had happened, proved enough to close the door to her memory?

There had been a government inquest. Arden had testified against Harris, and he'd finally admitted that there had been some problems with Project TAKE, and that he'd put Harley in the tank in order to deprogram him.

DNA linked Harley to the murder of Vera Thompson and the Oklahoma case. They never came to a satisfactory conclusion about Noah's death and how the blood ended up on his clothes. Arden's theory was that he'd been running the halls when he'd come upon the murder scene. In his newfound state of mental confusion, he'd convinced himself that he'd killed Vera. He couldn't live with that knowledge, so he'd jumped.

Harris would probably end up with a prison sentence of a few years—hardly more than a slap on the wrist, as far as Arden was concerned.

Her cell phone rang. She'd had it only a week, and still didn't immediately respond to the ring.

It was the deputy assistant director of the FBI's National Center for Analysis of Violent Crime.

"Just checking in," he said.

Meaning, he was checking to see if she was still coming.

"I'll be there tomorrow," she assured him.

"Good." She could hear the smile in his voice. "I have an interesting case for you, if you want it. If you're ready. A triple homicide in Georgia."

She was returning to work.

She could never make things right, but she could use her knowledge, however tainted and ill gained, to help other people.

They were nervous about having her back. That was understandable.

"If you'd rather start out on something easier," the assistant director said, "I can arrange it."

"The Georgia case will be fine."

She told him good-bye and disconnected.

She sometimes dreamed she was in the tank. And she still got confused. Sometimes she thought she'd killed Eli and her own parents. Then she had to tell herself that no, it was Harley. No, it was just a promising experiment that had gone wrong.

She still felt hope for Project TAKE. In the right hands, with restrictions and careful monitoring. With stronger subjects.

The gentler, weaker personalities had been no match for French. French had overpowered Harley. And he would have eventually overpowered Noah.

"It's getting late," Franny said.

They'd all come for the weekend, but now Franny and Daniel were anxious to get back to their apartment in Fairfax, Virginia. Some people might think they'd moved in together too soon, but intense bonds were often forged in the most dire of circumstances. Together, they'd lived years in a matter of hours.

Arden stood up and stepped off the porch.

Her memories of previous visits to the cabin were foggy. She recalled a picnic by a stream, with wine and bread. She remembered making love with Fury outside, then inside, in front of the fire.

But were the memories real? Had the events really happened?

Maybe it didn't matter. The memories were hers. Maybe that's what was important.

As someone once told her—you are what you remember.

Behind her, the cabin door opened—and Nathan Fury stepped out. "Forget me again?"

After all this time, he was still recovering from his injuries and four surgeries. But he was alive.

Arden smiled, and then she laughed out loud.

Sometimes hearts stopped beating. Sometimes they started again.

And sometimes a stranger wasn't really a stranger. Sometimes a stranger was a loved one who'd been bleached from your mind.

It was a lot to think about.

ANNE FRASIER

SLEEP TIGHT

"There will be no sleeping tight after reading this one...Guaranteed to keep you up all night."*

> A female FBI profiler is up against a killer who may have ties to her own tragic past.

"A riveting thriller...laced with forensic detail and psychological twists, Anne Frasier's latest intertwines the hunt for a serial killer with the personal struggles of two sisters battling their own demons and seeking their own truths. Compelling and real—a great read."
—*Andrea Kane

0-451-41077-7

Available wherever books are sold or at
www.penguin.com

O042/ Frasier

Penguin Group (USA) Inc. Online

What will you be reading tomorrow?

Tom Clancy, Patricia Cornwell, W.E.B. Griffin,
Nora Roberts, William Gibson, Robin Cook,
Brian Jacques, Catherine Coulter, Stephen King,
Dean Koontz, Ken Follett, Clive Cussler,
Eric Jerome Dickey, John Sandford,
Terry McMillan...

You'll find them all at
http://www.penguin.com

*Read excerpts and newsletters, find tour
schedules, and enter contest.*

Subscribe to Penguin Group (USA) Inc. Newsletters
and get an exclusive inside look
at exciting new titles and the authors you love
long before everyone else does.

PENGUIN GROUP (USA) INC. NEWS
http://www.penguin.com/news